W9-BNS-592

SPQR IV

THE TEMPLE
OF THE
MUSES

SPQR

Senatus PopulusQue Romanus

The Senate and People of Rome

Free Public Library
Township of Hamilton
1 Municipal Drive
Hamilton, NJ 08619

SPQR IV

THE TEMPLE OF THE MUSES

JOHN MADDOX ROBERTS

THOMAS DUNNE BOOKS
ST. MARTIN'S MINOTAUR
NEW YORK

FIC
Robe
c1

3 1923 00373025 2

THOMAS DUNNE BOOKS.
An imprint of St. Martin's Press.

THE TEMPLE OF THE MUSES. Copyright © 1992 by John Maddox Roberts. All rights
reserved. Printed in the United States of America. No part of this book may be
used or reproduced in any manner whatsoever without written permission except
in the case of brief quotations embodied in critical articles or reviews. For information, address St. Martin's Press, 175 Fifth Avenue, New York, N.Y. 10010.

Design by Heidi Eriksen

Library of Congress Cataloging-in-Publication Data

Roberts, John Maddox.
SPQR IV : the temple of the muses / John Maddox Roberts.
p.   cm.
ISBN 0-312-24698-6
1. Egypt—History—Greco Roman period, 332 B.C.–640 A.D. Fiction.
I. Title.
PS3568.023874T45   1999
813'.54—dc21   99–38764
CIP

First published in the United States by Avon Books, a division of the Hearst
Corporation

First St. Martin's Minotaur Edition: October 1999

10 9 8 7 6 5 4 3 2 1

Free Public Library
Township of Hamilton
1 Municipal Drive
Hamilton, NJ 08619

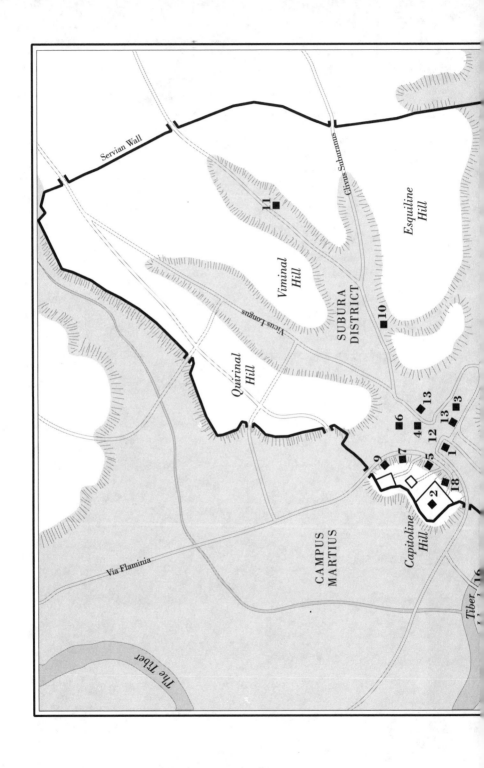

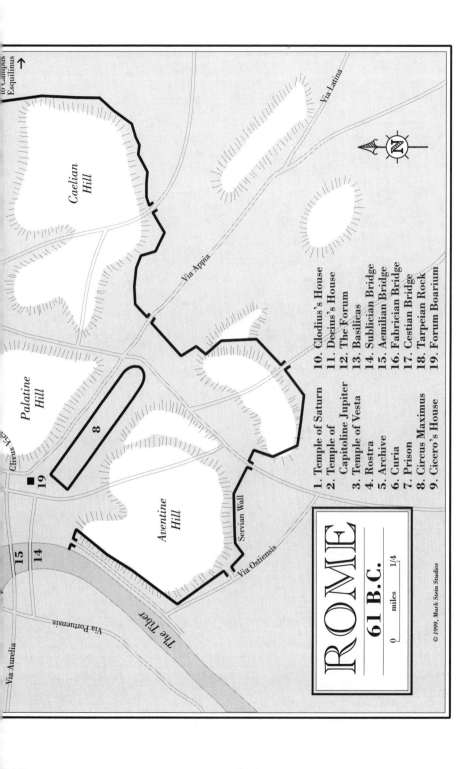

ROME
61 B.C.

0 — miles — 1/4

© 1999, Mark Stein Studios

Caelian Hill

Palatine Hill

Aventine Hill

The Tiber

Via Latina

Via Appia

Via Ostiensis

Via Portuensis

Via Aurelia

Servian Wall

Clivus N...

to Campus Esquilinus →

N

1. Temple of Saturn
2. Temple of Capitoline Jupiter
3. Temple of Vesta
4. Rostra
5. Archive
6. Curia
7. Prison
8. Circus Maximus
9. Cicero's House
10. Clodius's House
11. Decius's House
12. The Forum
13. Basilicas
14. Sublician Bridge
15. Aemilian Bridge
16. Fabrician Bridge
17. Cestian Bridge
18. Tarpeian Rock
19. Forum Boarium

1

I HAVE NEVER BEEN AMONG THOSE who think that it is better to be dead than to leave Rome. In fact, I have fled Rome many times in order to preserve my life. For me, however, life away from Rome is usually a sort of living death, a trans-Styxian suspension of the processes of living and a sense that everything important is happening far away. But there are exceptions to this. One of them is Alexandria.

I remember my first sight of the city as though it were yesterday, except that I remember nothing at all about yesterday. Of course, when you approached Alexandria by sea, you did not see the city first. You saw the Pharos.

It appeared as a smudge on the horizon while we were still a good twenty miles out to sea. We had cut straight across the sea like fools, rather than hugging the coast like sensible men. To compound the folly, we weren't in a broad-beamed merchantman that could ride out a storm at sea, but rather in a splendid war galley that carried enough paint and gilding to sink a lesser ship. On its bows, just above the ram, were a pair of bronze crocodiles that appeared to be foaming through their toothy jaws as the flashing oars propelled us over the waves.

"That's Alexandria," said the sailing master, a weather-beaten Cypriote in Roman uniform.

"We've made good time," grunted my high-placed kinsman, Metellus Creticus. Like most Romans, we both loathed the sea and anything having to do with sea travel. That was why we had chosen the most dangerous way to travel to Egypt. It was the quickest. There is nothing afloat swifter than a Roman trireme under all oars, and we had kept the rowers sweating since leaving Massilia. We had been on a tedious embassy to a pack of disaffected Gauls, trying to persuade them not to join the Helvetii. I detested Gaul, and was overjoyed when Creticus received a special commission from the Senate sending him to the Egyptian embassy.

The galley had a delightful miniature castle erected before the mast, and I climbed to its fighting platform for a better view. Within minutes the smudge became a definite column of smoke, and before much longer the tower was visible. From so far out there was nothing to give the thing scale, and it was hard to believe that this was one of the wonders of the world.

"You mean that's the famous lighthouse?" This from my slave Hermes. He had climbed after me, unsteadily. He was even more wretchedly seasick than was I, a matter of some satisfaction to me.

"I hear that it is more impressive up close," I assured him. It looked at first like a slender column, dazzling white in the noon sunlight. As we drew nearer, I could see that the slender shaft sat atop a stouter one, and that one on one broader still. Then we saw the island itself, and I began to get an idea of how huge the lighthouse was, for it dominated utterly the island of Pharos, which was itself large enough to conceal from view the entire great city of Alexandria.

The Pharos sat upon the eastern extremity of the island, and it was toward that cape that we steered, for we were bound for the Great Harbor. Around the western end of the island lay the Eunostos Harbor, the Harbor of Safe Return, where ships could enter the canal that connected the city to the Nile, or could proceed on to Lake Mareotis to the south. Hence the Eunostos was the favored commercial harbor. But we were on a government mission and therefore were to be received at the Palace, which was situated on the Great Harbor.

As we rounded the eastern end of the island, Hermes craned his neck to look up at the lighthouse. It was capped by a round kiosk from which smoke and flame billowed to the prevailing breeze.

"It *is* pretty tall," he admitted.

"More than four hundred feet, it's said," I affirmed. The old Successor Kings who followed Alexander built on a scale rivaling the Pharaohs. Their monster tombs and temples and statues weren't good for much, but they were impressive, which was the main idea. We Romans could understand that. It is important to impress people. Of course, we preferred useful things like roads and aqueducts and bridges. At least the Pharos was a truly useful structure, if a bit outsized.

When we passed between the Pharos and Cape Lochias, we came into view of the city, and it was breathtaking. Alexandria was situated on a strip of land separating Lake Mareotis and the sea, just to the west of the Nile Delta. Alexander had chosen the spot so that his new capital would be a part of the Greek world, rather than of priest-besotted old Egypt. It had been a wise move. The whole city was built of white stone and the effect was astonishing. It was like some idealized model of a city, rather than the real thing. Rome is not a beautiful city, although it has some beautiful buildings. Alexandria was incomparably beautiful. Its population was greater than that of Rome, but it had none of Rome's crowded, jumbled aspect. It had not just grown there like most cities. Instead it had been planned, laid out and built as a great city. On its flat spit of land, all the greater buildings were clearly visible from the harbor, from the huge Temple of Serapis in the western quarter to the strange artificial hill and temple of the Paneum in the east.

The greatest complex of buildings was the Palace, which stretched from the Moon Gate eastward along the sickle curve of Cape Lochias. There was even an Island Palace in the harbor, and a royal harbor attached to the Palace complex. The Ptolemies liked to live in style.

I went down to the deck and sent Hermes to fetch my best toga. The marines on deck were polishing their armor, but our mission was diplomatic, so Creticus and I would not be wearing military uniform.

Dressed in our best, flanked by our honor guard, we approached the dock nearest the Moon Gate. Above the gate was the figure of the beautiful but extremely elongated goddess Nut, the Egyptian goddess of the sky. Her feet stood upon one side of the gate, her long body overarched it and her fingertips rested on the opposite side. Her body was deep blue, spangled with stars, and slung beneath the arch thus formed was a huge brazen alarm gong, fashioned in the shape of a sun-disc. I was to see these reminders of Egyptian religion everywhere in Alexandria, which was otherwise a Greek city.

We sped toward the stone pier as if we intended to ram and sink it. At the last possible instant, the sailing master barked a command and the oars plunged into the water and stayed there, flinging forward a massive spray. The ship rapidly lost way and came to a gentle stop against the seawall.

"Could've tied a rose to the ram and she wouldn't've lost a petal," said the sailing master, with a certain justifiable exaggeration. The oars were shipped, lines were cast ashore and the trireme was drawn against the pier and made fast. The big boarding-bridge was lowered by its crane to the stone pavement and the marines arranged themselves along its railings, their old-fashioned bronze breastplates gleaming in the sun.

A delegation had come from the city to greet us, a mixed group, court officials in Egyptian garb and Romans from the embassy wearing togas. The Egyptian contingent had not neglected to bring entertainment. There were tumblers and trained monkeys and

4

several naked girls dancing through lubricious gyrations. The Romans were more dignified, but several of them swayed on their feet, already drunk at this early hour.

"I think I'm going to like this place," I said as we descended the bridge.

"You would," Creticus said. My family did not have a high opinion of me in those days. Drums thumped and pipes shrilled and sistra rattled while boys swung censers, engulfing us in clouds of fragrant smoke. Creticus bore all this with a becoming stoicism, but it all delighted me.

"Welcome to Alexandria, noble Senator Metellus!" cried a tall man dressed in a blue gown with a lot of gold fringe. He was speaking to Creticus, not to me. "Welcome, Quintus Caecilius Metellus, conqueror of Crete!" It wasn't much of a war, but the Senate had voted him the title and the triumph. "I, Polyxenus, Third Eunuch of the court of King Philopator Philadelphus Neos Dionysus, the eleventh Ptolemy, bid you welcome and give you freedom of our city and our Palace, in recognition of the deep love and respect which has for so long existed between Rome and Egypt." Polyxenus, like the other court officials, wore a black, square-cut Egyptian wig, heavy black makeup around his eyes and rouge on his cheeks and lips.

"What's a Third Eunuch?" Hermes asked me in a low voice. "Do Eunuchs One and Two have one ball each or something?" Actually, I'd been wondering that myself.

"On behalf of the Senate and People of Rome," Creticus said, "I am empowered and privileged to extend the great esteem which we have always cherished for King Ptolemy, the nobles and the people of Egypt." The courtiers clapped and twittered like so many trained pigeons.

"Then please accompany us to the Palace, where a banquet has been laid in your honor." That was more like it. No sooner had I felt solidity beneath my feet than my appetite had returned. To the accompaniment of drum and flute, sistrum and cymbal, we passed through the Moon Gate. Some of the Roman contingent fell in around us and I recognized a familiar face. This was a cousin of the Caecilian gens nicknamed Rufus for his red hair. He was not only red-haired but left-handed. With that combination he had no future in Roman politics, so he was always being sent out on foreign service. He clapped a hand on my shoulder and breathed wine in my face.

"Good to see you. Decius. Make yourself unwelcome in Rome again?"

"The old men decided it would be a good time for me to be away. Clodius finally got his transfer to the plebs and he's standing for the Tribuneship. If he gets it, that means I won't be able to go home next year either. He'll be too powerful."

"That's rough," Rufus said. "But you've just found the only place in the world where you won't miss Rome."

"That good?" I asked, brightening at the prospect.

"Unbelievable. The climate is wonderful all year, every debauchery in the world is to be had here cheap, the public spectacles are superb, especially the races, the high life doesn't stop just because the sun goes down, and, Decius my friend, you have absolutely never had your bottom kissed until you've had it kissed by Egyptians. They think every Roman is a god."

"I'll try not to disappoint them," I said.

"And the streets are clean. Not that you'll have to walk much if you don't want to." He gestured to the litters that awaited us just inside the Moon Gate. I gaped like a yokel who has just caught his first sight of the Capitol.

I had been carried around in litters before, of course. The sort we used in Rome were carried by two or four bearers and were a slow but dignified alternative to tramping through the mud and garbage. These were somewhat different. To begin with, each of them was carried by at least fifty black Nubians who shouldered poles as long as ships' masts. Each had seating accommodations for at least ten passengers which we reached by climbing a flight of stairs. Seated and hoisted, we were higher than the second-story windows.

The chair I was led to was made of ivory-inlaid ebony, draped with leopard skins. Overhead, a canopy protected me from the sun while a slave armed with a feather fan cooled me and kept the flies at bay. This was a definite improvement over Gaul. To my relief, Creticus and the eunuchs took the other litter. The musicians ranged themselves on the lower levels of the litters while dancers and tumblers frolicked along the poles, somehow managing to avoid the bearers. Then, like images of the gods carried in a sacred procession, we were off.

From my point of vantage, I saw immediately how such huge vehicles could traverse the city. The streets were broad and absolutely straight, a thing unknown in Rome. The one we were on ran right through the city, north to south.

"This is the Street of the Soma," Rufus told me, hauling a pitcher of wine from beneath his seat. He poured a cupful and handed it to me. "The Soma is Alexander's tomb. It's not really on this street, but it's close." We passed a number of cross streets, all of them straight but not as wide as the one we were on. All the buildings were of white stone and all of them of the same high quality, unlike Rome, where mansions and slums occupy the same block. I was later to learn that all the buildings in Alexandria were built completely of stone, with no wooden frames, floors or roofs. The city was all but fireproof.

We came to a cross street that was even wider than the one we were on. Here the litters turned east like ships tacking into the wind. The throngs in the streets cheered our little procession, all the louder, it seemed, when they saw the distinctive Roman garb. There were exceptions. The soldiers who seemed to be on every street corner regarded us sourly. I asked about these.

"Macedonians," said Rufus. "Not to be confused with the degenerate Macedonians of the court. These are barbarians right out of the hills."

"Macedonia's been a Roman province since Aemilius Paullus," I said. "How is it they have an army here?"

"They're mercenaries in the service of the Ptolemies. They don't much like Romans."

I held out my cup for a refill. "No reason why they should, considering how many times we've beaten them. They're still in rebellion, last I heard. Sent Antonius Hibrida packing."

"They're a tough lot," Rufus said. "Best to steer clear of them."

Aside from the sour-faced soldiers, the citizenry seemed to be a cheerful and cosmopolitan lot. I never saw such a combination of skin, hair and eye color except at a slave market. Greek dress predominated, but there was garb from every land under the sun, from swathing desert robes to jungle skins and feathers. The effect of all the white stone was somewhat softened by the masses of greenery that hung from balconies and rooftop gardens. Vases were filled with flowers and festal wreaths hung lavishly.

There were a great many temples to deities Greek, Asian and Egyptian. There was even a Temple of Roma, an example of that fundament-kissing at which the Egyptians excelled. The chief deity of the city, though, was Serapis, a god invented specifically for Alexandria. His temple, the Serapeum, was one of the most famous in the world. While the architecture was predominantly Greek, Egyptian decoration was much in evidence everywhere. The extraordinary Egyptian hieroglyphs were lavishly employed.

Ahead of us came a sound of musicians setting up an even louder racket than our own. From a side street emerged a frenzied procession, and the litter bearing the court faction halted to give it the right-of-way. A mass of ecstatic worshippers erupted across the great boulevard, many of them dressed only in brief goatskins, their hair unbound and whirling wildly as they beat tambourines. Others, less demented, wore gowns of white gauze and played harps, flutes and the inevitable sistra. I watched all this with interest, for I had yet to visit the Greek parts of the world, and the Dionysiac celebrations had long been forbidden in Rome.

"Them again," Rufus said disgustedly.

"In Rome they'd be driven from the city," said an embassy secretary.

"Are they Maenads?" I asked. "It seems an odd time of year to be holding their rites." I noticed that a number of them were brandishing snakes, and that now there were a number of young men among them, shaven-headed youths with the expression of one who has just been struck sharply at the base of the skull.

"Nothing so respectable," Rufus said. "These are followers of Ataxas."

"Is that some local god?" I inquired.

"No, he's a holy man out of Asia Minor. The city's full of his kind. He's been here a couple of years and acquired a great horde of these followers. He works miracles, foretells the future, makes statues speak, that sort of thing. That's another thing you'll find out about the Egyptians, Decius: They've no sense of decency when it comes to religion. No *dignitas*, no *gravitas*; decent Roman rites and sacrifices have no appeal to them. They like the sort where the worshippers get all involved and emotional."

"Disgusting," sniffed the secretary.

"They look like they're having fun," I said. By now a great litter was crossing the street, even higher than ours, carried by yet more of the frenzied worshippers, which couldn't have done much for its stability. Atop it was a throne on which sat a man who wore an extravagant purple robe spangled with golden stars and a tall headdress topped by a silver crescent moon. Around one of his arms was wrapped a huge snake and in the other he held a scourge of the sort one uses to thrash recalcitrant slaves. I could see that he had a black beard, a long nose and dark eyes, but little else. He stared slightly ahead as if unaware of the churning frenzy being staged on his behalf.

"The great man himself," Rufus sneered.

"That's Ataxas?" I asked.

"The very same."

"I find myself wondering," I said, "just why a procession of high officials gives way to a rabble that would have been chased from Rome with Molossian hounds at their heels."

Rufus shrugged. "This is Alexandria. Under this skin of Greek culture, these people are as priest-ridden and superstitious as they were under the Pharaohs."

"There is no shortage of religious charlatans in Rome," I pointed out.

"You'll see the difference before you've been at court for very long," Rufus promised.

When the frantic procession was past, we resumed our stately progress. I learned that the street we were on was the Canopic Way, the main east-west thoroughfare in Alexandria. Like all the others, it was straight as a chalk-line and ran from the Necropolis Gate in the west to the Canopic Gate in the east. In Rome, it was a rare street where two men could pass each other without having to turn sideways. On Canopic two litters such as ours could pass easily, while leaving plenty of room for pedestrian traffic on either side.

There were strict rules regarding how far balconies could protrude from the facades of buildings, and clotheslines over streets were forbidden. This in its way was refreshing, but one raised in Rome acquires a taste for chaos, and after a while all this regularity and order became oppressive. I realize that it seems a good idea at first, laying out a city where no city has been before, and making sure that it does not suffer from the ills that afflict cities that just grew and sprawled like Rome. But I would not care to live in a city that was a veritable work of art. I think this lies at the heart of the Alexandrians' reputation for licentiousness and riotous living. One forced to live in surroundings that might have been devised by Plato must seek relief and an outlet for the human urges despised by philosophers. Wickedness and debauchery may not be the only answers, but they are certainly the ones with the widest appeal.

In time we turned north along a great processional way. Ahead of us were several clusters of impressive buildings, some of them within battlemented walls. As we proceeded northward, we passed the first of these great complexes on our right.

"The Museum," Rufus said. "It's actually a part of the Palace, but it lies outside the defensive wall."

It was an imposing place, with wide stairs ascending to the Temple of the Muses, which gave the whole complex its name. Of far greater importance than the Temple was the cluster of buildings surrounding it, where many of the world's greatest scholars carried on their studies at state expense, publishing papers and giving lectures as they pleased. There was nothing like it in all the world, so it took its name from its temple. In later years, other such institutions, founded in imitation, were also called museums.

Even more famous than the Museum was the great Library attached to it. Here all the greatest books of the world were stored, and here copies were made and sold all over the civilized world. Behind the Museum I could see the great pitched roof of the Library, dwarfing all surrounding structures. I commented upon its immensity, and Rufus waved a hand as if it were a trifle.

"That is actually the lesser Library. It's called the Mother Library because it's original, founded by Ptolemy Soter himself. There's an even bigger one, called the Daughter Library, attached to the Serapeum. It's said that, between them, they contain more than seven hundred thousand volumes."

It seemed unbelievable. I tried to picture what 700,000 books must look like. I imagined a full legion plus an extra auxiliary cohort. That would be about 7,000 men. I imagined such a body of men, having looted Alexandria, filing out, each man carrying 100 books. Somehow, it still did not convey the reality. The wine probably didn't help.

Once past the Museum, we passed through yet another gate and were within the Palace itself. The Palace of Alexandria displayed the by-now familiar urge of the Successor Kings to build everything bigger than anyone had built before. Its lesser houses were the size of ordinary palaces, its gardens were the size of city parks, its shrines were as big as ordinary temples. It was a veritable city within a city.

"They've done well, for barbarians," I said.

We were set down before the steps of a sprawling stoa that ran the length of an apparently endless building. A crowd of court functionaries appeared at the top of the steps. In the middle of them was a portly, pleasant-faced man I recognized from his previous visits to Rome: Ptolemy the Flute-Player. He began to descend the Palace steps just as Creticus descended from his towering littler. Ptolemy knew better than to await him at the top of the steps. A Roman official climbs stairs to meet no one but a higher-ranking Roman official.

"Old Ptolemy's fatter than ever," I noted.

"Poorer than ever, too," Rufus said as we made our unsteady way to the mosaic pavement. It was a matter of constant amazement to us that the king of the world's richest nation was also the world's most prominent beggar. Not that we failed to take advantage of the fact.

The previous generation of Ptolemies had assassinated one another nearly out of existence, and an irate Alexandrian mob had finished the job. A royal bastard, Philopator Philadelphus Neos Dionysus, who was, in sober fact, a flute-player, had been found to fill the vacant throne. For more than a century Rome had been the power broker in Egypt, and he appealed to Rome to help shore up his shaky claim and we obliged. Rome would always rather prop up a weak king than deal with a strong one.

On the pavement Ptolemy and Creticus embraced, Creticus making a sour face at the scent Ptolemy wore. At least Ptolemy did not affect the Egyptian trappings so favored by the court. His clothing was Greek, and what remained of his hair was dressed in the Greek fashion. He did, however, make lavish use of facial cosmetics, to disguise the ravages of time and debauchery.

While Creticus and the king went into the Palace for the formal reception, I sneaked off with Rufus and a few others to the Roman embassy, where we would be staying. The embassy occupied a wing of the Palace and came complete with living quarters, banqueting facilities, baths, a gymnasium, gardens, ponds and a mob of slaves who might have staffed the biggest plantation in Italy.

I found that my own quarters were far more spacious than my house in Rome and that I was to have twenty slaves for my personal service.

"Twenty?" I protested when I was presented with my staff. "I already have Hermes, and the little wretch hasn't enough to do as it is!"

"Oh, take them, Decius," Rufus insisted. "You know how slaves are; they'll find something to do. Do the quarters suit you?"

I surveyed the lavish suite. "The last time I saw anything like it was when I visited Lucullus's new town house."

"It is a bit better than being a junior official back home, isn't it?" Rufus said with satisfaction. Obviously, he had found the best possible dead end for his career.

We went into a small courtyard to sample some of the local vintages and catch each other up on the latest doings in our various spheres. It was delightfully cool beneath the palms, where tame monkeys gamboled among the fronds. In a marble-bordered pool, bloated carp swam up to be fed, their mouths gaping like the beaks of baby birds.

"Did you stop by Rome on your way here?" the secretary asked eagerly.

"No, we came by way of Sicily and Crete. Your news from the Capitol is probably more recent than mine."

"What of Gaul, then?" Rufus asked.

"Trouble. The Helvetii are making warlike noises. They resent the Roman presence and they're talking about taking back the Roman Province."

"We can't let them do that!" someone said. "It's our only overland connection to Iberia!"

"That's just what we were trying to prevent," I said. "We called on a number of tribal leaders and reminded them of our old friendships and alliances and we passed a few bribes."

"Do you think they'll stay peaceful?" Rufus asked.

"You can never tell with Gauls," I said. "They're an emotional people, and they do love to fight. They could jump either way. When we left, most of them seemed to be content, but tomorrow some fire-raiser could make a speech accusing them of being women for accepting Roman authority, and the next day all Gaul could be in revolt just to prove their manhood."

"Well, we've beaten them many times before," said the secretary, who was a safe distance from Gaul.

"And they've whipped us a few times," I reminded him. "A tribe or two at a time, they're no danger. But if every tribe in Gaul decides to throw us out, I don't see that we could do much about it. They outnumber us about fifty to one, and they're on their own home ground."

"We need another Marius," someone said. "He knew how to handle Gauls and Germans."

"He knew how to handle Romans, too," I said sourly. "Mainly by massacring them."

"Only people of senatorial rank," the obnoxious little secretary pointed out. "But then, you Metelli were Sulla's supporters, weren't you?"

"Pay no attention to him," Rufus said affably. "He's a freedman's son, and the common herd were Marians to a man. But seriously, when does the proconsulship for transalpine Gaul change?"

"It will be one of next year's Consuls," I said, "which means some amiable dolt will undoubtedly be on the spot when the Gauls finally rise up and start wiping out every Roman citizen they can lay hands on." If I could have known what was happening back in Rome that year, I would have been far more alarmed. We faced something a great deal worse than a trifling military disaster in Gaul. But I was blissfully unaware of it, as was Rome in general.

"Now what of Egypt?" I asked. "There must be some problem, or the Senate wouldn't have ordered Creticus all the way from Gaul."

"The situation here is a chaotic shambles, as usual," Rufus told me. "Ptolemy is the last living male adult of the line. The question of the succession is growing urgent, because he will drink himself to death before long and we must have an heir to support or we'll have a whole civil war to sort out, and that could take a number of years and legions."

"Who are the contenders?" I asked.

"Just one, an infant born a few months ago, and sickly at that," the secretary said.

"Let me guess. Would his name be Ptolemy?" The only other name they used was Alexander.

"However did you get that idea?" Rufus said. "Yes, another little Ptolemy and one in for a lengthy minority, from the look of things."

"Princesses?" I asked. The women of that line were usually more intelligent and forceful than the men.

"Three," Rufus said. "Berenice is about twenty and she's the king's favorite. Then there's little Cleopatra, but she's no more than ten, and Arsinoe, who is eight or so."

"No Selene in this generation?" I asked. That was the only other name bestowed on the Ptolemaic daughters.

"There was one, but she died," Rufus said. "Now, if no other girls are born, Cleopatra is probably the one little Ptolemy will marry, if he should live that long. There's already a court faction supporting her." The Ptolemies had long ago adopted the quaint Egyptian custom of marrying their sisters.

"On the other hand," said the secretary, "should the king turn toes-up any time soon, Berenice will probably marry the infant and rule as regent."

"Would that be a bad idea?" I asked. "On the whole, the Berenices and Cleopatras have been a pretty capable lot, even if the men have mostly been clowns."

"This one's a featherbrain," Rufus said. "She falls into every loathsome foreign cult that comes along. Last year there was a Babylonian revival and she devoted herself to some Asiatic horror with an eagle's head, as if the native Egyptian gods weren't disgusting enough. I think she's over that one, but if so, she's just found another even worse."

15

Courts are never simple, but this was getting truly dismal. "So who supports Berenice?"

"Most of the court eunuchs favor Berenice," Rufus said. "The satraps of the various nomes are divided, and some of them would like to see an end to the Ptolemies altogether. They've become like little kings on their estates, with private armies and so forth."

"So we must pick somebody to back so that the Senate can vote on it, and then we'll have a constitutional justification should we have to intervene on behalf of our chosen heir?" I said.

I sighed. "Why don't we just annex this place? A sensible Roman governor would do it a world of good."

That evening there was a magnificent banquet, at which the centerpiece was a whole roast hippopotamus. I put the same question to Creticus, and he set me straight on a few matters.

"Take over Egypt?" he said. "We could have done that any time in the last hundred years, but we haven't and for good reason."

"I don't understand," I said. "When did we ever turn down a chance for a little loot and some more territory?"

"You aren't thinking it through," he said as a slave spooned some elephant-ear soup into a solid gold bowl supported by a crystal stand sculptured as a drunken Hercules. I dipped an ivory spoon into the mess and tried it. It would never replace chicken soup in my esteem.

"Egypt doesn't represent just a little loot and territory," Creticus explained patiently. "Egypt is the richest, most productive nation in the world. The Ptolemies are always impoverished only because they mismanage things so badly. They spend their wealth on frivolous luxury, or on projects that bring them prestige rather than prosperity or might." The Flure-Player was already snoring gently at Creticus's elbow, and so did not resent these comments.

"All the more reason for some good Roman reorganization," I said.

"And just who would you trust with this task?" Creticus asked. "Let me point out that the general who conquers Egypt will become, instantly, the richest man in the world. Can you imagine the in-fighting among our military gentry should the Senate dangle such a prize before them?"

"I see."

"There's more. Egypt's grain production surpasses that of all other nations by a factor so huge that it staggers the mind. The Nile obligingly delivers a new load of silt every year and the peasants work far more productively than our slaves. Two crops a year in most years, and sometimes three. In a time of famine for the rest of us, Egypt can feed our whole Empire, by stretching the rations a little."

"So the Roman governor of Egypt could have a stranglehold on the Empire?"

"And be in a position to set himself up as an independent king, with the wealth to hire all the troops he needs. Would you like to see Pompey in a position of such power? Or Crassus?"

"I understand. So this is why it's always been our policy to back one degenerate weakling after another for the crown of Egypt?"

"Exactly. And we always help them: with loans, with military aid, with advice. Not that they take advice very well. Caius Rabirius is working heroically to sort out Ptolemy's financial problems, but it could be years before he makes much progress." Rabirius was a famous Roman banker who had lent huge sums to Ptolemy, who in turn had named him minister of finance for Egypt.

"So who do we back this time?" I asked.

"It'll have to be the infant," he said, lowering his voice even further. "But no need to let that be known too soon." He favored me with a conspiratorial grin. "The other parties will court us lav-ishly as long as they think they have a chance to win Roman favor."

"The princesses are out of the question?" I said. I had yet to see these ladies. They were living at country estates at that season.

"The Senate has never favored the support of female rulers, and these are too surrounded by predatory relatives and courtiers.

I suppose the brat will have to marry one of them, but that's for the benefit of his Egyptian subjects. As far as the Senate is concerned, he can marry one of the sacred crocodiles."

"That having been decided," I said, "just how do we occupy ourselves here?"

"Like all the other Romans here," he said. "We have a good time."

2

For two months i lived the wonderfully idle existence of a Roman official visiting Egypt. I made the inevitable journey to all the most famous sites: I saw the pyramids and the nearby colossal head that is supposed to have an equally huge lion's body beneath it. I saw the statue of Memnon that hails the rising sun with a musical note. I toured some very odd temples and met some very odd priests. Wherever I went, the royal officials went into transports of servility until I began to expect them to erect little shrines in my honor. Perhaps they did.

Once you are out of Alexandria you are in Egypt proper, the Egypt of the Pharaohs. This Egypt is a curious and unchanging place. In any of the nomes, you would see a spanking new temple erected by the Ptolemies to one of the ancient gods. A mile or two away you would see a virtually identical temple, except that it would be two thousand years old. The only difference would be the somewhat faded paint on the older temple.

At the great ceremonial center of Karnak there is a temple

complex the size of a city, its great peristyle hall a forest of columns so massive and so tall that the mind wearies in its contemplation, and every square inch of it carved with that demented picture-writing the Egyptians delight in so. Over countless centuries the Pharaohs and priests of Egypt drove the populace to finance and build these absurd piles of rock, apparently without a murmur of protest in return. Who needs slaves when the peasants are so spiritless? Italians would have reduced the place to rubble before those pillars were head-high.

There can be no more agreeable way to travel than by barge upon the Nile. The water has none of the alarming instability of the sea, and the land is so narrow that you can see almost everything from the river itself. Walk a mile from the riverbank, and you are in the desert. And drifting downstream under a full moon is an experience out of a dream, the quiet broken only by the occasional bellow of a hippopotamus. On such nights the ancient temples and tombs gleam like jewels in the moonlight and it is easy to believe that you are seeing the world as the gods once saw it, when they walked among men.

It has been my experience that periods of ease and tranquility are invariably followed by times of chaos and danger, and my prolonged river idyll was no exception. My time of ease and idle pleasure changed as soon as I returned to Alexandria.

It was the beginning of winter in Egypt. And despite what many people say, there *is* a winter in Egypt. The wind grows cool and blustery, and on some days it even rains. My barge reached the delta and then took the canal that connected that marshy, rich country to Alexandria. It is wonderful to be in a country where one rarely has to walk for any great distance and there are no steep slopes to be negotiated.

I left the barge at one of the lake harbor docks and hired a litter to carry me to the Palace. This one was carried by a modest four bearers, but Alexandria is a beautiful city even at street level.

Our route took us by the Macedonian barracks, and I ordered a halt while I looked over the place. Unlike Rome, Alexandria had no ban on soldiers within the city. The Successors were always foreign despots, and they never thought it amiss to remind the natives of where power lay.

The barracks consisted of two rows of sprawling, three-story buildings facing each other across a parade ground. The buildings were predictably splendid, and the soldiers on parade went through their drill with commendable smartness, but their gear was old-fashioned to Roman eyes. Some wore the solid bronze cuirass now worn only by Roman officers, others the stiff shirt of layered linen, faced with bronze scales. The better-off Roman legionaries had gone over to the Gallic mail shirt generations before, and Marius had standardized it throughout the legions. Some of the Macedonians retained their long spears, although they had more than a century before discarded their old, stiff phalanx formation and had adopted an open order on the Roman model.

At one end of the field a troop of cavalry practiced its maneuvers. The Macedonians had found cavalry to be useful in the broad eastern lands that made up so much of the old Persian Empire they had conquered. We Romans had only a tiny cavalry force and usually hired horsemen when we felt the need.

At the other end of the field some engineers were erecting some sort of siege machine, a massive thing of ropes and timber. I had never seen such a device and ordered the bearers to take me nearer. Now, any foreigner would know better than to wander freely about a Roman camp or barracks, but I had become so accustomed to the unfailing toadying of the Egyptians that it did not occur to me that I might be intruding.

At our approach, a man who had been bawling at the engineers whirled and stalked toward us, the sunlight flashing from his polished greaves and cuirass. He carried a plumed helmet under one arm.

"What's your business here?" he demanded. I knew the breed: a long-service professional with slits for eyes and a lipless mouth. He looked like every centurion I ever detested. The arrow and spear gouges on his armor matched the scars on his face and arms, as if he had asked the armorer for a matching ensemble.

"I am Decius Caecilius Metellus the Younger, of the Roman diplomatic mission," I said, as haughtily as I could manage. "Your machine piqued my interest and I came for a closer look."

"That so?" he said. "Bugger off."

This was not going well. "See here," I protested, "I don't believe you appreciate the uniquely intimate relations between the Palace and the Roman mission."

"Bring old Flute-Face down here and we'll talk about it," the officer said. "Meantime, get away from my barracks and stay away!"

"You shall hear more of this," I promised. That is something one always says after being thoroughly intimidated. "Bear me to the Palace," I ordered grandly.

As we trotted thither, I fantasized punishments for the obdurate officer. He was perfectly within his rights to expel a foreign civilian, but that did not excuse him, in my estimation. After all, I was a Roman official, of a sort, and Egypt was a Roman possession, of a sort. But the man's insolence was quite driven from my mind by the news that greeted me when I reached the embassy.

I found Creticus in the atrium of the embassy and he beckoned me to him.

"Ah, Decius, this is convenient. We have some visitors from Rome. I was going to go greet them myself, but now you're here, so you can do it."

"*You* were going to greet them?" I said. "Who's that important?"

"A slave just brought this from the royal harbor." He held up a small scroll. "It seems that two ladies of important family have come to Alexandria for the salubrious climate."

"The climate?" I said, arching an eyebrow.

"This is a letter from Lucullus. He informs me that the climate in Rome is unhealthy, something involving political infighting and blood in the streets. He is sending his ward, the Lady Fausta Cornelia, and her traveling companion, another highborn lady, and asks me to extend all aid and courtesy."

"Fausta!" I said. "Sulla's daughter?"

He glared impatiently "What other lady has ever borne that name?"

"I was just making sounds of astonishment," I assured him. "I've met the lady. She is betrothed to my friend Titus Milo."

"All the better. Round up some slaves, they'll have a lot of baggage. And arrange for quarters. I'll speak to the court eunuchs about a reception for them." Romans would never make this sort of fuss for visiting ladies, no matter how highborn, but the Egyptian court, dominated by eunuchs and princesses, was different.

"Who is the other lady?" A horrible thought struck me. "It isn't Clodia, is it? She and Fausta are rather close."

He smiled. "No, you won't be displeased to see this one. Now go. They're fretting at the dock."

I barked loudly and a gaggle of slaves appeared from nowhere. I ordered litters to be brought and they appeared as if by magic. It was really the most extraordinary place. I climbed into one and we trooped off to the royal harbor. This was a tiny enclosure within the Great Harbor where the royal yachts and barges were kept. It was bounded by a stone breakwater, and the opening in this was further protected by the island bearing the jewellike Island Palace, rendering it proof against the most violent storms.

Among the royal barges the little Roman merchantman looked humble, indeed, but the ladies who stood at the rail radiated arrogance the way the sun radiates light. These were not only Roman ladies, but patricians to boot, with that special assurance of superiority that comes only of centuries of inbreeding.

The slaves set down the litters and I clambered from mine as they abased themselves before the ladies descending the gangplank. The German-blond hair of Fausta Cornelia was unmistakable. She possessed the golden beauty of the Cornelians to an extent matched only by her twin brother, Faustus. The other lady was smaller and darker, but just as radiant. A good deal more so, to my eyes.

"Julia!" I cried, gaping. It was, indeed, Julia Minor, younger daughter of Lucius Caesar. Not long before this, a meeting of our families had been held and we had been formally betrothed. That we had desired this betrothal was, of course, immaterial as far as the families were concerned, but was regarded as a rather fortunate happenstance. At that time the Metelli were in a frenzy of fence-mending with the contending power blocs. Creticus had married off his daughter to the younger Marcus Crassus. Caius Julius Caesar was the rising star of the Popular Assemblies, and a connection with that ancient but obscure family was desired. Caius Julius's own daughter was already promised to Pompey, but his brother Lucius had an unmarried younger daughter. Hence, we were betrothed.

"Welcome to Alexandria!" I cried. I took Fausta's hand briefly; then Julia presented her cheek to be kissed. I obliged.

"You've put on weight, Decius," she said.

"What a flatterer you are," I said. "These Egyptians feel they've failed their gods if they allow a Roman to walk a step more than necessary, and who am I to interfere in their devotion to piety?" I turned to Fausta. "Lady Fausta, your beauty adorns this royal city like a crown. I trust you had a pleasant voyage?"

"We've been heaving our guts out since we left Ostia," she said.

"I assure you, the accommodations here will more than make up for the rigors of a winter voyage." The slaves had been unloading their baggage during all this. By the time it was all ashore, the ship rode a foot higher in the water. The ladies were attended by their personal maids, of course, and a few other slaves. They would be lost among the multitude at the embassy.

"Is Alexandria as fabulous as I've always heard?" Julia asked, excited despite her rather drawn and haggard appearance.

"Beyond your wildest imaginings," I vowed. "It shall be my greatest pleasure to show it all to you."

Fausta smiled obliquely. "Even those low dives where you've no doubt been disporting yourself?"

"No need," I said. "The very basest of amusements are to be

had at the Palace." At that even the notorious Fausta looked a bit nonplussed.

"Well, I want to see the more elevated sights," Julia said, crawling wearily into her litter and inadvertently treating me to a flash of the whitest thigh I had ever seen. "I want to see the Museum and converse with the scholars and attend lectures by all the famous, learned men." Julia had that tiresome love of culture and education that infected Roman ladies.

"I shall be only too happy to introduce you," I said. "I am intimate with the faculty." Actually, I had been there only once, to visit an old friend. Who wants to consort with a pack of tiresome old pedants when some of the finest racehorses in the world are exercising in the Hippodrome?

"Really?" she said, eyebrows going up. "Then you must introduce me to Eumenes of Caria, the logician, and Sosigenes, the astronomer, and Iphicrates of Chios, the mathematician. And I must tour the Library!"

"Libraries," I corrected. "There are two of them, you know." I sought to change the subject and turned to Fausta. "And how is my good friend Milo?"

"Busy as ever," she said. "Fighting all the time with Clodius. He's secured a quaestorship, you know."

"I heard," I said, laughing. "Somehow I can't picture Milo working away in the Grain Office or the treasury." Milo was the most successful gangster Rome had ever seen.

"Don't bother. He works out of his headquarters as always. I think he's hired somebody to carry out his duties as quaestor. He sends you his warmest regards, by the way. He says you'll never amount to anything if you spend all your time lazing away in foreign lands instead of working in Rome."

"Well, dear Titus has always extolled the benefits of hard work and diligence. I, on the other hand, have always felt these to be virtues proper to slaves and freedmen. Look at how hard these litter-bearers work. Does it do them any good?"

"I knew you would say something like that," Julia said, sitting up and craning her neck to take in the magnificence through which we were carried.

"The men destined for greatness are all fighting it out in Rome right now," Fausta said.

"And every one of them will die on a battlefield, or from poison or the dagger of the assassin," I maintained stoutly. "I, on the other hand, intend to expire of old age with the rank of Senior Senator."

"I suppose every man must have his own ambition," she sniffed.

"Oh, look!" Julia said. "Is that the Paneum?" The weird, artificial hill with its spiral path and its circular temple was just visible in the distance.

"That it is," I said. "It has the most outrageous statue in it. But here's the embassy."

"Is this all part of the Palace?" Julia asked as I helped her from the litter. I was forced to kick a slave aside in order to perform even this simple, agreeable task.

"It is. In fact, for all matters involving practical power, the Roman embassy *is* the court. Come along, I'll see you to your quarters."

But I was not to be permitted even this. No sooner had we reached the atrium than a mass of courtiers entered, complete with riotous musicians, oiled Nubians leading leashed cheetahs, a tame lion, a pack of baboons dressed in livery, chiton-clad adolescent girls bearing baskets of rose petals which they scattered promiscuously, and, in the midst of them all, a young woman to whom all deferred.

"I hear that we have visitors," the young woman said. "If I had heard sooner, I would have come to the royal harbor to welcome you!"

I bowed as deeply as Roman dignity permitted. "You honor us with your presence, Princess Berenice. May I present the lady Fausta Cornelia, daughter of the late, illustrious Dictator Lucius Cornelius Sulla, and the lady Julia Minor, daughter of the reverend

Senator Lucius Julius Caesar." She embraced both ladies while the courtiers cooed and twittered.

The Roman ladies displayed creditable aplomb, accepting these royal embraces with coolness and dignity. Aplomb was called for, as Berenice was one of the Ptolemies who favored Egyptian fashions. On her upper body she wore only a cape of gauze, which was quite transparent. What she wore below that would have got a dancing-girl drubbed out of Rome for indecency. Her jewelry, on the other hand, would have rivaled a legionary's armor for weight and bulk.

"We are at a disadvantage, Highness," Fausta protested. "We are not prepared to receive royalty."

"Oh, think nothing of that," Berenice said. "I *never* get interesting women to entertain, just tiresome men with their politics and their foolish intrigues." She waved a hand that took in the whole Roman embassy, me included.

"And the foreign queens and princesses who come here are all ignorant and illiterate, no more than well-dressed peasants. But two genuine patrician ladies all to myself! Come along, you aren't staying here. You're going to stay in my palace." Yes, there was yet another palace within the Palace, this one belonging to Berenice. And so she shepherded them out like two new additions to her menagerie. I wondered if she would try to leash them as well.

Creticus came in just as the mob disappeared. "What was that all about?" he asked.

"Berenice has spirited away our ladies," I said. "They may never see Rome again."

"Well," he said practically, "that takes care of that problem. New toys for the princess instead of a headache for us. They'll need to be squired about the city by a Roman male of high lineage, though. Wouldn't be proper otherwise. That's your job."

"I shall be diligent," I promised.

Berenice was thoughtful enough to give her two new acquisitions an evening to recover from their ordeal at the hands of Neptune; then she threw a lavish reception for them, inviting all the luminaries of the Museum as well as the most fashionable people of Alexandria. As you might expect, this made for a fairly grotesque mixture. Since the Museum was owned and financed wholly by the Palace, Berenice's invitation had the authority of a summons. Thus every last star-gazing, number-torturing, book-annotating scholar in Alexandria was there, along with actors, charioteers, foreign ambassadors, cult leaders and half the nobility of Egypt, who were as decadent a pack of lunatics as one could wish for.

As they assembled, I spotted the one face I knew well. This belonged to Asklepiodes, physician to the gladiators of the school of Statilius Taurus in Rome. We had a long history together. He was a small man with clean-shaven cheeks and a jawline beard of the Greek sort, wearing the robes and hair-fillet of his profession. He was delivering a course of anatomical lectures that year. I took him aside.

"Quick, Asklepiodes, who are some of these people? Julia expects me to know them all!"

He grinned. "Ah! So at last I get to meet the beauteous Julia? Is she so deficient in perception that she thinks you a scholar?"

"She thinks I'm improving. Who are they?"

He looked around. "To begin with the most distinguished, there"—he nodded toward a tall, sharp-featured man—"is the illustrious Amphytrion, the Librarian. He is in charge of all things concerning the Library and Museum."

"That's a start," I said. "Who else?"

He nodded toward a burly, wild-haired man who stared around him like a wrestler challenging all comers. "That's Iphicrates of Chios, the mathematician, foremost champion of the school of Archimedes."

"Oh, good. She wants to meet him."

"Then perhaps her feminine charms will succeed where so many others have failed. He is a most irascible man. Let me see . . ." He picked out another dusty old Greek. "There is Doson the Skeptic, and Sosigenes, the astronomer, and . . ." and so on. I committed as many names as I could to memory, enough to fake knowledgeability. As soon as I had a chance, I went over to Julia and introduced Asklepiodes. She was polite but cool. Like many well-taught persons, she was only marginally interested in medicine, which is concerned with the real world.

"Would you care to meet some of the great scholars?" I asked her.

"Lead on," she said, with that maddeningly superior smile of hers. I escorted her to the ferocious-looking mathematician.

"Julia, this is the famed Iphicrates of Chios, foremost exemplar of the Archimedean School."

His face turned to oil and he took her hand and kissed it. "Utterly charmed, my lady." Then he turned and glared at me, an expression lent force by the Jupiter-like prominence of his forehead. "Don't think I know you."

"Perhaps it's slipped your mind, what with all that deep thinking. I attended your talk on the siege of Syracuse." I pulled this right out of the air, knowing that Archimedes had designed the defensive siege machinery of that city, but it seemed that I had struck my mark.

"Oh." He looked confused. "Perhaps you're right. There were a great many auditors at that lecture."

"And I've read your work, *On the Practical Applications of Geometry*," Julia said, looking worshipful. "*Such* a stimulating and controversial book!"

He grinned and nodded like one of the trained baboons. "Yes, yes. It shook up some people around here, I can tell you." Insufferable twit, I thought. And here was Julia, mooning over him as if he were a champion charioteer or something of the sort. I pried her away from the great man and took her to meet the Librarian. Amphytrion was as gracious as Iphicrates was crude, and I had an easier time of it. Berenice swept her off to meet some perfumed fools, and I was left with the Librarian.

"I noticed you speaking with Asklepiodes," he remarked. "Do you know him from Rome?"

"Yes, I've known him for years."

Amphytrion nodded. "An estimable man, but a bit eccentric."

"How is that?" I asked.

"Well . . ." He looked around to see if any eavesdroppers lurked nearby. "He is rumored to practice surgery. Cutting with the knife is strictly forbidden by the Hippocratic oath."

"Apollo forbid it!" I said, scandalized.

"And"—he lowered his voice even further—"it is rumored that he does *his own stitching*, something even the lowest surgeon leaves to his slaves!"

"No!" I said. "Surely this is some scurrilous rumor spread by his enemies!"

"Perhaps you're right, but the world isn't what is used to be. I noticed you've met Iphicrates. That wild man also believes in *practical* applications." He pronounced the word like something forbidden by ritual law.

Now, I knew these rumors about Asklepiodes to be true. Over the years, he had sewn up about a mile of my own hide. But he always did this in strict secrecy, because these Plato-crazed old loons of the academic world thought that it was blasphemous for a professional philosopher (and physicians accounted themselves philosophers) to *do* anything. A man could spend his whole career pondering the possibilities of leverage, but for him to pick up a stick, lay it across a fulcrum and employ it to shift a rock would be unthinkable. That would be *doing* something. Philosophers were only supposed to think.

I extricated myself from the Librarian, looked around and saw Berenice, Fausta and Julia talking to a man who wore, among other things, an enormous python. The purple robe with its golden stars and the towering diadem with its lunar crescent looked familiar. Even in Alexandria one didn't see a getup like that every day. It was Ataxas, the future-foretelling, miracle-working prophet from Asia Minor.

"Decius Caecilius," Berenice said, "come here. You must meet the Holy Ataxas, Avatar on Earth of Baal-Ahriman." This, as near as I could figure it, was a combination of two if not more Asiatic deities. There was always something like that coming out of Asia Minor.

"On behalf of the Senate and People of Rome," I said, "I greet you, Ataxas."

He performed one of those Eastern bows that require much fluttering of the fingers.

"All the world trembles before the might of Rome," he intoned. "All the world marvels at her wisdom and justice."

I couldn't very well argue with that. "I understand you have an . . . an establishment here in Alexandria," I said lamely.

"The Holy One has a splendid new temple near the Serapeum," Berenice said.

"Her Highness has graciously endowed the Temple of Baal-Ahriman, to her everlasting glory," Ataxas said, fondling his snake.

And used Roman money to do it, I'd no doubt. This was ominous. Obviously, Ataxas was the latest in Berenice's long chain of religious enthusiasms.

"Tomorrow we sacrifice fifty bulls to consecrate the new temple," the princess said. "You must come."

"Alas," I said, "I've already promised to take Julia to see the Museum." I looked desperately at her for affirmation.

"Oh, yes," she said, to my great relief. "Decius is intimate with the great scholars. He's promised to give me the whole tour."

"Perhaps the next day, then," Berenice urged. "The priestesses will perform the rite of self-flagellation and worship the god in ecstatic dance."

That sounded more like it. "I think we can—"

Julia trod on my toe. "Alas, that is the day Decius has promised to show me the sights of the city: the Paneum, the Soma, the Heptastadion . . ."

"Oh, what a pity," Berenice said. "It is a sublime spectacle."

"There's Fausta," Julia said, "I must speak with her. Come along, Decius." She took my arm and steered me away. Ataxas looked after us sardonically.

"I don't see Fausta," I said.

"Neither do I. But I don't know how long I could keep dodging invitations to that fraud's odious temple."

"What savages!" I said. "Fifty bulls! Even Jupiter only demands one at a time."

"I noticed you weren't all that averse to watching a bunch of barbarian priestesses flogging themselves into a frenzy and dancing like naked Bacchantes."

"If you're asking whether I prefer a brothel to a butcher shop, I confess that I do. I'm not entirely without taste."

In the course of the evening, we were invited to the rites of at least a dozen loathsome Oriental deities. Most of these were touted by transient religion-mongers much like Ataxas. As Rufus had predicted, I had discovered that the place of these religious frauds was quite different in Alexandria. In Rome, the followers of crackpot cults were drawn almost exclusively from the slaves and the poorest of plebeians. In Alexandria, the wealthiest and highest persons lavished money and attention on these disreputable fakes. They would adopt them as matters of fashion and rave about the latest unwashed prophet as the leader to the one true path of enlightenment. For a few months, anyway. Few of the nobility of Egypt had the tenacity of attention possessed by a ten-year-old child.

The scholars were nearly as tiresome. Before the reception was over, Iphicrates of Chios had managed to get into arguments with at least six guests. Why anyone would argue over abstract matters escaped me. We Romans were ever an argumentative lot, but we always argued over important things like property and power.

"Nonsense!" I heard him shout once in his obnoxiously loud voice. Indeed, his conversational tone could be heard all over the reception hall, and in several other rooms besides. "That story about a crane that picked up Roman ships and set them down inside the city walls is patent foolishness!" He had an Armenian ambassador backed into a corner. "The mass of the counterweights would be prohibitive, and the whole thing would be so slow that any ship could easily avoid it!" He went on about weights and masses and balances, and the other scholars looked deeply embarrassed.

"Why do they tolerate him?" I asked Julia's latest catch, an editor of Homeric works named Neleus.

"They have to. He's a great favorite of the king. Iphicrates makes toys for him: a pleasure-barge driven by rotating paddles instead of oars, a moving dais in the throne room to elevate the king above the crowd, trifles like that. Last year he devised a new system of awnings for the Hippodrome that can be spread, altered as the sun moves and then rolled up, all from the ground instead of sending sailors up on ropes to haul them around."

"Makes sense to me," I said. "If the king is going to finance this Museum, he might as well get some good out of it."

"But, Decius," Julia said patiently, "this reduces him to the status of a mere mechanic. It's unworthy of a philosopher."

I snorted into my excellent wine. "If it weren't for 'mere mechanics,' you'd be hauling water from the river to your house instead of having it delivered from the mountains by way of an aqueduct."

"Roman accomplishments in applied philosophy are the marvel of the world," Neleus said. Greeks may despise us as their intellectual inferiors, but they have to toady to us because we're powerful, as is fitting.

"Besides," I said to Julia, "I thought you admired Iphicrates."

"I do. He is unquestionably the finest mathematician alive."

"But having met him," I said, "you find your enthusiasm dimmed?"

"His manner is abrasive," she confessed. By this time the man was talking with Ataxas, of all people, and keeping his voice down for a change. I couldn't imagine what those two could find to talk about, but I knew a few Pythagoreans in Rome, and they had contrived the almost inconceivable feat of confusing mathematics and religion. I wondered what monstrous, Minotaur-like cult might emerge from a fusion of Archimedes and Baal-Ahriman.

We finally did encounter Fausta. She was naturally the center of much attention. Everyone wanted to meet the daughter of the

33

famous Dictator, whose name was still feared throughout much of the world. Julia, as a mere Caesar, was not so assiduously courted. If only they had known.

For this was the year of the famous First Triumvirate. Back in Rome, Caesar, Pompey and Crassus had decided that they owned Rome and the world. People now write as if this were some great, world-shaking event. In fact, nobody was even aware of it save the three involved. It was merely a highly informal agreement among the three to watch out for one another's interests while one or more of them had to be away from Rome. It was a portent of things to come, though.

But that evening we were blissfully unaware of such intriguing. We were free of tiresome politics, and we had time on our hands and all of Alexandria in which to enjoy ourselves.

3

"THE MUSEUM," I SAID, "WAS founded in the reign of Ptolemy I, surnamed Soter, 'the Savior,' two hundred thirty-five years ago." I had bribed a tour guide to teach me his spiel, and I now delivered it to Julia as we mounted the steps to the main hall. "It was planned and directed by the first Librarian, Demetrios of Phaleron. The Library, of worldwide fame, is actually an adjunct of the Museum. Since the time of Demetrios, an unbroken chain of Librarians has overseen the institution and its collections. The successors of Demetrios have been Zenodotus of Ephesus, Callimachus of Cyrene, Appolonius of Rhodes, Eratosthenes of Cyrene, Aristophanes of Byzantium, Appolonius the Eidograph, Aristarchus of Samothrace—"

"I can read, Decius." Julia said, cutting me off in mid-genealogy.

"But I still have a hundred years of Librarians to impart," I protested. It had been a considerable feat of memorization on short notice, but we noble youth of Rome had that sort of rote learning flogged into us from an early age.

"I read everything I could find on the Museum and the Library during my journey. You can learn a great deal between bouts of seasickness."

At the top of the stair one passed between a pair of gigantic obelisks. Beyond them was a courtyard paved with polished purple marble, dominated by beautiful statues of Athena, Apollo and Hermes. The greatest buildings of the Museum complex faced on this courtyard: the Library, the magnificent dining hall of the scholars and the Temple itself, a modest but exquisite structure sacred to the Muses. Beyond these were a good many more buildings: the living quarters, lecture halls, observatories, colonnades and so forth.

Julia did much exclaiming over the architectural marvels. In truth, Rome had nothing to touch it. Only the Capitol had anything like the splendor of the great edifices of Alexandria, although our Circus Maximus was a good deal larger than their Hippodrome. But the Hippodrome was made of marble, where the Circus was still mostly of wood.

"This is sublime!" she said excitedly.

"Exactly the word I would have chosen," I assured her. "What would you like to see first?"

"The lecture halls and the refectory," she said. "I want to see the scholars as they go about their philosophical labors."

Someone must have sent word ahead of us, because Amphytrion appeared at that moment. "I will be most happy to escort our distinguished guests. The Museum is at your disposal."

The last thing I wanted was to have some dusty old Greek coming between me and Julia, but she clapped and exclaimed what a privilege this was. Thus robbed of a graceful way to sidestep his unwanted intrusion, I followed the two into the great building. In the entrance peristyle he gestured toward the rows of names carved into the walls.

"Here you see the names of all the Librarians, and of the

famous scholars and philosophers who have ornamented the Museum since its founding. And here are the portrait busts of the greatest of them." Beyond the peristyle was a graceful colonnade surrounding a pool in which stood a sculptural group depicting Orpheus calming the wild beasts with his song.

"The colonnade of the Peripatetic philosophers," Amphytrion explained. "They prefer to converse and expound while walking, and this colonnade is provided for their convenience. The Orpheus was sculpted by the same hand that created the famous *Gigantomachia* at the altar of Zeus in Pergamum."

This I was prepared to admire to the fullest. It was an example of that flowering of late Greek sculpture that I have always preferred to the effete stuff of Periclean Athens, with its wilting Apollos and excessively chaste Aphrodites. Orpheus, caught in mid-note, was the very embodiment of music as he strummed his lyre. The beasts, obviously stopped at the moment they were about to spring, were carved with wondrous detail. The lion's fanged mouth was just relaxing from a terrifying snarl, the wolf lapsing into doglike friendliness, the bear standing on his hind legs looking puzzled. In real life no one is ever attacked simultaneously by such a varied menagerie, but this was myth, and it was perfect.

But Julia wanted to see the philosophers at their labors, so we went in search of some. The problem was that, when they aren't talking, philosophers aren't doing much at all. Mostly they stand around, or sit around, or in the case of the Peripatetics, walk around, pondering matters and looking wise.

We found Asklepiodes in a lecture hall, speaking to a large audience of physicians about his discoveries concerning the superiority of stitching lacerations rather than searing them with a hot iron. One of the attendees ventured to question whether this was properly the concern of physicians, and Asklepiodes parried him neatly.

"Before even the divine Hippocrates, there was the god of healing, Asklepios. And do we not read in the *Iliad* that his own son, Machaon, with his own hands tended the wounds of the Greek heroes, even withdrawing an arrowhead in one instance?" I applauded this point vigorously, and there were learned murmurs that this was a valid point.

From the lecture halls we passed into a large courtyard filled with enigmatic objects of stone: tall spindles, slanted ramps, circles with gradations marked off in inscribed lines. A few of the smaller instruments I recognized as similar to the *gnomon* that engineers use to lay out building sites or camps for the legions.

"Welcome to my observatory," said a man I recognized as Sosigenes, the astronomer. He grinned engagingly as Julia went through her now-customary gush of enthusiasm.

"I shall be most happy to explain something of my studies, my lady," he said, "but I confess that there are few things more useless than an astronomer in the daytime." And this he proceeded to do. Sosigenes had a redeeming sense of humor that was notably absent in most of the philosophers there. I found myself actually listening attentively as he explained the purpose of his instruments, and the importance of recording the movements of the stars and planets in calculating positions in navigation, and in determining the real date as opposed to the slippery dates of conventional calendars. The reliable calendar we now use was the invention of Sosigenes, although Caesar took the credit by making it the legal calendar through his authority as Pontifex Maximus. I resolved to return to the observatory some night when he could explain more effectively the mysteries of the stars.

In another courtyard we found the redoubtable Iphicrates of Chios, bossing a crew of carpenters and metal workers as they assembled a complicated model of stone, wood and cable. At our arrival he turned frowning, but smiled and bowed when he saw that Rome had come calling.

"And what do you work on now, Iphicrates?" Amphytrion asked.

"His Majesty has asked me to solve the long-standing problem of silting in the great canal that links the Mediterranean with the Red Sea," he proclaimed proudly.

"A daunting prospect," I said. "But its solution would do much to facilitate traffic between the West and India."

"It's good to see that someone from outside these walls has a grasp of geography," he said.

"It's one of the things we Romans find important," I answered. "What is your solution?"

"The basis of the problem is that the canal is at sea level, and therefore a noticeable current flows through it from west to east, just as water enters the Mediterranean from the Ocean through the Gates of Heracles, and from east to west through the Hellespont." In explaining the mysteries of his art, his voice lost its accustomed belligerence and he actually communicated a bit of his own excitement at solving these thorny natural problems.

"I have designed a series of waterproof gates and dry docks at each end of the waterway. By means of these, the dry docks can be flooded to raise or lower shipping to the proper level, and it can sail, row or be towed the intervening distance without a constant current. The amount of silt admitted will be minimal, and the waterway will need to be dredged no more often than every fourth or fifth year."

"Most ingenious," I acknowledged. "Worthy of the successor to Archimedes."

"I thank you," he said with poor grace. "But the revered Archimedes did not fare so well at the hands of the Romans." Greeks are always carrying some sort of grudge.

"Yes, well, it was an unfortunate incident, but it was his own fault. You see, when Roman soldiers have just broken into your city after a lengthy siege, and are rampaging about, looting the city and massacring anyone who shows resistance, why, the last thing you want to do is speak insolently to them. If he had just kept his mouth shut and abased himself, he would have been spared. As it was, Marcellus felt awfully bad about it and he gave the old boy a very nice tomb."

"Just so," Iphicrates said through gritted teeth.

"But, learned Iphicrates," Julia said hastily, "what other marvelous works occupy your mind? In your books you have said that you always have a number of projects under study at any time."

"If you will come this way," he said, ushering us into a spacious room adjoining the courtyard where the workmen assembled his water gate. The room was full of cupboards and tables, and the tables were littered with models in varying stages of assembly. Most of the machines, as he explained them, had something to do with raising weights or water. I pointed at one that displayed a long, counterweighted arm tipped with a sling.

"A catapult?" I inquired.

"No, I never design engines of war. That is an improved crane for lifting great stones. A number of your Roman engineers have shown interest in it. It will prove most helpful in your great bridge and aqueduct projects."

While he spoke to Julia and the Librarian, I wandered about the room, admiring his amazingly lucid drawings and diagrams, every one of them applying geometry and mathematics to the accomplishment of some specific task. This was a sort of philosophy that I could appreciate, even if I found the man himself odious. The open cupboards were filled with more papyri and scrolls. On one table was an oversized scroll of dark, oiled olive wood, its handles stained vermilion. Even a glance told me that it was not made of Egyptian papyrus, but of the skin-paper of Pergamum. I picked up the massive scroll and began to unroll it, but Iphicrates made a massive, throat-clearing sound.

"Excuse me, Senator," he said, hastily taking it from my hands. "This is the unfinished work of a colleague, lent to me on the understanding that no one else should see it until he has finished it and made it public." As he locked the thing in an ornate cupboard, I wondered what sort of colleague would trust Iphicrates of Chios with anything.

"That scroll reminds me," Julia said, adroitly smoothing things over. "I have yet to see the famous Library. And who better to show it to me than the Librarian himself?" We bade farewell to the difficult mathematician and received his churlish goodbyes in return.

I had already toured the Library, and once you have seen one tremendous warehouse of books, you have seen them all. Besides, it was a noisy place, with hundreds of scholars reading at the top of their lungs. Romans read at a polite, dignified murmur, but not Greeks or, worse, Asiatics. I left Julia and Amphytrion to the dubious pleasures of the Library while I idled about in the great outer courtyard, admiring the splendid statues. I had been there no more than a few minutes when my slave Hermes appeared bearing the most welcome of sights: a bulging wineskin and a pair of cups. I had left him with our litter with strict orders to stay where he was. Naturally, he had ignored me. He was an unregenerate young criminal, but he made up for it by anticipating my needs with mystical precision.

"Didn't think you'd be able to take too much culture at once," he said, pouring me a cup. "I went out to a wineshop and picked us up some first-rate Lesbian."

I took the cup gratefully. "Remind me to flog you sometime for disobedience." I raised the cup in toast to the statue of Sappho that stood just inside the portico of the Temple. She had this place of honor because the old Greeks had named her "the tenth Muse." I took a long drink and addressed the statue.

"Now I know what your inspiration was, old girl." The many tourists made scandalized noises to see someone drinking in such a place. That was all right. A Roman Senator can do whatever he likes, and we're used to snooty foreigners calling us barbarians. Hermes poured himself a cup.

"I trust you have some valuable information for me," I said. "There are limits to the insolence I will tolerate."

"I got this straight from the queen's personal maids," he assured me. "She's pregnant again." This was one of the ways that Hermes served me.

"Another royal brat!" I said. "This is going to complicate

things, especially if it turns out to be a boy. Another princess won't matter much, with three already underfoot."

"They say Pothinus, the Number One Eunuch, is not pleased." Hermes was privy to more privileged information than the whole diplomatic corps.

"No reason why he should be. It just complicates his life, too. Not to mention that eunuchs as a rule don't take much satisfaction in human fertility. How far along is she?"

"Three months. Berenice is furious, Cleopatra seems to be happy about it and Arsinoe's too young to care. As far as I know, young Ptolemy hasn't been told yet."

"What about the king?" I asked.

"I don't move in such exalted circles. You're the great Roman official."

"Much good does that do me. I'm a glorified tour guide these days."

"At least you're in agreeable company. Would you rather be in Rome, dodging Clodius and being poisoned by his sister and worrying about what Caesar has planned for you? Enjoy the vacation, is what I say."

"Hermes," I said, "here we stand in the midst of the greatest assemblage of philosophers in the world. I don't need your worldly advice."

He snorted. "I've seen plenty of these philosophers since we've been here. You know why they all have slaves to wipe their bottoms for them? Because they're too crackbrained to do it for themselves."

"You shouldn't speak that way of your betters." I tossed him the empty cup. "Take this back to the litter. That skin had better not be noticeably flatter when we leave here."

Still at loose ends, I went into the Temple itself. I had never visited the Temple, and so I was completely unprepared for its breathtaking beauty. It was circular, thus giving equal place to each of the nine Muses, whose statues stood around its periphery.

In Rome we had our fine Temple of Hercules and the Nine Muses, but there the pride of place is given to Hercules, a Roman favorite. The images of the Muses are not of the highest quality.

These were worthy of Praxiteles. They were carved from the finest white marble, adorned with only the subtlest tints, unlike so many garishly painted statues. This gave them a spectral, almost transparent presence, like spirits seen in a dream. Before each burned a vessel of frankincense, wreathing them in smoke and contributing to their divine appearance. Only their eyes, delicately inlaid with shell and lapis lazuli, shone forth with more than mortal intensity.

I realized then how little I knew of the Muses. I daresay I could have named two or three of them: Terpsichore, because everyone likes dance, and Polyhymnia, because we all sing praises of the gods, and Erato, because she is the Muse of love poems and her name is similar to Eros. But the others were hazy to me.

The proportions of the Temple were perfect. It was not numbingly huge like so many of the Alexandrian buildings, but rather of human scale. The statues of the Muses were only slightly larger than life-size, just enough to emphasize that these were not mere mortals. The polished marble of which it was built was of many colors, but all of it pale, accentuating the aetherial nature of the place.

Outside of Rome, I have encountered only a few temples, shrines or sanctuaries that seemed to me genuinely holy. Alexandria's Temple of the Muses was one of them. Being there was like falling under the spell of the sublime goddesses.

"You like our Temple, Senator?" I turned to see a small, bearded man dressed in a simple white, Dorian chiton and a hair-fillet of plain white cloth.

"It is sublime," I said in a low voice. To speak loudly in this place would be a desecration. "I want to sacrifice to them."

He smiled gently. "Here we do not sacrifice. On their festivals, we offer the goddesses wheat kneaded with honey, and we pour

43

libations of milk and honey and water, that is all. We burn incense to their honor. They are not deities who love the blood of sacrifice. Here we work to their glory."

"Are you a priest?" I asked.

He bowed his head slightly. "I am Agathon, Archpriest of the Muses. Are you familiar with our goddesses?"

"Just slightly. They aren't well known in Rome."

"Then allow me to introduce you." He led me to the first, who stood to the right of the doorway. As we walked, he spoke, or rather intoned, the names, qualities and attributes of each. The Muses differed little in face, figure or garments, so they were known by their attributes.

"Clio, the Muse of history Her attributes are the trumpet of heroes and the clepsydra.

"Euterpe, Muse of the flute, and bearer of the flute.

"Thalia, the Muse of comedy, who bears the mask of comedy.

"Melpomene, the Muse of tragedy. Her attributes are the tragic mask and the club of Heracles.

"Terpsichore, bearer of the cithara, Muse of lyric poetry and the dance.

"Erato, the Muse of love poetry, who alone of the Muses has neither attribute nor attitude.

"Polyhymnia, Muse of heroic hymn, but also of mime, whose finger touches her lips in the attitude of meditation.

"Urania, the Muse of astronomy, whose attributes are the celestial globe and the compass.

"Greatest among them all, Calliope, Muse of epic poetry and eloquence, who bears the stylus and tablets."

All the Muses were portrayed standing except for Clio and Urania, who were seated. I never gave them the study they merited, for my times were mostly times of civil war and violence, unsuited to cultivation of the gentler arts. But from that day to this I have never forgotten their names and attributes, and whenever my steps took me near their temple by the Circus Flaminius, I never omitted to toss a bit of incense into their braziers.

I thanked the priest with deepest appreciation. The experience had been unexpected and was one I somehow knew I would cherish all my days. When I left the Temple it somehow seemed odd to me that everything outside was exactly as I had left it. A few minutes later Julia and Amphytrion emerged from the Library, and she looked at me strangely.

"Are you drunk?" she asked. "It seems awfully early."

"Just one cup, I swear it," I said.

"Then why do you look so strange?"

"The gentleman looks like one who has been given a vision from the gods," Amphytrion said seriously. "Has this happened?"

"No," I said hastily. "At least, I don't think so. Julia, let's go back to the Palace."

"I wanted to see more," she said, "but perhaps we'd better."

We thanked Amphytrion and returned to our litter. I tried to cover my odd mood with small talk, and soon Julia was chattering away about the stupendous collection of books in the Library, which was sufficient to make the whole city smell of papyrus. I promised to show her the Paneum the next day. I had been there before, and expected no unusual experiences as a result.

"Oh, by the way," Julia said. "Amphytrion has invited us to a banquet to be given tomorrow evening in the Museum. It is an annual affair, in honor of the founding of the Museum."

"Oh, no!" I groaned. "Couldn't you beg off? The last thing I want to do is go to a learned banquet and endure a lot of elevated talk from men who don't know how to have a good time."

"Berenice is going," she said firmly, "and she'll want me and Fausta to attend. You may do as you like."

I knew what that tone meant. "Of course I'll go, my dear. Where is Fausta, by the way?"

"She went to see all those bulls sacrificed. She likes that sort of thing."

"She would. Hermes has been asking around about that temple. It seems the bulls are to be castrated and their testicles will be made into a cloak to drape over the god's shoulders, like they do for the image of Diana at Ephesus."

She made a face. "The stories that boy picks up. I don't know why you tolerate him."

"He's amusing, which is more than you can say for most slaves, and he steals very little considering his opportunities."

When we were back in the Palace, I looked up Creticus, who was conferring with the others in the embassy over some newly arrived papers. When Rufus saw me, he picked up one of the papers and waved it at me.

"These just came in this morning by a fast cutter, Decius. The elections have been held in Rome. Caius Julius Caesar's to be Consul next year."

"Well, there was never much doubt," I said. "Now perhaps his creditors will have some hope of getting repaid. Who's the other?"

"Bibulus," Creticus said disgustedly. "They might as well have elected an oyster."

"It'll be a one-man Consulship, then," I said. "Oh, well, at least Julia will be happy."

We looked over the election results, looking for friends and enemies. As usual, there were plenty of both. Creticus jabbed a finger at a name on the list of new Tribunes.

"Vatinius," he said. "He's Caesar's man. That means Caesar's laws are likely to make it through the Popular Assemblies."

"What are the proconsular provinces to be?" I asked. Creticus mumbled his way down a page; then his mouth fell open.

"For both of them it's to be the supervision of rural roads, cattle-paths and pastures in Italy!" We all rocked with laughter

"That's a deadly insult!" I said. "It's war between Caesar and the Senate."

Creticus waved the thought away. "No, Caius Julius will find a way out of it. He'll get the Popular Assemblies to vote him a rich province. The Tribunes can override the Senate easily enough these days. Remember, he gave up his right to a triumph to return to

Rome and stand for Consul. That counts for a lot with the commons. They think he's been cheated and they'll be on his side."

The astonishing rise of Caius Julius in Roman politics was the wonder of the age. Rather late in life, he had emerged from obscurity to reveal himself as an accomplished politician, a gifted governor and, recently in Spain, a more than adequate military leader. For one who had been noted only for debauchery and debt, his career was doubly amazing. His tenure in Spain had been profitable enough for him to clear the most crushing of his debts. As Consul he couldn't be harassed by his remaining creditors, and if he could secure a rich province, he would be among the most redoubtable men in Rome. He was a man whom all thought they knew but whom no man had ever fathomed.

"Maybe you can go home soon, Decius," Rufus said. "You're betrothed to Caesar's niece, so he'll keep Clodius reined in while he's Consul."

"I'm not afraid of Clodius," I said, not quite truthfully.

"The sight of you two fighting in the Forum is embarrassing to the family," Creticus said. "Fear is immaterial. You'll go home when the family calls you back."

"Oh, well, so much for that," I said. "By the way, I've just learned that the queen is pregnant." I told them what I had learned from Hermes.

"A gentleman should not listen to slave gossip," Creticus snorted.

"Slave gossip has kept me not only informed but, on more than one occasion, alive," I retorted. "I think this is reliable."

We talked over the likely implications. Predictably, all bemoaned the likelihood of another son, which would complicate Roman-Egyptian relations. The gathering broke up on that sour note.

The next day I escorted Julia to the Paneum. This was one of Alexandria's more eccentric sights, an artificial hill with a spiral path ascending it and the Paneum itself at the top. It was not a true temple. That is to say, there was no priesthood, and no sacrifices were offered there. Rather, it was a shrine to the much-beloved god.

The climb up the spiral path was a long one, but it was beautifully landscaped, with the path paralleled by a strip of well-planted ground adorned with tall poplars, studded with odd little grottoes and alive with statues of Pan's woodland followers. Fauns capered, satyrs chased nymphs, dryads disported themselves all the way up the hill.

At the top was a shrine without walls, consisting of a roof supported by slender pillars, for who would confine a sylvan god like Pan within walls? Beneath the roof was a bronze statue of the god, half again as tall as a man, horned and cloven-hoofed, goat-legged, dancing ecstatically with his syrinx in one hand.

"How beautiful!" Julia said as we passed between the pillars. And then: "Goodness!" She was staring at the god's far-famed attribute; a rampantly erect penis which, on a man, would have somewhat exceeded his forearm in size.

"Surprised?" I said. "Every herm in every garden is similarly equipped."

"But not so heroically," Julia said, her eyes wide. "I pity the nymphs."

"Now, Fausta would have said that she envied them." That lady had decided to spend the day among the self-flagellating priestesses of Baal-Ahriman. She had an altogether livelier breadth of interest than Julia.

"Fausta places an excessive value on physical things," Julia said. "Hence her interest in your odious friend Milo."

"Milo is intelligent, eloquent, forceful, ambitious and is destined for great things in Roman politics," I pointed out.

"Others have the same qualifications. He is also violent, unscrupulous and balks at nothing to advance himself. Also common qualities, I grant you. What makes him unique, and desirable as far as Fausta is concerned, is that he has the face and body of a god."

"Is that his fault? And Cornelian standards are rather high in that area. In all of Rome, who is a match for Fausta but Milo?"

She snorted a delicate, patrician snort. "Why should she bother? It's not as if they are going to be seen in public. Roman husbands won't even sit with their wives at the Circus. They do make a striking couple, though. She is so fair and delicate, he is so dark and brawny. And his bearing is as arrogant as hers, even though his birth is so much lower."

I smiled to myself. Even Julia admired Milo, although she would never admit it directly. Virtually every woman in Rome did. Serving-girls scrawled his name on the walls as if he were some reigning gladiator or charioteer. "Handsome Milo," they called him, declaring that they were soon to expire of passion for him, frequently going into indecent detail. Julia would never be so shameless, but she was not immune to his charm.

"Birth no longer means much in Rome," I said. "Power these days is in the Tribuneship and with the Popular Assemblies. A patrician like Clodius transfers to the plebs so that he can stand for Tribune, and even your uncle Caius Julius, who is as patrician as Romulus, has become a man of the people because that's where the power is."

"My uncle Caius wishes to restore the ancient dignity of the Senate, a task in which he says that Sulla failed. If he must go to the commons for the authority to do so, it is merely because that is how corrupt the times have become. He is willing to endure this indignity for the good of the state."

Her family loyalty was touching, but it was misplaced. The veriest political dunce knew that Caius Julius had no interest in restoring the dignity of the Senate. Restoring the monarchy was more like it, with Caesar as king. We had no idea then how close he would come to doing it, though.

"The view from here is extraordinary," she said, changing the subject. And indeed it was. The Paneum was not exactly a lofty eminence, but Alexandria was so flat that no great altitude was required to see all of it. I resumed my character of tour guide.

"The Palace complex you know by now," I said. "Over there"—I pointed to the southeastern section of the city—"is the

Jewish Quarter. It is said that there are more Jews in Alexandria than in Jerusalem." I pointed to the western side of the city, dominated by the immense bulk of the Serapeum, a single temple that rivaled the entire city Museum complex in size. "That's the Rakhotis, the Egyptian quarter, so called because there was a native town of that name when Alexander founded the city here. The city is cut up into perfectly rectangular blocks, and these in turn form greater blocks, each named for one of the letters of the Greek alphabet."

"It's so odd," Julia said, "being in a city all made up of straight lines and right angles. I suppose it contributes to public order."

"I feel the same way," I said. "It's like being in a city planned by Plato."

"Plato favored circles," she informed me. "But I doubt that circles work very well in city planning. What's all that beyond the city wall to the west?"

"That's the Necropolis. They're very keen on tombs in Egypt. All burial grounds are on the west bank and necropolises are always to the west of the cities. I suppose it's because that's where the sun goes down. People have been dying for a number of centuries in Alexandria, so the Necropolis is almost as big as the city itself."

"And yet Alexandria has been here for a tiny span of time, by Egyptian standards. According to Herodotus, the list of Pharaohs goes back for nearly three thousand years. Even Rome is an infant by comparison. Do you think Rome will last as long?"

"Of course," I said. Ridiculous question.

But even the most pleasant day must give way to evening, and this one was committed to the banquet at the Museum. We returned to the Palace to bathe and change raiment. A welcome custom among the Romans in Alexandria was to dispense with the cumbersome toga when dining out, wearing instead the light, casual *synthesis*. The practice was so eminently practical that Caesar introduced it to Rome a few years later. Since by that time Caesar was arbiter of all that was correct, it caught on.

We were carried through the cool evening to the Museum, our

body slaves walking behind us, carrying our dining needs. There was quite a crowd of slaves, as Fausta and Berenice were among us. I nudged my bearers to trot up alongside the litter shared by these two.

"How did the flogging go?" I called across to Fausta.

"It was enthralling!" she said. "There were at least a hundred of the priestesses dancing before the statue of Baal-Ahriman, and before the service was over, some of them passed out from shock and blood loss."

"That sounds like more fun than a Saturnalia riot," I said, ignoring Julia's elbow, which nearly cracked one of my ribs. "I wish we had entertainment like that in the Roman temples."

"It was a very proper religious ceremony," Berenice insisted. "The Holy Ataxas has revealed the sublime nature of the great god, and the value of religious ecstasy in his worship. During the holy trance, one enters mystic communion with the divinity. The Holy Ataxas has promised that, when his followers have achieved the perfection of devotion, the god will speak to us."

"*Speak?*" I said. "You mean, manifest himself in some mystical fashion, as gods have been wont to do?"

The princess shook her head. "No, he will speak, in his own voice, and all will be able to hear."

"Fascinating," I mumbled, astonished as always by the unplumbable depths of human gullibility. At last I yielded to Julia's elbow and sat back in the litter.

"It is not socially correct to ridicule someone else's religion!" she hissed when the others were out of earshot.

"I wasn't ridiculing," I protested. "I merely asked some questions. Besides, this is not a true religion. It's a foreign cult. And no educated person, whatever his nation, should lend credence to such fraudulent drivel."

"So what? She is a princess, and certain allowances are always made for royalty. It's not as if this were Rome and Ataxas were challenging Jupiter for supremacy."

In such deep theological discussion did we pass the time as

our bearers sweated our way to the Museum. The litter lurched a bit as they carried us up the great stairway; then they deposited us in the anteroom of the dining hall. There we were greeted by the luminaries of the place. Which is to say that they groveled to Berenice and graciously acknowledged us as part of her entourage.

We passed into the refectory, which had been laid out for a banquet suitable for scholars, which is to say simple, austere and elegant. But the presence of royalty improved matters. The wine was first-rate, as was the food, although ostentatious sauces and bizarre presentation were out. For entertainment, a lengthy passage from Homer was recited by Theagenes, the greatest tragic actor of the Alexandrian theater. We all sat through this with becoming dignity. The excellent wine helped.

In fact, the general air of quiet and self-possession made me a bit suspicious. Something seemed to be missing. Then I noticed that Iphicrates of Chios wasn't there. I turned to Amphytrion.

"Where's old Iphicrates? He's missing a good feed and he might liven things up a bit."

The Librarian looked slightly pained. "He was in his study this afternoon. Perhaps I should send to see that all is well with him." He summoned a slave and sent him off to check on Iphicrates. The old man couldn't come right out and say that he was overjoyed with Iphicrates's absence.

I knew that the after-dinner chat would consist entirely of learned discussion, and this I wished to avoid at all costs. If I couldn't get away, the best I could hope for was argument and vituperation. This I knew Iphicrates could supply in abundance. As the dishes were cleared away, a white-bearded old gentleman stood.

"Your Highness, honored guests, I am Theophrastus of Rhodes, chairman of the Department of Philosophy. I have been asked to lead the discussion for this evening. With your permission, I have chosen as subject the concept first articulated by the Skeptic philosopher Pyrrho of Elis: *acatalepsia*. That is to say, the impossibility of knowing things in their own nature."

This was even worse than I had feared. The slave reappeared and whispered something urgently to Amphytrion, at which a look of great consternation crossed the Librarian's face. He stood hurriedly.

"I am afraid I must interrupt the evening's festivities," he said. "It seems there has been some sort of—of accident. Something has happened to Iphicrates and I must go see what is wrong."

I turned and snapped my fingers. "My sandals." Hermes slipped them on my feet.

"Sir," Amphytrion said, "it is not necessary for you to—"

"Nonsense," I said. "If there is trouble, I wish to be of any assistance I may." I was desperate to get out of there.

"Very well, then. Esteemed Theophrastus, please continue."

We left the dining hall with the old boy's voice droning away behind us. The Museum was strangely dark and quiet at night, with its small slave staff gone off to their quarters, except for a boy whose sole task was to keep the lamps filled and trimmed.

"What seems to have happened?" I asked the slave who had been sent to find Iphicrates.

"You'd better see for yourself, sir," he said, sweating nervously. Slaves often get that way when something bad has happened. They know that they are most likely to be blamed. We crossed the courtyard where I had seen the workmen assembling Iphicrates's model canal mechanism the day before. It looked unreal in the moonlight. The slave stopped outside the study where we had seen his drawings.

"He's in there."

We went in. Six lamps provided decent illumination, enough to see that Iphicrates lay on his back in the middle of the floor, dead as Hannibal. A great vertical gash divided his lofty brow almost in two, from the bridge of his nose to his hairline. The room was a shambles, with papers scattered everywhere and cabinets thrown open, their contents adding to the mess on the floor.

"Zeus!" Amphytrion cried, his philosophical demeanor slipping a bit. "What has happened here?"

"For one thing," I said, "there has been no accident. Our friend Iphicrates has been most thoroughly murdered."

"Murdered! But why?"

"Well, he was rather an abrasive sort," I pointed out.

"Philosophers argue a great deal," Amphytrion said stiffly, "but they do not settle their arguments with violence."

I turned to the slave, who still stood without the door. "Go and bring the physician Asklepiodes."

"I think it is somewhat too late even for his skills," Amphytrion said.

"I don't require his healing skills, but his knack for reading wounds. We have worked together on a number of such cases in Rome." I went to look at the cabinets. The locked one had been pried open and its contents scattered.

"I see. But I must immediately report this incident to his Majesty. I imagine that he will wish to appoint his own investigating officer."

"Ptolemy? He'll be in no condition to hear any reports or appoint any officers until late tomorrow morning at the very earliest." I looked at the lamps. One had burned low, its wick smoking. The others flamed brightly.

"Nonetheless, I shall send word," Amphytrion said.

From without we could hear the voices of a number of people approaching. I went to the door and saw the whole mob from the banquet crossing the courtyard.

"Asklepiodes, come in here," I said. "The rest, please stay outside for the moment."

The little Greek came in, beaming all over his bearded face. He loved this sort of thing. He walked to the corpse and knelt beside it, placing his hands beneath his jaw and moving the head this way and that.

"Even the best lamplight is inadequate for really good analysis of this sort," he pronounced. "Dedius Caecilius, would you place four of the lamps around his head, no more than three or four inches away?" He got up and began rooting about in the mess. I did as he

54

requested and within a minute he found what he was looking for. He returned with what looked like a shallow, very highly polished bowl of silver. He turned to the little group of scholars who peered in through the door.

"Iphicrates was doing research on the use by Archimedes of parabolic reflectors. A concave mirror has the power to concentrate the light it reflects." He turned the open end of the bowl toward Iphicrates, and sure enough, it cast a beam of concentrated light upon the ghastly wound. From outside came murmurs of admiration at this philosophic cleverness.

While Asklepiodes made his inspection, I went to the doorway.

"Your colleague Iphicrates has been foully murdered," I announced. "I ask all of you to think whether you have seen any strange persons in this area just before the banquet." I said this primarily to keep them occupied so that they wouldn't interfere with my investigation. I wouldn't have trusted this lot to notice if their robes were on fire. Sosigenes was the only one I would have thought a reliable observer. Except for the late Iphicrates, who was unavailable for comment.

Fausta came close and peered in. "A murder! How thrilling!"

"If you really marry Milo," I said, "murders will get to be old stuff to you, too." I turned back to Amphytrion. "Is there any sort of inventory of Iphicrates's things? It would help greatly to know what is missing, since the murderer or murderers clearly were looking for something."

He shook his head. "Iphicrates was a secretive man. Nobody but he knew what he possessed."

"No students? Personal slaves?"

"He did all his work alone save for such workmen as he requested. He had a valet, a slave owned by the Museum and assigned to him. Few of us feel the need for a staff of slaves."

"I would like to question the valet," I said.

"Senator," he said, his patience wearing thin, "I must remind you that this is an affair to be investigated by the crown of Egypt."

"Oh, I'll clear things with Ptolemy," I said confidently. "Now, if you will be so good, I think it would be best if you were to assign a secretary to make an inventory of every object in this room: papers, drawings, valuables, everything right down to the furniture. If items known to have belonged to Iphicrates prove to be missing, it could be helpful in determining the identity of the murderer."

"I suppose it would do no harm," he grumped. "The king's appointed investigator might find it useful as well. Is this some new school of philosophy of which I was previously unaware?"

"It's my own school. You might call it 'applied logic.' "

"How very . . . Roman. I shall assign competent personnel."

"Good. And be sure that they list the subjects of all the drawings and papers."

"I shall be sure to do so," he fumed. "And now, Senator, if you do not mind, we have funeral arrangements to make on behalf of our departed colleague."

"Asklepiodes?" I said.

"I have seen enough." He rose from beside the corpse and we went aside to a corner of the room.

"How long has he been dead?" I asked first.

"No more than two hours. He probably died about the time the banquet was starting."

"And the weapon?"

"Most peculiar. Iphicrates was killed with an axe."

"An axe!" I said. This was exceptional. No common dagger for this murderer A few barbarian peoples favored the axe as a weapon, mostly in the East. "Was it a woodman's axe, or a soldier's *dolabra?*"

"Neither. Those have straight or gently convex edges. This weapon has a rather narrow and very deeply curved edge, almost a crescent."

"What sort of axe is that?" I wondered.

"Come with me," he said. I followed him from the room, mystified. As far as I knew, he had left his extensive collection of weapons back in Rome. There was a great deal of subdued muttering from the crowd outside as it drew aside for us. Someone fell in beside us.

"You've found congenial activity, I see." It was Julia.

"Yes. Extraordinary luck, don't you think? Where is Fausta?"

"She and Berenice went back to the Palace. A murder scene is not the proper place for royalty."

"I hope they don't start blabbing when they get there. I want to persuade Ptolemy to assign me to the investigation tomorrow."

"Decius, must I remind you that this is Egypt, not Rome?"

"Everybody wants to tell me that. It's not as if this were really an independent nation. Everybody knows that Rome calls all the tunes here."

"And you're with the diplomatic mission. You have no business interfering in an internal police matter."

"But I feel I owe Iphicrates something. If it hadn't been for him, I'd be listening to a discussion on *acatalepsia* right now."

"You're just bored," she insisted.

"Utterly." An inspiration seized me. "I'll tell you what: How would you like to help me in this?"

She paused. "Help you?" she said suspiciously.

"Of course. I'll need an assistant. A *Roman* assistant. And it wouldn't hurt to have one who can talk to the highborn ladies of Alexandria and the court."

"I'll consider it," she said coolly. I knew I had her. She was usually eager to take part in my disreputable snooping, but back in Rome it was not a respectable activity for a patrician lady. Here she could do as she liked, within reason.

"Good," I said. "You might start by getting Berenice to persuade Papa to assign me to the case."

"I knew you had some low motive. Where are we going?" We were in a wing of the Museum I hadn't yet seen, a gallery of statues and paintings, fitfully illuminated by lamps.

"Asklepiodes has something to show us," I said.

"The axe has been little used as a weapon in modern times," he said. "Although in antiquity it was not considered to be an unfit weapon even for noblemen. In Book Thirteen of the *Iliad*, the Trojan hero Peisandros drew an axe from behind his shield to engage Menelaos, not that it did him much good."

"I remember that part," I said. "Menelaos stabbed him through the top of his nose and both his eyeballs fell bleeding to the dust beside his feet."

"That would be the part you remember," Julia said.

"I love those passages. Asklepiodes, why the art gallery?"

"In art, the axe is usually depicted as a characteristic weapon of the Amazons."

"Surely," I said, "you aren't suggesting that Iphicrates was done in by an Amazon?"

"I rather think not. But look here." He had stopped before a large, splendid black-figure vase standing on a pedestal that identified it as the work of the famous vase-painter Timon. It depicted a battle between Greeks and Amazons, and Asklepiodes pointed to one of those martial ladies, mounted, dressed in tunic and Phrygian bonnet, raising on high a long-handled axe to smite a Greek who was dressed solely in a large, crested helmet and armed with spear and shield.

Julia fetched a lamp from a wall sconce and brought it close so that we could study the weapon. Although the handle was long, the head was quite compact, rather narrow and widening slightly to a half-circular cutting edge. The opposite side of the head bore a sharp, stubby spike.

"It's something like the sacrificial axe the *flamine*'s assistant uses to stun the larger sacrificial animals," Julia noted.

"Ours aren't quite that deeply curved on the edge," I said.

"In parts of the Orient," Asklepiodes said, "axes of this very form are still in use for religious purposes."

"Have you seen any here in Alexandria?" I asked him.

He shook his head. "No. But there is certainly at least one such axe in the city."

We took our leave of him and returned to our litter, where we found the bearers sound asleep, a defect I quickly remedied. We crawled into the litter and lay back on the cushions.

"Why would anyone murder a scholar like Iphicrates?" Julia wondered sleepily.

"That's what I intend to find out," I told her. "I hope it isn't anything as common as a jealous husband."

"Your superiors won't like you taking a hand in this, you know. It could complicate their work."

"I don't care," I said. "I want to find out who did this and see that he's punished."

"Why?" she demanded. "Oh, I know that you're bored, but you could cure that by escorting me on a boat trip down the Nile to the Elephantine Island, showing me the sights along the way. You have no real interest in Alexandria and you certainly didn't like Iphicrates. What is it?"

I always hated it when she was so penetrating and insightful. "It's nothing you need to bother yourself about," I insisted.

"Come on, tell me." She sounded amused. "If I'm to be your assistant, I want to know."

"Well," I said uneasily, "it's something about the place. Not the Museum or Library so much, but the Temple itself."

"And?" she prodded.

"And it's wrong to commit murder in a temple. Even the place where Iphicrates was killed is a part of the Temple complex."

Her eyebrows went up. "Even a foreign temple?"

"The Muses are legitimate goddesses," I maintained. "We worship them in Rome."

"I never thought you all that pious, Decius," she said.

"This Temple is different," I stubbornly insisted.

She lay back on the cushions. "I'll accept that. But I want you to show me this Temple." She said nothing more the rest of the way back to the Palace.

I had more than enough to occupy my mind.

4

"WHAT'S ALL THIS ABOUT A MUR-
der?" Creticus demanded.

So I told him all about it, at least what little I knew so far.
We were taking breakfast in the shaded courtyard of the embassy:
flat Egyptian bread, dates, figs in milk and honey.

"Local matter, then," he said when I'd finished. "Nothing to
concern ourselves about."

"Still, I want to look into it," I said. "It's bad form to kill
someone when royalty and Romans are present. Especially Romans. They ought to show more respect to a Senator and two visiting
patrician ladies."

"I'm sure the slight was unintended," Creticus said, spreading
honey on a scrap of bread, to the delight of the hovering flies. "Still,
if it amuses you, I see no harm in it. It can't amount to anything,
though. He was just a scholar."

"Thank you, sir. These Egyptians are a touchy lot where their supposed authority is concerned, though. If they give me trouble, may I count on you for support?"

He shrugged. "As long as it doesn't cause me too much difficulty."

After breakfast I hurried to the royal quarters, where my toga and senatorial insignia quickly got me admitted to the royal presence.

I found Ptolemy enjoying a far more substantial breakfast than I had just left. There were whole roast peacocks and Nile fish the size of pigs, oysters by the bucket and a roast gazelle. Those were only the main courses. How he could face any sort of food in his condition was something of a mystery.

When I entered he looked up from his platter with eyes like ripe cherries. His nose looked as if it had been carved and lovingly polished from the finest porphyry. The rest of his face was veined somewhat less luridly. He had once been a fine-looking man, although a certain leap of imagination was required to discern this.

"Ah, Senator . . . Metellus, is it?"

"Decius Caecilius Metellus the Younger, your Majesty. I am with the Roman embassy."

"Of course, of course. Come, sit down. Have you eaten yet?"

"Just minutes ago," I assured him.

"Well, have some more. More than I can eat here, anyway. Have some wine, at the very least."

It was early to be drinking, but you don't get to sample a king's private stock every day, so I partook.

"You've heard about the murder at the Museum, sir?" I began.

"Berenice mentioned something about it earlier, but I was still a little fuzzy. What happened?" So I gave my account yet another time. I was used to this sort of repetition. When dealing with the Senate and its committees, you render your report in full to the lowest committee chief, who listens with a serious expression until you've finished and then sends you to the next higher-up to do it all over again, and so forth until you address the full Senate, most of whom snore through it.

"Iphicrates of Chios?" the king said. "Designed cranes and water wheels and catapults, didn't he?"

"Well, he said he didn't work on war machines, but that was the sort of work he did. The others seemed to think it was undignified, doing truly useful work like that."

"Philosophers!" Ptolemy snorted. "Let me tell you something, Senator. My family owns that Museum and we support everyone in the place. If I want costumes and masks designed for my next theatricals, I send an order there and they put their artists to work on it. If I want a new water-clock, they design it for me. If I need a new Nile barge, they will design and have it built for me, and if one of my officers comes back from a campaign with an arrow lodged in him, those physicians will damned well come and get that arrow out, even if they have to get their philosophical fingers bloody in the process."

This was illuminating. "So their philosophical detachment from the real world is a pose?"

"Where I and my court are concerned it is. They may think they're some sort of Platonic sages, but to me they're just workmen in my employ."

"So if you tell them to cooperate in my investigation of this murder, they'll be sure to comply?"

"Eh? Why should you investigate?" The old sot was a bit sharper than I had anticipated.

"For one thing, I was present, as were two patrician ladies, and therefore Rome is involved." This was a stupendously tenuous connection, but I needed something. "And, in Rome, I have a certain reputation for getting to the bottom of these matters."

He squinted at me with his reddened eyes. "You mean it's your hobby?"

"Well, yes, I suppose so." This was truly lame.

"Why didn't you say so in the first place? A man ought to be allowed to indulge his hobbies. Go ahead."

I couldn't believe it. "You mean you'll give me your official authorization?"

"Certainly. Have your secretary draw up the proper document and send it to my chamberlain for my lesser seal."

"Thank you, your Majesty," I said.

"Odd sort of hobby, looking into who killed somebody. Well, a man finds his pleasures where he can. Sometime I must tell you about the satrap of the Arsinoene Nome and his crocodile."

"Perhaps another time," I said hastily, finishing the excellent wine and getting to my feet. "I'll have the requisite document here shortly."

"Sure you won't have some smoked ostrich?"

"You are too generous. But duty calls."

"Good day to you, then."

I hurried back to the embassy and browbeat a scribe into composing a document making me official investigating officer for Ptolemy. That is the good thing about dealing with a king if he's favorable to you: He doesn't have to justify himself to anybody. If the Flute-Player wanted to name a foreign embassy official investigator in a murder, he could do it and nobody could contradict him.

I took the document personally to the chamberlain's office. That functionary, the eunuch named Pothinus, looked at it skeptically.

"This is most irregular." He was a Greek wearing Asiatic jewelry and an Egyptian wig, not an uncommon Alexandrian combination.

"I have yet to see anything regular at this court," I said. "Be so good as to append the king's lesser seal. He has agreed to this arrangement."

"It is unethical to approach his Majesty so early in the morning. It is not the hour of his most discriminating discernment."

"I found his Majesty to be most perspicacious and in fullest command of his mental faculties," I said. "You speak disloyally, sir."

"I . . . I . . . I protest, Senator!" he sputtered. "Never would I offer the slightest disloyalty to my king!"

"See that you don't," I said coldly, and no one can speak as coldly as a Roman Senator. One must always maintain a firm hand with eunuchs. He appended the seal without further back talk and I left with it clutched happily in my fist. I was official now.

I found Julia and Fausta waiting for me in the courtyard of the embassy. I held up my royal commission triumphantly. Julia clapped her hands.

"You got it! Don't take full credit. I talked to Berenice and she went to the king when he rose this morning."

"He had very little memory of the event, but enough stuck in his mind to accomplish my ends," I said.

Fausta arched a patrician eyebrow. "Do you think that if you find the murderer, that will put Ptolemy in your debt?" Being who she was, Fausta could only assume that I sought some sort of political advantage.

"When did the gratitude of a Ptolemy ever do anyone any good?" I asked. "He barely knew who Iphicrates was, and I doubt he cares who the murderer might be."

"Why, then?" She was genuinely puzzled.

"Just being in Alexandria I have caught the fever of philosophy," I explained. "I am now developing my own school of logic. I propose to demonstrate the validity of my theories by uncovering the culprit."

She turned to Julia. "The Metellans are such a dull, plodding lot as a whole. It's good that they have a madman to lend them a bit of color."

"Isn't he amusing? He's better than Berenice's entourage."

I was outnumbered. "Jest as you will," I said, "but I am going to be doing something infinitely more interesting than sorting out the problems of a pack of brainless Macedonian bumpkins who masquerade as the royalty of Egypt." I stalked off haughtily, bellowing for Hermes to show himself. He came running.

"Here are the things you asked for," Hermes said. I took my dagger and *caestus* and tucked them inside my tunic. My sightseeing idyll was over and I was ready for serious business.

"Where are we going?" he asked.

"To the Museum," I said.

He looked around. "Where's the litter?"

"We are going to walk."

"Walk? Here? You'll cause a scandal!"

"I can't set my mind to serious work if I'm being carried around like a sack of meal. It's all right for decadent, inert foreigners, but a Roman should have more *gravitas*."

"If I could be carried about, I'd never wear out another pair of sandals," Hermes said.

Actually, I wanted a closer look at the city. Prowling the streets and alleys of Rome had always been one of my choicest amusements, but I had as yet had no opportunity to do the same in Alexandria. The attendants and guards at the Palace gate stared in amazement to see me walking out attended only by a single slave. I half expected them to come chasing after me, begging to carry me wherever I wanted to go.

It was a strange, disorienting experience to walk in a city made up of straight lines and right-angled intersections. Merely crossing one of the wide streets gave me an odd sensation of exposure and vulnerability.

"It must be hard to elude the nightwatch in a city like this," Hermes observed.

"They might have been thinking something of the sort when they designed it. A bad place for a riot, too. See, you could line up troops at one end of the city and sweep through the whole town. You could herd rioters down the side streets, separate them into little groups or crowd them into one place, wherever you want."

"It's unnatural," Hermes said.

"I agree. I can see the advantages, though."

"All made of stone, too," Hermes said.

"Timber is scarce in Egypt. It's comforting, knowing you aren't likely to be incinerated while you sleep."

The people who thronged the streets were of all nations, but the bulk of them were native Egyptians. The rest were Greeks,

Syrians, Jews, Sabaeans, Arabs, Galatians and people whose features and dress I did not recognize. There were Nubians and Ethiopians in every shade of black, most of them slaves but some traders. Everyone spoke Greek, but other languages formed a subcurrent beneath the predominant Greek tide, especially Egyptian. The Egyptian language actually sounds the way those hieroglyphs look. At every street corner there were mountebanks to be seen, dancing, tumbling and performing magic tricks. Trained animals went through their paces, and jugglers kept unlikely objects in the air with uncanny skill. Hermes wanted to gawk at all of these, but I tugged him past them, my mind set on greater matters.

We could have entered the rear of the Museum complex from the Palace itself, but I preferred to get a feel of the city. One raised in a great city has a feel for cities, as a peasant has a feel for arable land and a sailor for the sea. I had grown up in Rome and had urban bones. These people were foreigners, but they were city-dwellers, and all such have certain things in common.

My bones told me that this was a fat, happy, complacent populace. Whatever discontent there might be was minor. Had there been a riot or insurrection brewing, I would have known it. Alexandrians were known to riot from time to time, even killing or expelling a king or two, but these people were too busy making money or otherwise enjoying themselves to represent a threat. Civil discontent is always a menace in polyglot cities like Alexandria, where tribal antipathies sometimes override respect for law and authority. Not that Rome has place of pride in that respect. Our civil disorders tend to involve class rather than national divisions.

"Don't even think it, Hermes," I said.

"How do you know what I'm thinking?" he said, all wounded innocence. I knew when he said it that I was right.

"You're thinking: 'Here's a place where a presentable lad can fade into the population, and who's to notice? Here I can pass myself off as a free man, and no one will know I was ever a slave.' Isn't that what you were thinking?"

"Never!" he said vehemently.

"Well, that is good to hear, Hermes, because there are many cruel, brutal men in this city who do nothing but look for runaways to haul back to their masters for the reward, or to sell off to new masters. Should you disappear some morning, I would only have to pass the word and you would be back before nightfall. This is a large city, but the accents and inflections of the Roman streets aren't at all common here. So forget such fantasies and apply yourself to my service. I'll free you one of these days."

"You've never trusted me," he complained. I could understand why he thought so, since I delivered that same speech, with minor variations, every few days. One can never truly trust slaves, and some, like Hermes, are less trustworthy than others.

The day was a pleasant one, as most are in Alexandria. The climate was not as ideal as that of Italy, but then, no place save Italy has such a climate. The throngs were lively and cheerful, and the scent of incense mixed with the pervasive smell of the sea. In most respects Alexandria was a more pleasantly aromatic city than Rome.

Armed with my royal commission, I mounted the steps of the Museum. I wanted to pay another visit to the Temple, but on this morning I had more urgent business. I passed through the entrance and made my way past the lecture halls that resounded with the droning of the philosophers, down the long colonnade of the Peripatetics, back to the courtyard where Iphicrates's marvelous canal lock sat forlornly, unattended. This, I thought, was a project that might not see completion for a while.

I went into Iphicrates's quarters, which had been tidied up. The blood had been scrubbed from the floor and a pair of secretaries were scribbling away, collating the writings and drawings on a large desk. A third man wandered around the study with a puzzled expression.

"Is the inventory nearly complete?" I asked.

"Almost, Senator," said the elder of the two secretaries. "We will soon be finished with the drawings. This"—he indicated a papyrus lying on the table—"is the list of his writings and this"—

he pointed to another—"is a listing of all the objects we found in these quarters." I began to study the latter. It would have helped immeasurably to know what had been there *before* the murder, but this was better than nothing.

"And what might be your business?" I asked the third man. He was a Greek with a long nose and a bald head, dressed like the Librarians I had seen.

"I am Eumenes of Eleusis, Librarian of the Pergamese Books. I came here to find a scroll that the late Iphicrates borrowed from my department."

"I see. Was it by any chance a large scroll, of Pergamese skin-paper, with olive wood rollers, the handles stained vermilion?"

He looked surprised. "Why, yes, Senator. Have you seen it? I've been looking all morning."

"What is the subject of this book?" I asked, ignoring his question.

"Forgive me, Senator, but Iphicrates borrowed this book in strictest confidence."

"Iphicrates is dead, and I have been appointed to investigate. Now tell me—"

"Who are you?" interrupted someone from the doorway. Annoyed, I turned to see two men standing in the doorway. The one who had spoken I did not recognize. Just behind him stood a man who looked familiar.

I drew myself up. "I am Senator Decius Caecilius Metellus and I am investigating the murder of Iphicrates of Chios. Who might you be?"

The man came into the room, followed by the other. Now I remembered where I had seen that one. He was the hatchet-faced officer who had shooed me away from the parade ground.

"I am Achillas," said the first man, "Commander of the Royal Army." He wore studded boots and a rich, red tunic. Over that he wore one of those leather strap-harnesses that military men sometimes wear to give the appearance of armor, without having to endure its weight. His hair and beard were trimmed close all around.

"And I'm Memnon, Commander of the Macedonian Barracks," said the other. "We've met." They were both Macedonians, a nation of men who simply use their names, without the of-this-or-that the Greeks delight in so.

"So we have. And what are you two doing here?"

"By whose authority do you investigate?" demanded Achillas. I was ready for that one.

"The king's," I said, holding out my sealed document. He studied it through slitted eyes.

"That damned, drunken fool," he muttered. Then, to me: "What is your interest in this matter, Roman?"

"Rome is the friend of Egypt," I said, "and we are always pleased to render aid to King Ptolemy, Friend and Ally of the Roman People." I always loved this sort of diplomatic hypocrisy. "I am known in Rome as a skillful investigator of criminal acts, and I am more than happy to place my expertise at the service of the king." I refolded my commission and placed it inside my tunic, leaving my hand there for the nonce. Memnon pushed forward, glaring at me. He wore cuirass and greaves, but no helmet. I was intensely aware of the short sword belted at his side.

"You aren't wanted here, Roman," he growled. "Go back to your embassy and drink and fornicate like the rest of your worthless countrymen. This is Egypt."

At our first encounter we had been on his ground, surrounded by his soldiers. This was different.

"I am in the service not only of the Senate and People of Rome, but of their ally, your king. I believe that I am far more loyal to him than you are."

They always get that look in their eyes when they go for their weapons. With a strangled sound of rage he gripped his sheath with one hand and his hilt with the other. I was ready for that, too.

The blade was halfway out of its sheath when my own hand emerged from my tunic, now gripping my *caestus*. I fed him a good one, the spikes on the bronze knucklebar catching him on the jaw just in front of the ear. He staggered back with a grunt of amazement. I was amazed, too. I had never struck a man with my *caestus* without knocking him down. So I hit him again, on the same spot. This time he toppled amid a crash of bronze, like those heroes sung of by Homer.

The secretaries and the Librarian wore round-eyed expressions of surprise and fear. Hermes grinned happily, like the bloody-minded little demon that he was. Achillas looked very grave.

"You go too far, Senator," he said.

"*I* go too far? He attacked a Roman Senator, an ambassador. Kingdoms have been destroyed for that."

He shrugged. "A hundred years ago, perhaps. Not now." Well, that was true enough. With a visible effort, he calmed himself. "This is not a matter worth provoking a diplomatic crisis. You must understand, Senator, that it always vexes us to see Romans come here and assume authority as if by right."

"I quite understand," I said. "But I am here by authority of your king." On the floor, Memnon groaned.

"I had better see him to a physician," Achillas said.

"I recommend Asklepiodes," I said. "He's nearby. Tell him I sent you." He summoned a few slaves and they bore the fallen hero away. I still did not know why the two were there. They had been reluctant to say, and I thought it unwise to press the matter.

I turned back to the Librarian. "Now, you were about to tell me the nature of the missing book, were you not?" I slipped off my *caestus* and tossed it to Hermes. "Go wash the blood off that." I told him.

"Why . . . ah . . . that is . . ." Eumenes took a deep breath and calmed himself. "Actually, Senator, it is one of the more valuable works in the Library. It was written by Biton and dedicated to King Attalus I of Pergamum more than one hundred years ago."

"And its title?" I asked.

"*On Engines of War.*"

Hermes handed back my *caestus* as we left the Museum.

"That was as good as an afternoon in the amphitheater," he said. "But that was one tough Greek."

"Not Greek," I corrected. "Macedonian. An altogether tougher breed."

"I knew he was some sort of foreigner. You should have killed him. Now he'll be coming for you." Hermes had a delightfully simple way of looking at things.

"I'll talk to the king. Maybe I can get him posted up the river someplace. I am more concerned about Achillas. He's the ranking man in the royal army. See what you can find out about him."

I do some of my best thinking while walking, and I had much to think about. So, Iphicrates never designed military machines, did he? Obviously, he had been lying. Typical Greek. But I wondered why all the secrecy. It was not as if the activity were unlawful. There had to be more to it.

Before long, we found ourselves in the quarter of the Jews, an odd race with a paucity of gods. Other than that, they were much like other Easterners. Many thought it strange that their god had no image, but until a few centuries ago, there were no statues of Roman gods, either. The early Ptolemies had favored the Jews as a balance against the native Egyptians. There was some sort of ancient antipathy between the two. As a result, Jews had flocked to the city.

The streets were quiet and almost deserted, an odd thing in Alexandria. I asked at one of the open stalls and found that it was a day of religious observance for the Jews, one that they spent at home rather than in a temple. This was commendable piety but boring for the observer.

"There's other places in this city more lively," Hermes said.

"Unquestionably," I answered. "Let's go to the Rakhotis."

The Rakhotis was the Egyptian quarter, the largest in this most cosmopolitan of cities. It was easily the size of the Greek, Macedonian and Jewish quarters combined. In its own way, it was the oddest, to Roman eyes.

The Egyptians are the most ancient of peoples, and so profoundly conservative that they make the most reactionary Romans appear wildly mutable. The common subjects of the Ptolemies are identical to the ones you see painted in the temples of the oldest Pharaohs. They are short, sturdily built people, dark of skin, although not as dark as Nubians. The usual garment of the men is a kilt of white linen, and most wear short, square-cut black wigs. They rim their eyes with kohl for its supposed beneficial effects, believing that it protects the eyes. The old Egyptian nobility, of whom there are still a few specimens here and there, is of a different race, taller and fairer, although darker than Greeks or Italians. Their language is spoken nowhere outside Egypt.

To see them now makes it difficult for one to believe that these were the people who built the mind-stunning pyramids, but then the Greeks of today aren't much like the heroes of Homer, or even like their more recent ancestors of the Persian wars. The Egyptians take their religion very seriously, despite having some of the most supremely silly-looking gods in the world. Everybody thinks the animal-headed gods are hilarious, but my personal favorite is the one who is depicted dead and wrapped up like a mummy except for his face but who stands upright with an erect penis protruding from his wrappings.

In the Rakhotis we found the usual uproarious street scene, with hawkers plying their wares, animals being led to the markets, and the endless religious processions that are an inescapable part of Egyptian life. Here I was not simply sightseeing. I had a specific destination, but I didn't want to look as if I were investigating in this district.

Our first stop was the Great Serapeum. It was another example of the Cyclopean architecture that so delighted the Successors. Almost as large as the Temple of Diana at Ephesus, the Serapeum was dedicated to the god Serapis, who was himself an Alexandrian invention. The Successors thought they could do everything better than anyone else, including god-making. Alexandria was a new sort of city, and they wanted a god for their city who would blend Egyptian and Greek religious practice, so they concocted a god with the majestic, serene countenance of Pluto and melded him with the Egyptian gods Osiris and Apis, hence the name Serapis. For some reason this cobbled-together deity proved to be popular, and now he is worshipped throughout much of the world.

The Serapeum, like the Palace, forms a veritable city within a city, with livestock pens for the sacrificial animals, several cohorts of priests and attendants, rooms full of paraphernalia and treasures, fabulous art objects and even an arsenal and a private army to guard it all.

The temple itself was typical of the type, which is to say a standard Greek temple, only bigger. It sat on a lofty, man-made hill of stone, and the upper, visible part was always open to the public. It contained the statue of the god, which was surprisingly modest in its proportions. All this was for show. Since Serapis was an agglomeration of Chthonic deities, the actual worship was carried out in a series of underground crypts.

I strolled among these wonders, gawking like any other foreign tourist, but my attention was elsewhere. It was directed toward a smaller temple two streets south of the Serapeum. From it rose smoke as from a minor volcano, and the breeze carried the sounds of wailing song and clashing musical instruments. I stopped one of the priests, a man dressed in Greek sacerdotal garments, but with a leopard skin thrown over his shoulders in the Egyptian fashion.

"Tell me, sir," I said, "what god might be worshipped in that noisy temple over there?"

From the lofty eminence of the Serapeum he stared down his equally lofty nose at the temple in question.

"That is the Temple of Baal-Ahriman, although in better days it was a respectable temple of Horus. I would recommend that you avoid it, Senator. It is a cult brought here by unwashed foreigners, and only the lewdest and most degraded of Alexandrians frequent it. Their barbarous god is worshipped with disgusting orgies."

Hermes tugged at my arm. "Let's go! Let's go!"

"We shall, but only because it is within the scope of my investigation," I said.

We descended the majestic steps of the Serapeum and crossed two blocks to the Temple of Baal-Ahriman, which was thronged with worshippers, sightseers and idlers. It seemed that the inaugural festivities were still in progress. People danced to the clanging of cymbals and the rattle of sistra, the wailing of flutes and the thumping of drums. Many lay inert, worn out by their sanctified exertions.

Incense burned in huge bronze braziers all over the temple and its courtyards. It was needed, too. Fifty bulls produce a great deal of blood when they are sacrificed, far more than the gutters and drains of the temple were designed to cope with. The incense deadened the smell and kept down the flies a bit. The heads and hides of the bulls were mounted on stakes, facing inward toward the temple.

Like most Egyptian temples, it was rather cramped inside, what with the thick walls and the usual forest of squat pillars. At the utmost end was the statue of the seated god. Baal-Ahriman was about as ugly as a god can get without turning viewers to stone. His head was that of a lion that appeared to suffer from some form of leonine leprosy. The body was that of an emaciated man with withered female breasts, a little difficult to discern because he was still wearing his cloak of bulls' testicles. The flies were especially numerous in this inner sanctum.

"You have come to pay your respects to the great Baal-Ahriman?" I turned to see Ataxas, still draped with his snake.

"A Roman official always gives due respect to the gods of the lands he visits," I said. I took a pinch of incense from a huge bowl and tossed it onto the coals that glowed in a brazier before the disgusting thing. The resultant puff of smoke did very little to allay the stench.

"Excellent. My Lord is pleased. He harbors only the greatest love for Rome, and would like to be numbered among the gods worshipped in the greatest city in the world."

"I shall speak to the Senate about it," I said, mentally vowing to start a major war before allowing his ghastly death-demon to set a diseased paw within the gates of Rome.

"That would be splendid," he said, beaming greasily.

"Am I to understand," I inquired, "that the god is soon to speak to the faithful?"

He nodded solemnly. "That is true. Upon several occasions of late, my Lord has come to me in visions and has told me that he will soon make himself manifest among his worshippers. He will speak forth in his own voice, requiring no intermediary."

"I take it, then, that he will speak oracular pronouncements, which you will then interpret for the ears of the vulgar?"

"Oh, no, Senator. As I have said, he will require no intermediary. He will speak plainly."

"Since his original home was in Asia," I hazarded, "I presume that he will speak in one of the Eastern tongues?"

"My Lord has now made his home in Alexandria, and it is my belief that he will therefore speak in Greek."

"And the subject of his pronouncements?" I asked.

He shrugged. "Who may know what is the will of a god, until that will is made manifest? I am but his priest and prophet. Doubtless my Lord shall say that which he deems meet for men to hear."

Typical priestly prevarication.

"I shall look forward to his advent among men," I assured the scoundrel.

"I shall send word to the embassy should my Lord tell me that he is preparing to speak."

"I would appreciate that."

"Now, please be so good as to come with me, Senator. I am sure that you have not yet seen much of our new temple." Taking my arm, he gave me a tour of the building, explaining that the papyrus-headed capitals of the pillars were symbolic of Lower Egypt, as lotus capitals symbolized Upper Egypt. I already knew this, having taken the Nile tour, but I wanted the man in a forthcoming mood.

We passed through the back of the temple into the rear courtyard, where a feast was in progress. Great carcasses turned on spits over glowing coals. Like so many thoughtful gods, Baal-Ahriman desired only the blood of the sacrifice, and left the flesh for his worshippers.

"I beg you to partake of our feast," Ataxas said hospitably. "My calling forbids me the eating of flesh, but my Lord wishes his guests to enjoy themselves."

Sweating slaves stood beside the carcasses wielding curved, swordlike knives. As the spits rotated slowly, they shaved off papyrus-thin slices of the flesh and piled them on flat loaves of Egyptian bread. Hermes looked at me longingly and I nodded. He rushed off to snatch up one of the cakes, which he brought back to me rolled up around its dripping contents. Then he dashed back to get one for himself. A slave girl brought a tray laden with wine-cups and I took one. She was barely nubile, wearing one of those delightful Egyptian slave outfits consisting of a narrow belt worn low on the hips, from which depended a tiny apron of beaded strings. Aside from that, she wore a good many ornaments. This was one fashion I knew I would never succeed in transferring to Rome.

"Excellent wine," I commented.

"A gift from her Highness," Ataxas explained.

It had been a long time since breakfast and I had been re-gretting passing up Ptolemy's invitation to share his own, so the bread and sacrificial meat were doubly welcome.

"I take it you have heard about the murder of Iphicrates of Chios?"

He paused. "Yes, I have. It was most upsetting. Who would want to kill him?"

"Who, indeed? At Princess Berenice's reception the other evening, I noticed that the two of you were conversing. What were you talking about?"

He looked at me sharply. "Why do you ask?"

"The king has commissioned me to investigate the murder. I was wondering if Iphicrates might have said something to indicate that he had an enemy."

77

He relaxed. "I see. No, we had met at a number of royal receptions where we discussed the relative merits of our callings. He, a Greek philosopher and mathematician of the school of Archimedes, had a great disregard for the supernatural and the divine. He was known to say so loudly. We were merely carrying on a debate of long duration. I fear that he said nothing to indicate who might have had reason to kill him." He bowed his head and passed a few moments in what appeared to be deep thought. Then: "He did say one odd thing. He said, 'Some believe in the power of the gods, and some believe in magic, but when the kings of the East want to defy Rome, they consult with me, for in geometry lies the answer to all things.'"

"That is a curious statement," I said.

"Isn't it? I thought it was merely more of his philosophical pompousness, but perhaps not, eh?" He shook his head, making his long, oiled locks and curled beard sway. "Perhaps he was involved in things a philosopher ought to avoid. Now, Senator, I must prepare for the evening sacrifice. Please, stay and enjoy yourself. All that we have is yours." He gave that fluttering, Eastern bow and left. By this time Hermes had returned to my side and was tearing away at the bread-wrapped sacrificial meat.

"What do you think of him?" I asked Hermes.

"He's done well for himself," Hermes said, his mouth half full.

"Have you ever eaten beef before?"

"Just scraps, out at your uncle's country estate. It's tough, but I like the taste."

"Take some of the fruit and olives as well. Too much meat is bad for the digestion. But how does Ataxas impress you? It seemed to me that his Asiatic accent slipped a little while I was questioning him." One of the priestesses gyrated by us, clashing her tiny cymbals in time to the music. Her robes were shredded and her back was colorful with red stripes from the previous day's flogging.

"He still has chalk between his toes."

I paused in the middle of a bite. "He was a slave? How do you know?"

Hermes smiled with superior knowledge. "You saw that big ear-bangle he was wearing?"

"I saw it."

"He wears it to cover a split earlobe. In Cappadocia, a slave who runs has a notch cut out of his left earlobe." There is a whole world of slave lore most of us never learn.

5

"IT SOUNDS LIKE NONSENSE TO ME,"
Julia said. We stood on the steps of the Soma, the tomb of Alexander
the Great. She was beautifully dressed as a Roman lady, but she
had already started to use Egyptian cosmetics. It was a bad sign.

"Of course it's nonsense," I said. "When everybody is lying,
as they usually do when you're investigating a crime, the art is to
sort through the nonsense, and especially the things they *don't* say,
to find the truth."

"And why are you so sure Ataxas is lying? Just because he
was once a slave? Many freedmen have done well after earning
their freedom, and they usually don't brag about their former
status."

"Oh, it's not that. But he said that they were carrying on a
dispute of long standing. But I saw them together and it was the
only time that evening that Iphicrates kept his voice down. During
a *dispute!* You heard him. He bellowed at the top of his lungs
anytime anyone questioned him in the slightest fashion." And that

reminded me of something else: another man I would have to question.

"I admit it seems unlikely," she said. "Now what's this I hear about you assaulting the Commander of the Macedonian Barracks? Someone was complaining to the king about it. Are you incapable of staying out of trouble, even in Egypt?"

"The man was insolent, and he tried to draw his sword on me. You can't let foreigners get away with that sort of behavior."

"It isn't a good idea to make enemies, either, especially in a land where you have no stake in the status quo and where the local politics are unfathomable."

"Cautious good sense sounds strange coming from the niece of Julius Caesar."

"When Roman men are so reckless, sanity becomes the province of women. Let's go inside."

The Soma, as with so many of the marvels of Alexandria, was not a single building but rather a whole complex of temples and tombs. All of the Ptolemies were buried there, along with a number of other distinguished persons. At least, they were famous in their lifetimes. I had never heard of most of them. The Soma proper was the central structure, a magnificent house in the form of an Ionic temple that stood atop a lofty marble platform populated with an army of sculptured gods, goddesses, Macedonian royalty, soldiers and enemies. The kings Alexander had conquered were depicted on their knees in chains with collars around their necks. The roof was plated with gold, as were the capitals and bases of the columns. All was built of colorful marble drawn from all the lands Alexander had conquered.

At the entrance we found a small group of foreign visitors waiting to be shown the place. This tomb was sacred to the Ptolemies and you couldn't just go wandering through on your own. Before long a shaven-headed priest appeared. Instantly, he caught sight of Julia and me and he hurried over to us.

"Welcome, Senator, my lady. You are just in time for the next tour." I should hope so, I thought. You'd better not keep us waiting out here. The others showed him their appointments. We, of course, needed no such thing. It was a mixed group: a wealthy spice merchant from Antioch, a historian from Athens, an overpainted dowager from Arabia Felix, a priest or scholar of some sort from Ethiopia, nearly seven feet tall. This sort of gathering was not at all unusual in Alexandria. We passed through the massive, gold-covered doors into the interior.

The first thing to greet our eyes within was a huge statue of Alexander, seated on a throne and looking very lifelike but for the odd addition of a pair of ram's horns growing from his temples. In Egypt, Alexander was worshipped as the son of the god Ammon, whose tutelary animal was the ram. The boy-king was depicted as about eighteen years old, his long hair overlaid with gold. His eyes were extraordinarily blue, an effect I later learned the artist had achieved by inlaying the irises with layer on layer of granulated sapphire.

"Alexander of Macedon, surnamed the Great," the priest intoned, his voice echoing impressively, "died at Babylon in his thirty-third year, the 114th Olympiad, when Hegesias was Archon of Athens." I tried to remember who the Consuls of that year might have been, but I couldn't. "Before he went to join the immortal gods, he conquered more land than any other man in history, adding to the empire of his father the entirety of the Persian Empire and miscellaneous other lands. When he died his lands stretched from Macedonia to India to the Nile cataracts." Match that, Pompey, I thought.

"He died in mid-June," the priest went on, "and since the godlike Alexander had no adult heir, his body lay in state for a month, during which his generals settled the future of the Macedonian Empire. Then skilled Egyptians and Chaldeans were called in to embalm his mortal remains."

"They left him there for a *month?*" I said. "In *June?* In *Babylonia?*"

Julia dug an elbow into my ribs. "Shh!"

"Er, well, it may be that some thoughtful person drained the, ah, bodily fluids to aid the preservation and placed the king in some cool part of the palace. In any case, undoubtedly the body of Alexander was not as that of other men. He had joined the immortals, and it is likely that, as when the corpse of Hector was dragged behind the chariot of Achilles, his fellow gods preserved his body from deterioration."

"I would hope so," I said. "Must've made the whole palace uninhabitable, otherwise." Another jab from Julia.

"The body," the priest went on, "was swathed in Sidonian linen of the finest quality and then, as you shall soon see, was completely encased in plates of gold exquisitely wrought so as to preserve and display the exact contours of both frame and features. This was encased in a coffin, also of gold, with the spaces between filled with rare spices. The lid of the coffin, likewise of gold, was also wrought in the exact likeness of the late king.

"A funeral carriage was prepared, of a splendor never seen before or since. It was cunningly crafted to endure the shocks of travel through Asia. Its superstructure combined the elegance of Greece with the barbaric magnificence of Persia. On a throne base covered with a Tyrian carpet of fabulous weave lay the sarcophagus of Pantalic marble, carved by a master sculptor with episodes of the king's heroic life. The sarcophagus was protected by a cover of gold, over which was spread a purple robe, heavily embroidered with gold thread. Atop this were placed the arms of the king.

"Housing the sarcophagus was a mortuary chamber ten cubits by fifteen cubits in the shape of an Ionic temple, its proportions identical to the temple in which we now stand. Its columns and roof were of gold, embellished with precious gems. At each corner of the roof stood a statue of the winged victory wrought of gold. Instead of celia walls, the temple-chamber was surrounded with a golden net, so that the king's subjects could see his sarcophagus as the funerary procession passed by. The netting bore painted tablets, taking the place of an Ionic frieze. The tablet on the front portrayed Alexander in his state-chariot, with his Macedonian bodyguard on one side and his Persian bodyguard on the other. The tablet on one side displayed war-elephants following the king and his personal entourage. That on the other, cavalry in battle formation. The rear tablet showed ships of war ready for battle. Golden lions stood at the entrance of the mortuary chamber."

I was beginning to wonder whether there was any gold left in Alexander's empire. But there was more to come.

"Over the roof was a huge golden crown in the form of a conqueror's wreath. As the great vehicle moved, the rays of the sun were dashed from it like the lightning of Zeus. The car had two axles and four wheels. The Persian-style wheels were shod with iron, their spokes and naves overlaid with gold, the axles terminating in golden lions' heads, with golden arrows in their mouths." This, I was sure, had to be the end of it. But such was not to be.

"The funeral car was drawn by sixty-four selected mules. The mules wore gilded crowns, and golden bells on each cheek, and collars of precious cloth adorned with gold and gems. The carriage was accompanied by a staff of engineers and roadmenders and was protected by a select body of soldiers. The preparations for Alexander's last journey required two years.

"From Babylon the king traveled through Mesopotamia, into Syria, down to Damascus and then to the Temple of Ammon in Libya, where the god might behold his divine son. From there the funerary carriage was to proceed to Aegae in Macedonia, there to rest among the tombs of the former Macedonian royalty, but in crossing Egypt the procession was met by the king's former companion, Ptolemy Soter, who persuaded the leader of the procession to allow him to perform the final rites instead, at Memphis."

"Hijacked the body, eh?" I said. "Good for him. You wouldn't catch me letting that much gold leave my kingdom, either." Jab.

"The king lay at Memphis for a number of years," the priest went on, ignoring me, "until this splendid mausoleum could be completed. Then, amid much rejoicing and solemn ceremony, the king, Alexander the Great, found his final resting place in the city named for him."

He let us contemplate all this splendor for a while, then signaled for us to follow him again. We entered a room where Alexander's robes and armor were displayed, then another which held the marble sarcophagus the priest had described, along with the outer coffin with its wonderfully carved golden lid. After a few minutes of contemplation, he led us into the final chamber.

This was a room of relatively modest dimensions, perfectly circular, with a domed ceiling. In its middle lay Alexander, sheathed in thin, perfectly molded gold, looking as if he might wake up at any moment. After the Macedonian custom, he was laid out on a bed, this one carved from alabaster. I leaned toward Julia and whispered in her ear:

"Short little bugger, wasn't he?"

Unfortunately, the chamber was one of the magical sort that magnifies sound. My whispered words boomed out as if shouted by a herald. The priest and the other tourists glared at us as we made our embarrassed way out, bestowing effusive thanks and proclaiming our appreciation.

"Have you been drinking early again?" Julia demanded.

"I swear I haven't!"

I thought she was going to attack me, but she couldn't keep it up, and by the time we fell into our litter we were both laughing helplessly.

"Must be a lot more fun in there than it looks like from out here," Hermes said.

"To the Heptastadion!" I said, and the bearers hoisted us to their shoulders and off we went.

"Have you learned anything?" I asked Julia as we drifted through the streets.

"It's difficult to get Alexandrian ladies to talk about anything except religion and clothes. Nobody talks about politics in a monarchy."

"Forget the Alexandrians," I advised. "Work on the wives or other womenfolk of the foreign ambassadors, specifically the ambassadors of those yet independent nations that fear being the next additions to Rome's empire."

She looked at me sharply. "What have you learned?"

"Very little," I admitted, "but I suspect that Iphicrates, despite his protestations, ran a profitable sideline in designing weapons for our enemies or those who expect to become our enemies soon. Parthia would be a good place to start. Now that the nearer East is subdued, King Phraates is the one who has Pompey and Crassus and, forgive me, your uncle barking at the gates like so many starving Molossian hounds. The last truly rich kingdom left independent."

"Except for Egypt," she said.

"Egypt isn't . . . well, Egypt is nominally independent, but that's a joke."

"Perhaps it isn't funny to the Egyptians. They're only poor because the recent generations of Ptolemies have been stupid. Once they were the mightiest nation in the world. The Pharaohs ruled in Egypt when the Greeks besieged Troy. What nation that has fallen from power doesn't dream of regaining it?"

"A good question. That would explain Achillas's interest in Iphicrates. But whatever the military gentry is up to, it's still stuck with the Ptolemies. Everyone except Egyptians considers brother-sister marriage an abomination. Such matings seem to work well enough with horses, but not with humans. It certainly hasn't improved the Ptolemaic line."

"Degenerate dynasties are easily toppled by strong men who have the army behind them," she said. Leave it to a Caesar to take the pragmatic view of power politics.

"But the Egyptians are awfully conservative. They prize their royalty even if they weren't Egyptian to begin with. An Alexandrian mob toppled the Ptolemy before this one just because he murdered his rather aged wife, one of the Berenices. What would they do to a usurper, who wasn't even a part of the family?"

"I'll look into his pedigree," she said practically. "I'll wager he has some sort of family connection. And the traditional way for a usurper to legitimize his power is to marry into royalty. There is a selection of princesses, you'll recall. Besides, he could ease his way into power by acting as regent for young Ptolemy."

Caesars can be frightening people. She had worked all this out since hearing of my run-in with Achillas and Memnon, while I was sniffing around the Serapeum, eating sacrificial beef and ogling bloody-backed priestesses. These absorbing speculations were interrupted by our arrival at the Heptastadion.

"It's the longest bridge in the world," I told her as we were carried across. "Almost a Roman mile." It divided the Great Harbor to the east from the Eunostos Harbor to the west. We paused over the central arches and marveled as several ships passed from one harbor to the other without having to lower their masts.

Back in our litters, we traversed the rest of the causeway to the island of Pharos, which had its own small town, complete with several lovely temples, including the one to Poseidon and another to Isis. At the extreme eastern spit of land we climbed from our litters at the base of the lighthouse. Seen up close, it was oddly unimpressive. That was because the step-back of its construction made its great height invisible. All one could see was a rather massive wall that did not at first seem to be terribly high. We went inside and were shown the dizzying central shaft, which terminated in a tiny dot of light so far overhead that it seemed that the tower was in danger of scraping the underside of the sun. Amid a great mechanical clatter a huge basket of iron and timber was lowered at intervals to be filled with wood for the fire basket overhead. Since Egypt was so poor in native wood, most of it was shipped in from the islands and from the mainland to the west. Ashes were dumped down a chute into a waiting barge, which took them out to sea for disposal.

We turned down an offer to ride up in the wood basket and instead climbed an endless ramp that wound up the inner sides of the base. For Julia, recently arrived from the hilly terrain of Rome, it was an easy climb. I had been living the soft life and was puffing and sweating by the time we walked out onto the first terrace. Even on this lowest section of the lighthouse we stood higher than the highest temple roofs of the city. The stone spire soared interminably above us, its peak sending up smoke into the clear air. Julia leaned back and shaded her eyes, trying to see the top.

"I almost wish I'd had the courage to ride up," she said wistfully.

"It isn't natural for people to ascend so high," I said. "However, if you want to climb the steps up there, I'll wait for you here."

"No," she said, "the view from here is splendid enough. You can see the whole city, from the Hippodrome to the Necropolis. You can see all the way to Lake Mareotis. It's all so orderly, like a picture painted on a wall."

"It does seem so," I said. "It's hard to believe that in the midst of all that order, something very peculiar and dangerous is happening. At least Rome *looks* like a place where awful things are happening all the time."

"I wouldn't have put it that way."

"Julia, I want to get to know Princess Berenice better."

"Why?" she said suspiciously.

"We need to talk religion."

That evening we were rowed from the royal harbor in the curve of Cape Lochias to the gemlike palace on the Antirrhodos Island. This was an even more frivolous place than the Great Palace, strictly a pleasure retreat, wanting even a throne room or any other place for conducting public business. Berenice was throwing another of her endless parties for the fashionable set. Ptolemy and Creticus weren't attending, but I went, along with Julia, Fausta and a number of the embassy staff. The parties on the island were legendary because they were without even such feeble restraints as the Great Palace insisted upon.

It was in full roar when we got there, as the setting sun made an imperial purple mantle of the western sky and the torches were being kindled. Music made the evening riotous, and we were helped from our boat by pseudo-Maenads costumed, if that is the word, in leopard skins and vine leaves, wearing masks. Men dressed as satyrs chased naked nymphs through the gardens while acrobats walked on tightropes stretched between the wings of the palace.

"My father would never approve," Julia said, wide-eyed. "But then, my father isn't here."

"That's the spirit," I commended her. "I wish Cato was here, just so I could watch him drop dead from apoplexy." Berenice came out to greet us, leading a half-dozen tame cheetahs on leashes.

The Egyptians are fond of cats of all sorts, from lions down to the little house cats that seem to own the towns. So devoted are they to these little beasts that, when one dies, it is mourned exactly as if a member of the family had died. The punishment for killing one was the same as for murder. It seemed odd to me that people would want little lions running around the house, but in recent years they have become popular even in Rome. They are said to be good at catching mice.

Berenice gushed the usual welcomes and compliments and urged us to loosen up and have a good time, something I was quite prepared to do. Instead of tables where guests could recline to eat, there were small tables everywhere heaped with rare delicacies. Slaves carried pitchers of wine and everyone stood or wandered about, eating, drinking and talking as long as they could remain upright. Besides the human servants, there were more of the liveried baboons. They were not very efficient as servers, but they were better behaved than many of the guests.

I wanted to speak with Berenice, but the big cats she led made me nervous. I knew that these tame cheetahs behaved like hunting dogs, but somehow they looked unnatural on leashes. So I left Julia and Fausta with the princess and made my way into the palace. It had all the marks of a long evening, so there was no rush about cornering the woman.

I had never been to the Island Palace before, and found it very much to my taste. The proportions were almost Roman in their acknowledgment of human stature. The rooms were not vast echoing halls, and their decoration was calculated to enhance rather than to overwhelm.

The same could not be said of the guests and the entertainment. In an open court was a pool in which a muscular youth wrestled with a medium-sized crocodile, splashing the guests almost as copiously as the pair of hippos who shared the water. Some guests, overcome with excitement, leapt into the pool and disported themselves after the fashion of naiads, diving beneath the surface and coming up to spout water on unsuspecting passersby. I watched for a while, hoping that the wrestler would lose his hold and the crocodile make a lunge for the naiads. That would have been even more exciting. However, the youth trussed up the reptile with cords and carried it off amid much applause.

In another courtyard a team of Cretan dancers, elaborately costumed, went through one of their famed productions concerning the scabrous doings of the Olympian deities, with startling realism. I climbed to a second-floor gallery for a better view. Below, on an elaborate stage, were being enacted the legends of Leda and the swan, Europa and the bull, Ganymede and the eagle, Danae and the shower of gold (an incredible piece of costuming), Pasiphae inside the artificial cow designed by Daedalus, and a few probably known only to Greeks. I managed to tear my eyes away from this edification long enough to notice that I wasn't alone. A girl of about ten leaned on the railing and watched all this with solemn interest.

She was a beautiful child, with skin like alabaster and the reddish hair that is common among Macedonians. Her garments and jewels were rich. Clearly, this was a daughter of a noble family, strayed from her keeper.

"Aren't you a little young for this sort of entertainment?" I asked. "Where is your nurse?" She turned and regarded me with enormous green eyes. They were the most beautiful eyes I ever saw in a human face.

"My sister says that I must learn how the noble peoples of many lands comport themselves. I have been attending these receptions of hers for some time now." Her speech was not the least bit childish.

"I take it, then, that you are the Princess Cleopatra?" She nodded, then turned back to the spectacle below.

"Do people really behave this way?" On the stage, something

91

that looked like a dragon was mounting Andromeda, who was chained to a rock. I didn't remember that part of the legend of Perseus.

"You shouldn't concern yourself with the doings of supernatural beings," I advised her. "You'll find that what goes on between men and women is quite confusing enough." She turned from the dancers and looked me over with a calculation disturbing to see in one so young.

"You're a Roman, aren't you?" she said in excellent Latin.

"I am. Decius Caecilius Metellus the Younger, Senator, presently attached to the embassy, at your service." I gave her the slight bow Roman officials are permitted.

"I never heard the name Decius used as a *praenomen*. I thought it was a *nomen*." She was inordinately well taught.

"It was introduced into my family by my grandfather, who was sent a vision by the Dioscuri."

"I see. I have never been granted a vision. My sister sees them all the time." I could well believe that.

"Your Latin is excellent, Princess. Do you speak other languages?"

"Besides Latin and Greek, I speak Aramaic, Persian and Phoenician. What is it like, being a Roman?" This was an odd question.

"I am not sure I understand, Princess."

"You rule the world. The Roman officials I've seen comport themselves as arrogantly as the kings of most lands. Does it feel different, knowing that the world lies at your feet?" I had never been asked such a question by a ten-year-old.

"We don't really rule the world, Highness, just a very great part of it. As for our arrogance, we prize the qualities of *dignitas* and *gravitas* highly. We of the governing class are taught them from earliest youth. We don't tolerate foolishness in public men."

"That is good. Most people tolerate any sort of behavior in one whose birth is high enough. I heard that you knocked Memnon down yesterday with a single blow."

"Word does get around. Actually, it took two to put him down."

"I am glad. I don't like him."

"Oh," I said.

"Yes. He and Achillas are too presumptuous for their station. They treat my family with disrespect."

This was something to ponder. At that moment some of the guests stormed the stage and began ripping the costumes from the dancers amid excited laughter and shouted encouragement.

"Princess, despite your sister's advice, I think you should retire. You are far too young to be here alone, and some of these people have taken leave of whatever senses they had."

"But I am not alone," she said, nodding slightly to the shadowed gallery behind her. Suddenly I was aware that someone stood there, still as a statue.

"Who are you?" I asked. A youth of about sixteen stepped forward, his arms folded.

"I am Apollodorus, Senator."

He was a fine-looking boy, with curly black hair and handsome features that bore the unmistakable stamp of Sicily. He wore a brief chiton belted with a short sword and had leather bands at his wrist and ankles. He had that relaxed, almost limp bearing that you only see in the most highly trained athletes, but this was no mere *palaestra*-trained pretty boy. He had the mark of the *ludus* all over him, although I had never seen them in one so young.

"What school?" I asked.

"The *ludus* of Ampliatus in Capua," he said. That made sense.

"A good choice. They teach boxing and wrestling there as well as swordsmanship. If I wanted a bodyguard for my daughter, that's where I would send him."

The boy nodded. "I was sent there when I was ten. The king had me brought back five months ago, when he decided that the princess was to move to Alexandria." He turned to Cleopatra. "The Senator is right, Highness. You had better go inside now." His tone was easy, but I could hear adoration in every inflection.

"Very well," she said. "I really can't understand why people act in such a fashion anyway." Just wait, I thought.

I bade her good evening and made my way down to the party once more. In later years Marcus Antonius was reviled for being so besotted with Cleopatra, forgetting Rome and everything else to serve her. They thought him weak and unmanly. But I knew Cleopatra when she was ten, and poor Antonius never had a chance.

I was beginning to feel the need of something to go with the wine. On a broad marble table was coiled a gigantic sausage, made from the intestines of an elephant stuffed with the sweet flesh of waterfowl. It smelled delicious, but the appearance was horrifying. A slave offered me a skewer strung with the bloated bodies of huge locusts. These are a great delicacy in the desert, but scarcely to Roman taste. Luckily, I encountered a tray of pork ribs simmered in *garum* before starvation set in. I feasted on these and other agreeable items and felt ready to face the balance of the evening.

The sound of clashing weapons drew me to a lawn where athletes were putting on an exhibition of swordsmanship. These were not true gladiators, for there were none in Egypt in those days. They were skillful and pleasant to watch, but none of them would have lasted a minute in an Italian amphitheater. I saw Fausta and Berenice watching them. To my relief, the cheetahs were gone.

"This is a most extraordinary event, Highness," I said to Berenice.

"We do our best. Fausta was just telling me about the gladiator fights she and her brother put on at her father's funeral games. Our priests and philosophers and such would never allow death-fights here, I'm afraid. They sound thrilling."

"The *munera* are an integral part of our religion," I told her. "Other people sometimes find the fights a bit strong for their tastes."

"We showed a thousand pairs fighting over a period of twenty days," Fausta said, "not to mention hundreds of lions and tigers and rhinoceroses, along with the more common bears and bulls. The Senate protested the extravagance, but who cares about them?" Spoken like a true daughter of Sulla. "Of course, women are supposed to be forbidden to attend the *munera*, but we do anyway. I find them far more enjoyable than the chariot races."

"Each has its advantages," I said. "You can bet openly on the races, for instance, while it's frowned on at the fights. Speaking of religious matters," I said cleverly, "I would be most interested in hearing the princess tell how she found the holy man Ataxas and his god, Baal-Ahriman." Fausta looked at me quizzically. This was the last subject she would have expected me to bring up.

"Ah, it was so marvelous! I was in my garden in my Alexandrian palace just before the last floods, when the image of Horus spoke to me."

"Spoke to you?" I said, with a conscious effort to keep my eyebrows level.

"Yes, very clearly. He said, 'Daughter, I proclaim the advent of a new god to rule over the Red Land and the Black. His prophet will appear in your court before the floods. Receive him as befits one sent by the immortal gods of Egypt.' "

"And that was all?" I asked. In most accounts, the gods are wordier.

"It was enough," she said.

"And did the god's mouth, or rather his beak, move as he spoke?" Perhaps I should explain that Horus is one of the less repellent of the Egyptian gods, having the noble head of a falcon.

"I did not notice. I prostrated myself at his feet the moment he began to speak. Even a princess must abase herself before a god."

"Quite understandable," I assured her.

"You can imagine my transports of joy when the Holy Ataxas arrived to proclaim the truth of Baal-Ahriman. He was quite modest and unassuming, you know. He was astonished when I told him that Horus had already announced his coming."

"Indeed, indeed. And has he manifested greater than normal powers since his arrival?"

"Of course. He has healed many believers of afflictions such as deafness and palsy. He has bidden other statues to speak, and they have, foretelling a brilliant future for Egypt. But he claims no special powers for himself. He says that he is the mere conduit for the glorious might of Baal-Ahriman." When she spoke of Ataxas, her eyes seemed to disengage from each other, as if seeing something infinitely far away, or else seeing nothing at all.

"You say a 'brilliant future.' Is there any indication of the nature of this brilliance?"

"No, but I believe that is to be the matter of the divine words we shall soon hear from Baal-Ahriman himself."

I had more questions, but at that moment the majordomo arrived, gasping for breath. Another eunuch.

"Princess, a hippo has left the pond and is attacking the Cretan dancers!"

"They probably think it's Zeus in disguise again," I said, "looking for another mortal woman to ravish. If he gets any volunteers, this might be worth seeing."

"Oh, I suppose I must attend to it," Berenice said. "Seti, summon the guards. Tell them to bring long spears. They can probably poke the beast back into the pond. It is not to be harmed. It is sacred to Taveret."

"There goes the reason why the gods frown upon incest," I said when she was gone.

"Rome is full of eccentrics, too," Fausta said. "It just seems sillier in foreign royalty."

"I suppose so. But if Horus wanted to proclaim the coming of a new god, why not to Ptolemy? Why choose his deranged daughter?"

"I take it you find her story difficult to accept?"

"Decidedly. Divine visitations are common enough in legend, but they always sound more plausible in the age of heroes. Mind you, my own grandfather was visited by the Dioscuri, but that was in a dream and I think he'd been drinking."

"Why this sudden interest in religion, Decius? Surely being in Egypt hasn't infected you with their odd passions?" A true daughter of Sulla, Fausta believed in very little save greed and the lust for power.

"Religion is powerful and dangerous, Fausta. That's why we Romans harnessed it to the service of the state centuries ago. That's why we made the priesthoods a part of the civil service. It's why we forbade consultation of the Sybilline Books except in extreme situations, and only then at the behest of the Senate."

"Your point being?"

"The most dangerous sort of religion is the volatile, emotional sort peddled by charismatic holy men like Ataxas. They have a way of making their short-term prophecies come true by inciting their fanatical followers to *make* them come true. People are unbelievably credulous. You notice that he heals deafness and palsy, afflictions easy to simulate. I'll wager he's never restored an amputated hand or foot."

"You wouldn't be interested if it was just some fraud enriching himself at the expense of fools," she asserted. "Do you detect a power play at work here?"

"I feel sure of it, although I am mystified as to its actual nature."

"Why do you care anything about the affairs of Egypt?" she asked.

"Because virtually anything that happens here touches upon Roman interests. Whatever Ataxas is up to, it can't be anything good. It would seem a pity to send in the legions to settle things here when a simple exposure of a plot might solve the problem."

Fausta smiled. "Julia says that you are mad but very interesting. I'm beginning to see what she means." No sooner had she pronounced this enigmatic statement than the lady herself showed up.

"This affair is getting utterly out of hand," Julia said. "Decius, I think we should return to the embassy."

"You talk as if the two of you were married already," Fausta observed.

"Will you come with us?" Julia asked Fausta, not bothering to inquire whether I wished to leave.

"I think I'll stay," Fausta said. "I've always heard about the debauchery of the Egyptian court, and this is a chance for a close look. Go on, you two. Enough of the Roman embassy staff remains for the sake of decorum." Actually, most of them had passed out or were well on their way, but I never doubted Fausta's ability to take care of herself.

We boarded a barge for the short row back to the Palace wharf.

"I've just had an interesting conversation with the concubine of the Parthian ambassador," Julia said.

"He didn't bring his wife, I take it?" I said.

"No. Wives and children must be left behind in Parthia against the ambassador's good behavior."

"The poor man. And what did this consolationary female have to say?"

"By great good luck she is a highly educated Greek *hetaira*. The ambassador's Greek is deficient, and she helps him with documents written in that language. Most of it is the usual tedious embassy business, but recently she read for him certain illustrated documents which he translated into Parthian. He sent the originals and translation to King Phraates in a locked chest under heavy guard."

I felt the familiar angling, the one I always get when an important bit of the puzzle clicks into place. "And the nature of these documents?"

"They were plans for war machines. She could make nothing of the drawings, and most of the text was in technical language she wasn't familiar with, but there was some sort of device for setting fire to ships, and others for breaching walls and hurling missiles. There was also a receipt for a large sum of money in payment for these plans. The money was paid to Iphicrates of Chios. She thought it a great coincidence that he was murdered so soon after."

"Remind me never to entrust my secrets to a talkative Greek woman. Did she recall anything else?"

"This came out in the middle of a great gush of words concerning all the details of her life. I thought it would be unwise to press her about it. Easterners never listen to women, and she was dying for somebody to talk to." This, as it turned out, was an unfortunate choice of words.

6

"THE MAN'S NAME IS EUNOS," Amphytrion said. "He is from Rhodes and was personal valet to Iphicrates for two years."

"Can he read?" I asked.

"Of course. All the Museum slaves assigned to personal service must meet certain standards of education. After all, if one must send a slave from a lecture hall to fetch a certain book, he must be able to recognize it."

"Sensible," I said. "Tell me, do you know whether the General Achillas or any other of the military nobles paid frequent visits to Iphicrates?"

He looked at me as if I had taken leave of my senses. "Meaning no disrespect to his Majesty's noble servants, the military men are an ignorant lot of Macedonian mountain bumpkins. Why would they consort with a scholar like Iphicrates?"

"Was Iphicrates ever absent for extended periods?" I asked.

"Why, yes. He took monthly trips by boat upon the river,

taking measurements of the water's rise and fall and observing the effects of flowing water upon the banks. He was deeply interested in the dynamics of water. You saw the canal lock he was designing."

"Yes, I did. What was the duration of these trips?"

"I fail to see the pertinence of these questions, but he always took six days at the beginning of each month for these journeys."

"Is that a common sort of arrangement here?" I asked.

"Within reasonable limits, our scholars have perfect freedom to pursue their studies as they see fit. They need not even give lectures if they do not wish to. Here in the Museum, our goal is pure knowledge."

"Most commendable," I murmured. I was beginning to have severe doubts concerning the purity of Iphicrates's knowledge. There was a knock at the door and a middle-aged Greek entered, dressed in the livery tunic of the Museum. He bowed to Amphytrion and to me, then waited with that dignified self-possession common to slaves conscious of their own superiority in slave society.

"Eunos, the Senator wishes to question you concerning the late Iphicrates of Chios."

"Eunos," I began, "did you attend Iphicrates on the night of his murder?"

"Yes, Senator. I helped him prepare to go to the banquet that night, then he dismissed me. As I was walking down the gallery toward my quarters, he called me back and told me to bring some extra lamps. I did as he directed and set the lamps in his study. I was about to light them, but he dismissed me and I left."

"Had you any indication why extra lamps were required when he was about to attend a banquet?"

"He had a visitor. I had not heard the man arrive."

"Did you get a look at him?" I asked.

"When I came in with the lamps, the man was sitting in the bedroom to the rear. The light was dim. He seemed to be medium-sized, with dark hair and beard trimmed in the Greek fashion. He did not look my way. That was all I saw."

"Do you remember anything else that might help to identify

this stranger? Anything else Iphicrates might have done that was unusual?"

"I am sorry, sir. No, there was nothing else." I dismissed him and sat pondering for a while. It didn't surprise me that the man had not come forth earlier. Any intelligent slave knows better than to volunteer information unless asked. Amphytrion had less excuse for not asking, but that was understandable, too. It would have been beneath his philosophical dignity to listen to a slave.

"I would like another look at Iphicrates's quarters," I told Amphytrion as I rose from my chair.

"Be my guest, Senator, but we must remove Iphicrates's belongings soon. The distinguished scholar of music, Zenodotos of Pergamum, is to arrive soon and we shall need those rooms."

I found Asklepiodes finishing up an anatomy lesson and persuaded him to accompany me. We found the study in good order, the completed inventory arranged neatly on the large table. I picked up one of the silver bowls.

"You said that Iphicrates was doing research into the properties of parabolic mirrors," I said. "Just what are the properties of these things, besides concentrating light?"

"They also concentrate heat," Asklepiodes said. "Come, I'll demonstrate." We went out into the courtyard and he squinted at the angle of the sun. With the reflector, he cast a disc of light against the side of the now-abandoned canal lock. Then he drew it back. As he did so, the disc shrank until it was an intensely bright spot the size of a copper *as*. "Put your hand there and you will see what I mean."

Gingerly, I slid my hand along the wooden surface until the tiny disc of light rested in my palm. It felt distinctly warm, but not hot enough to be distressing.

"To what use did Archimedes put these devices?" I asked.

"It is said that he set fire to Roman ships with them."

"Do you think that is possible? It doesn't seem to make all that much heat."

"These are miniatures. The ones Archimedes used would have

been larger than shields. And he used a great many, perhaps a hundred of them lined up atop the harbor walls of Syracuse. With that many concentrating their light, I believe they might well have succeeded in firing attacking ships. Ships are extremely combustible at the best of times."

So for a while we experimented with the four silver bowls. With the light of all four concentrated on a single spot, we managed to coax some faint wisps of smoke from the wood. Back inside, I went over the inventory lists, trying to find anything that might offer a clue to just what the infuriating pedant had been up to.

"Items: a box of miscellaneous rope samples, each sample labeled," I read. "What do you think that means?" So we rooted around until we found the box beneath the cable. It contained scores of pieces of rope, variously twisted and braided and of various materials, both animal and vegetable fibers being used. Each sample was about a foot long, and from each dangled a papyrus label adorned with shorthand lettering and strings of numerals.

Asklepiodes selected a handful. "These are made of human hair," he said. "What might be the use of such ropes?"

I studied the labels, trying to piece together their meaning. "Human hair is said to make the best rope for torsion-style catapults. The women of Carthage sacrificed their tresses to build war engines during the siege. Scipio conquered a city of bald-headed women. Look here: These abbreviations give the race and nation of each donor. The man was obsessive about detail."

"And the numbers?" For once, even Asklepiodes was at a loss.

I pondered them a while. "I think they measure the weight or tension at which the ropes finally broke. How he could determine such things I've no idea." If my guesses about his shorthand were correct, the hair of black Africans rated the lowest in this regard, while the hair of blond German women was the strongest and most resilient. None of the vegetable fibers or cords of animal hide were as good as hair. Even silk, while strong, had deficiencies in the torsion department because it was, if I translated correctly, "too stretchy." Besides, it was far too expensive.

I told Asklepiodes what the slave had said. "At least now we have a description of the killer, however sketchy."

"Medium-sized, dark hair and beard of Greek cut . . . that certainly narrows the field. Surely there can be no more than twenty or thirty thousand men of that description in Alexandria."

"And among them is General Achillas," I pointed out.

"A tenuous connection at best."

"It's enough for me," I maintained. "A man of that description is in Iphicrates's quarters on the evening of his murder. The next day, Achillas shows up without warning or reason and objects to my prying into the killing."

"Persuasive, but far from conclusive," Asklepiodes said.

"There's more. A few days ago, in a spirit of idle curiosity, I wandered into the parade ground of the Macedonian barracks. I noticed some sort of war engine under construction and went for a closer look. That lout Memnon ran me off, very rudely. I'll wager that, were we to go by the parade ground now, we would find that the engine has disappeared."

"If, as you seem to suspect, Iphicrates was designing engines of war for Achillas, why would he murder the man?"

"That has me puzzled," I admitted. "It could be because Achillas was approaching other kings with his designs. That could have violated some agreement the two had. I have learned that he accepted a large sum of money from Phraates of Parthia for certain designs."

"And yet," Asklepiodes said, "these activities of Achillas; are they illegal or understood to be some sort of provocation?"

"They could be so construed. Our foreign policy can be a complex matter. Once an allied king has accepted our help and protection, we assume leadership in military matters. That is our right as the greatest race of soldiers in the world. When we see such a king strengthening his defenses, we must assume that he is strengthening them against us since, with our aid, he has no one else to fear."

Asklepiodes made one of those throat-clearing sounds that denote skepticism. "It may be that, flying in the face of all reason, some kings are less confident in the security of Roman protection than are you."

"Oh, I'll admit that they sometimes suffer the odd massacre or city sacking before the legions can come to their aid, but overall, the system is reliable. Sometimes, as a gesture of confidence, we have them demolish a part of the capital city's walls. That way, when they begin to rebuild them without informing us first, we know they are up to something. The agreement with Egypt is not that formal, but this sudden interest in improved armaments is most suspicious."

"Are there no other enemies who might justify such preparations?"

"Now that old Mithridates is dead and Tigranes has had his teeth pulled, there is no one. Parthia is too far away."

"An uprising by disaffected nobles, perhaps? I have heard rumors that some of the nomes are in arms and defying Alexandria."

"That's a job for infantry and cavalry," I said. "I've toured much of the land down to the first cataract. There are no fortifications to speak of. That part of Egypt is protected by the desert from foreign invasion. The only walled towns are up here in the delta area, and all of them are under Ptolemy's control."

"It seems, then, that you have good reasons for your suspicions. Now, what do you propose to do about them? Your superiors are not the sort of men to take hasty action."

"No, I have to gather more evidence. I have an utterly unjustified reputation as a troublemaker, and they'll look with skepticism on anything I bring them that isn't more concrete than what I already have."

"And how do you propose to assemble this information?"

"I think a bit of travel is called for."

I took my leave of Asklepiodes and went to the Library. The

immense place was full of the dusty smell of books and the droning sound of scholars reading. Despite the size and massiveness of the building, the interior was not dim, abundant light being admitted by its extraordinarily large clerestory and numerous skylights of clearest glass. All the interior marble was white, to make best use of the admitted light. There were many statues of the various gods of learning: Apollo, Athena, ibis-headed Thoth and others, as well as busts of the great philosophers. The walls were lined up to the clerestory with lozenge-shaped cells holding scrolls like so many wine jars, each cell labeled with its contents.

By asking attendants, I was guided to the Wing of the Pergamese Books and found Eumenes of Eleusis overseeing the copying of some of his precious scrolls.

"May I help you, Senator?" he inquired politely.

"I hope that you may. The book that disappeared from the study of the late Iphicrates; you said it was by Biton, and entitled *On Engines of War?*"

"That is so."

"Might you have a copy?"

He nodded gravely. "Yes. We have copies made of every book that comes to the Library. This spares excessive handling of the more valuable originals."

"Yet Iphicrates insisted upon the original?"

"He was most insistent. He said that he did not wish to cope with the inevitable copier's errors."

"I see. Might I have a look at a copy?"

"Certainly, Senator." I followed him to a nook where scores of scrolls rested in their racks, labels dangling from their handles. He scanned the rack expertly and plucked a scroll from its resting place. It was a good deal smaller than the massive original I had seen in Iphicrates's study.

"Is it in a single volume?" I asked.

"Yes, it isn't a lengthy work. If you wish to peruse it, please unroll it carefully It probably hasn't been looked into since it was made here nearly a century ago."

"How does the Museum happen to have the original, since it was dedicated to Attalus I of Pergamum? I would think it would be among the Pergamese collection." The rulers of Pergamum had founded a library in imitation of the Alexandrian, and in those days it still had a reputation second only to the original.

"An earlier Ptolemy . . . ah . . . borrowed it in order to have a copy made. Through an oversight, an excellent copy was returned, rather than the original."

"Has this been a common oversight?" I asked.

"Well, we do have several thousand original manuscripts from that library."

It figured. King or foot soldier, all Macedonians are thieves.

"There are a number of vacant tables, Senator, if you wish to read the book now."

"Actually, I would rather take it to the embassy and read it at my leisure, if that is permitted."

"We really prefer not to lend volumes outside the Library, Senator. Now that the original has disappeared, this is the only copy we have."

"If my investigation is successful," I said, "I think it very likely that I will be able to return the original to you." I kept the scroll in a tight grip.

"Well, that being the case, and in view of our sovereign's eagerness to please Rome in any way he may, I think we can make an exception in this case."

"You have my heartiest thanks, and those of the Senate and People of Rome," I assured him.

Back at the embassy. I called on Creticus. I found him going over correspondence from Rome and elsewhere in the Empire.

"If you don't mind, sir, I think I'd like to take a few days to do some hunting."

He looked up suspiciously. "Since when did you like to do anything more strenuous than watch other people race chariots? What are you up to?"

"I just need a bit of exercise. Too much of the good life, as it were."

"It's not as if you do much necessary work around here. Will you take Julia with you?"

"I don't think that would be proper, sir. We're not married yet."

"You're concerned about *respectability?* Now I know you're hiding something. What happened to this murder investigation of yours?"

"It will hold for a few days."

"Go, then. Stay out of trouble."

Hermes was no less amazed when I told him.

"Hunting?" he said. "You mean, hunting *animals?*"

"What else is there to hunt? Except for runaway slaves?"

"You've never done this before."

"All the more reason to start now. Go find us some hunting gear. This place has clothing and equipment for every sort of activity. We leave tomorrow as soon as it's light enough to see." Muttering and shaking his head, he went to do my bidding.

I found a comfortable corner and a pitcher of wine and settled down to delve into Biton's book. I slipped off its stiff leather cover and carefully began to unroll the crackling scroll. Unlike the original, this copy was made on Egyptian papyrus, another reason for its reduced bulk.

Biton began with a disquisition upon the history of war machines. These had been relatively rare and simple among the Babylonians and Egyptians and even rarer among the early Greeks. The Greek army that besieged Troy had not used them except for the wooden horse, which was not the same thing. But as men increasingly fought over fortified cities, these engines became necessary. At first they were mere towers for storming walls, covered galleries on wheels to protect rammers, and the various forms of missile-hurling device. Alexander's battles had mostly been of the open-field sort, and he had rarely resorted to engines.

Then came the Successors. These men had no new land to conquer, but they fought interminably among themselves over the carcass of Alexander's empire. This consisted primarily of seizing each other's ports, fortresses and capital cities. Such warfare called for engines, and to this endeavor the Successors brought the same mania for size and complexity that they brought to building.

Most notable of these was Demetrius Poliorcetes, "the Besieger," son of Antigonus One-Eye and the greatest military hobbyist of all time. He designed some of the strangest and certainly the largest engines of war ever conceived. He mounted storming towers on yoked ships for assaulting harbor walls. He built towers a hundred feet high equipped with dozens of catapults and completely plated with iron.

Others were not far behind. Dionysus, tyrant of Syracuse, had formed a sort of academy of military arts where the best engineers worked on engines and new designs of warship and new types of weapons and armor.

All this military experimentation had come to an end with the ascendancy of Rome. We beat them all because we knew that the ultimate weapon is the Roman legionary and the organization of the Roman legion. With them, even mediocre generals turn in victory after victory with monotonous regularity. An inspired general like (even now I hate to admit it) Caesar could accomplish marvels. And the Successors cared only about fighting. It was all they were good for. Romans value law and sound rule. But somebody believed that this inevitable tide of Roman rule could be reversed, and they thought that possession of some magic weapon would give them victory over the invincible legions.

There followed a lengthy text, with drawings, of the various engines, including the fanciful monsters of Demetrius. A final section concerned the defenses designed for Syracuse by the great Archimedes. The incendiary reflectors were mentioned, although there was no description of them. The ship-lifting crane Iphicrates had ridiculed was not mentioned. That, apparently, was an invention of later tale-tellers. There was a cranelike device made to swing out over the harbor and drop heavy weights upon the attacking ships, smashing through deck and hull to sink them. Perhaps that was the origin of the story.

When I was finished, the light was dim and my pitcher was almost empty. It had been fascinating reading, but it had not explained some things. I still did not know why the murderer had taken the scroll. Surely he knew there was at least one copy, and doubtless there were others in other lands. Might Iphicrates have written in the original? That seemed unlikely. The Librarians would have regarded it as a desecration. The text and drawings would have been extremely useful to a captain of engineers with a city or a fort to besiege, but I saw nothing in the book that would convince even the most gullible would-be conqueror that here was something that would tip the balance against the might of Rome. There had to be more, and it had to be in the original manuscript of Siton, dedicated to Attalus more than a century before.

7

By LAMPLIGHT, I DRESSED IN THE hunting garments Hermes had found in the well-stocked embassy wardrobe. The tunic was a dark rust-red, with twin stripes of olive green running from the shoulders to the hem. The high boots of red leather were elegantly topped with spotted serval skin, with the dainty paws dangling over the shins. It made a dashing outfit, and I was sorry that Julia wouldn't have the opportunity to see me wearing it.

Hermes awaited me outside my door and followed me as I left the embassy. He was loaded with our other gear: short hunting spears, a roll of two cloaks, a satchel of travel food and an enormous wineskin.

"I won't have to carry this far, will I?" he groused.

"Hermes, how would you ever manage in the legions? Do you know what a soldier has to carry?"

"What of it?" he said. "The legions are for citizens. And I'll bet you never had to carry much. You were an officer."

"To answer your question, we are going to do most of our journeying by boat."

Even so, it was a long walk. The city was all but deserted so early. As we passed the Macedonian barracks, there was enough light to discern that, as I had predicted, the war machine was nowhere to be seen. We went to the Canopic Way and took it almost the whole length of the city until we reached the canal that cuts through the Rakhotis from north to south, connecting the Kibotos Harbor to the Nile canal and Lake Mareotis.

We stopped at the bridge over the canal and Hermes set down his burden, puffing away. I descended the stair by the bridge to the broad pavement that ran the length of the canal. It was crowded with boats and rafts, mostly those of farmers bringing produce to the city markets. Along one section I found a line of travel barges. The bargemen sat in their craft. At my approach a dockside foreman came to my, eying my attire.

"You wish to go hunting, sir? Not far from here can be found lion, gazelle, oryx . . ."

"What I shall hunt I have not yet decided," I told the man. "Is there a boatman here who took the philosopher Iphicrates of Chios on his monthly expeditions?"

The man looked puzzled, but he turned and addressed the bargemen in Egyptian. One man stood and stepped off his craft. He exchanged a few words with the foreman, who turned back to me.

"This man took Iphicrates out three times."

"Tell him I want to go where Iphicrates went." There was a bit more talk and we agreed upon a price. Hermes and the bargeman transferred our gear into the little vessel while I made myself comfortable in the prow. The man went to the stern and picked up his pole. Soon we were off, drifting silently by the awakening city.

The bargeman was a typical Egyptian of the riverine sort. He had short, bowed legs and had probably seldom ventured onto land in his life. His command of Greek was uncertain and he had not a word of Latin. He poled his craft along with quiet serenity, looking like a picture on a wall.

Soon we were in the tunnel that passed through the lake wall, its great double portcullis raised for the day. The bulk of the canal traffic was coming into the city at that hour. There was very little leaving it. We passed the entrance to the Nile canal and headed toward the lake. I turned and called out to the bargeman.

"Didn't Iphicrates go to the Nile to measure its rise and fall, and to examine the shores?" I wasn't sure he understood the whole question, but he understood enough.

"He went to the lake," he said.

Soon we were on the quiet waters of Lake Mareotis. Its shores were low and marshy, lined with papyrus. The reeds were alive with waterfowl, wild ducks and geese and gulls, herons and the occasional wading ibis. We passed wallows where hippos disported themselves, their smiling mouths and comically wiggling ears belying their essentially hostile and ill-tempered nature. Hermes's eyes grew round when he saw these huge, wild beasts so close.

"Will they attack us?" he asked.

"They never scared you before," I said.

"We were on a bigger boat then. Those things could swallow us with one gulp."

"If they were so inclined. But they eat grass. As long as we stay clear of them, they won't bother us. Now that"—I pointed at something that looked like a floating log—"will definitely eat you, should you fall in." As if hearing me, the thing turned and regarded us with a glistening eye. Hermes grew paler.

"Why don't they exterminate those monsters?" he said.

"Crocodiles are sacred to the god Sobek. They mummify them and put them in temple crypts."

"Egyptians! Is there anything they don't worship and make into mummies?"

"Slaves," I told him. "There is no god of slaves."

"Or Romans either I'll bet," was his rejoinder.

We drifted eastward in the direction of the delta until the sun was nearly noon-high. Then we came around a low headland to a place where a stone dock protruded into the water. The bargeman turned the nose of his craft toward the wharf.

"What is this?" I asked him.

"This is where the man from the Museum went."

In the distance I could see a large house amid tilled fields.

"Whose estate is this?"

He shrugged. "The king's, or some great noble's." A safe guess, since everything belonged to the king or some great noble.

"Keep going," I instructed him. "I'll tell you where to put in to shore."

He turned away from the wharf. I saw nobody manning the pier. As far as I could tell, we were unobserved. That was of little importance in any case, since we were far from the only watercraft on the lake that morning. Fowlers and fishers were at their work, and boats carried produce from the plantations fringing the lake. Barges like ours carried huge bundles of papyrus reeds for the paper factories of Alexandria. It was not exactly crowded, but one more boat should attract no attention.

About a mile east of the pier I saw a small inlet that cut through the reeds to the shore. "Put us in there."

The barge nosed aground on a sandy bank surrounded by palm trees. We unloaded our gear and set it among the trees. The bargeman looked around with a dubious expression.

"Not much hunting here, I think."

"We'll chance it," I told him. "Come back for us here at this time tomorrow and I'll pay you double what you got today."

It was all one to him, so he agreed. People everywhere assume that all foreigners are insane. Thus, when you are in a strange land, it is easy to get away with eccentric behavior. He poled his barge away from the shore and was soon out of sight. We carried our gear to a spot sheltered from view by high bushes and rested beneath the shade of the palms.

"All right," Hermes demanded. "Why are we here? It certainly isn't for hunting." He started at a sound in the nearby bushes. When he saw that it was just an indignant ibis, he relaxed.

"Iphicrates was in the habit of taking monthly journeys, supposedly to measure the Nile waters and observe the banks. As I've just learned, he went nowhere near the river. He came instead to this estate, and I propose to find out what he was doing here."

"If he was lying about where he went, he had a reason for it," Hermes said, with a slave's grasp of subterfuge. "Couldn't this be dangerous?"

"It most certainly is. That is why I am taking as few chances as possible. Many travelers go hunting in the Egyptian wilds, so our leaving the city should have aroused no suspicion. I intend to explore this estate, but I shall do it cautiously. It's too early now. We'll set out when the sun gets lower."

"We?" Hermes said.

"Yes, we. You'll enjoy this, Hermes, it's just your sort of activity."

"You mean I should enjoy getting caught and tortured for spying?"

"No, Hermes. *Not* getting caught is what you like."

So we made ourselves as comfortable as possible and dozed away the forenoon and a good part of the afternoon. In the cool of early evening we kindled a small fire in which I charred some pulpy, rotted palm-wood. Then we immediately extinguished the fire lest the smoke betray our presence.

Some years before, I had served under my kinsman Quintus Caecilius Metellus Pius in Spain, during the rebellion of Sertorius. I had seen no open, set-piece battles, but instead had fought guerrillas in the mountains. This was considered poor campaigning by most, since conventional leadership of soldiers in glorious battles was considered a necessity for political advancement at home. But it had taught me some valuable skills. Our Iberian mountaineer scouts had taught me the rudiments of their craft, and these skills I was about to put to good use in Egypt.

By the time we made our preparations, Hermes was eager to

go. He had spent hours in a near-panic. A true child of the metropolis, he was certain that open country was alive with wild, ravenous beasts hungering for his flesh. Every disturbance in the water was a crocodile coming ashore. Every quiet rustle in the bushes was a cobra. The louder rustles had to be lions. The scorpions that infested Alexandria probably represented a far greater danger to him, but they were commonplace. For some reason, most people fear being slain in an exotic manner. This is not peculiar to slaves.

With soot from the charred wood I streaked my face, arms and legs and directed Hermes to do the same. Then we daubed ourselves liberally with reddish clay from the bank. Egyptians divide their nation into the Red Land and the Black Land. The Red Land is Upper Egypt, to the south, but anywhere in Egypt away from the river and the delta is tolerably red. With our streaked limbs and faces and our dark red tunics, we would blend well with our surroundings in the fading light.

I picked up one of the short hunting spears and told Hermes to do likewise. He held it as if it were an asp that might bite him, but I thought it might give him a bit of confidence. We smeared the points with soot and clay to dampen any gleam, and we set off.

The first half-mile was easy, the reeds and brush so high that we could walk upright. There was a good deal of wildlife, and these were hard on my slave's nerves. We disturbed a family of ugly little pigs, and a pair of hyenas lurked back in the bush, watching us. A jackal cocked its huge ears in our direction. These last are rather attractive little beasts, somewhat like foxes.

"Hermes," I whispered at about the twentieth time he jumped, "the only really dangerous beasts are still well ahead of us. You'll know them because they will be carrying weapons." That quieted him.

With startling abruptness, we were out of the dense lakeside growth and at the edge of the cultivated land. At the limit of the tall grass there was a sloping earthwork dike, perhaps ten feet high. This presumably was a barrier against the occasional overflow of the lake. We went up this on hands and knees. At the crest I slowly raised my head until I could see over the top.

On the other side stretched cultivated fields, but these had been left fallow, sown with grass and made into pasture for at least the past year or two, from the look of them. A few head of the piebald, lyre-horned Egyptian cattle munched placidly on the rich forage. On the far side I could vaguely descry some buildings and odd shapes, including what appeared to be a high watchtower. I wanted a closer look, but it was still too light to risk crossing the pasture, where we could easily be seen. A few hundred paces to the left I saw an orchard of date palms. I ducked back down below the crest of the dike, and Hermes did the same.

"We're not going to cross that field, are we?" he said. "It's all full of cowshit and those animals have sharp horns."

"I didn't see any bulls," I told him. "But don't worry. We're going over to that date orchard and work our way closer through the trees." He nodded excitedly. He was naturally sneaky and underhanded, and all this appealed to him, except for the animals.

We walked the short distance and crossed the dike, descending its opposite slope into the cool dimness of the orchard. Like the fields, this, too, was neglected. Last season's fruit lay on the ground, food for pigs and baboons, while monkeys swarmed overhead, eagerly devouring this season's growth.

"Some of the finest farmland in the world here," I said, "and someone is letting it go to ruin. That's not like Egyptians." Indeed, the sight offended the remnants of my rustic Roman soul. Hermes was unmoved, but then, slaves do the actual work of farming, while we landowners practice a sort of agrarian nostalgia, fed by stories of our virtuous ancestors and pastoral poetry.

We progressed cautiously through the orchard, scanning the surroundings for observers. At one point a tribe of baboons screamed and hooted at us, pelting us with dung and dates. These were quite unlike the tame baboon-servants of the court, but rather were nasty, bad-tempered beasts like hairy dwarfs with long, befanged snouts.

"Do you think all that noise gave us away?" Hermes asked when we were past them.

"Baboons sound like that all the time. They scream at intruders and at each other. Everyone here will be used to it."

At the extremity of the orchard we could see the roofs of the buildings, but the grass had grown too high to see anything else, except for the exceedingly high tower, which gleamed a lurid red in the rays of the setting sun. Hermes pointed up at it.

"What's that?" he whispered.

"I think I know, but I want a closer look," I whispered back. "From here on, be very quiet and move very slowly. Watch me and do what I do." With that, I lay down on my belly and began to crawl slowly forward on knees and elbows, dragging my spear along the ground by my side. It was a painful means of progression, but there was no remedy for that. I elbowed my way through the grass, keeping a wary eye out for the snakes that are so abundant in Egypt. I was not as nervous as Hermes, but only a fool discounts the creatures. After all, when you slither on your belly like a reptile, you intrude on the domain of snakes, so to speak, and had best be ready to answer their challenges.

A few minutes of this crawling brought me to the edge of the high grass and I paused while Hermes crawled up beside me. Slowly, like actors in a mime, we parted the grass before our faces and looked into the field beyond.

Surrounded by large farm buildings of the usual Egyptian mud-brick architecture was a broad field of hard-packed dirt, rather like a parade ground. In fact, it *was* a parade ground, for its inhabitants were soldiers. I could tell they were soldiers because, even though none of them bothered with armor or helmet in this place, still they wore their military boots and their sword-belts, without which they would have felt naked. They were a mixed group of Macedonians and Egyptians, and they were drilling on the most fanciful battery of war engines seen since the siege of Syracuse.

One team operated a contraption that looked like six giant crossbows yoked together. It looked ridiculous, but with a startling crash it shot six heavy javelins across the field to smash through a formation of wicker dummies. The machine rocked with the violence of its discharge, and some of the spears went through four or more of the dummies before slowing down.

On another part of the field men worked at a huge, counterweighted catapult with a long, cranelike arm terminating in a sling instead of the usual basket. Soldiers placed a ponderous stone in the sling and stood back. At a shouted signal the counterweight dropped and the long arm swept through a graceful arc. It stopped against a rope-padded horizontal bar and the sling whipped around in an ever-accelerating half-circle and its free end released, hurling the stone an unbelievable height and distance, so far that we did not hear its crashing fall.

There were more conventional-looking weapons as well, moving tortoises slung with battering rams, their heads actually cast in the shape of bronze ram heads with curling horns: giant augurs to bore through walls; small, fast-firing catapults for rocks and javelins; and many others. But the centerpiece, dwarfing all the others, was the tower.

It was at least two hundred feet high, and completely plated with iron. That was the reason for its strange ruddy gleam. At various levels balconies protruded from the main structure, equipped with catapults protected by movable shields. Once in a while a plate would swing forward and up from the forward face and a missile would arch out, after which the plate immediately dropped.

"That," I said, "to answer your earlier question, is something very like the 'city-taker' of Demetrius the Besieger. It was the biggest siege tower ever built, and I think this one may be even bigger."

Then, amid a hideous groaning and squealing, the colossal thing began to *move*. Slowly, painfully, it lurched forward a foot at a time as the men inside it and atop it cheered. Of course, one expects siege towers to move, else they would be of little use, but they are always pushed by oxen or elephants or at least a crowd of slaves or prisoners. But this outrageous device moved with no visible means of propulsion. Besides, there was something unnatural about anything so large moving at all. If I had not already been as low as I could get, my jaw would have dropped.

"Magic!" Hermes squealed. He tried to get up, but I grabbed his shoulder and held him fast.

"It's not magic, you young idiot! It's driven by some sort of inner mechanism, a windlass or capstan of some sort, a thing of gears and wheels and teeth. I was studying drawings of such things just last night."

Actually, I had only the vaguest idea of what it might be. Even the simplest waterwheel seemed intolerably complex to me. Still, I preferred to think that there was some mechanical explanation. I had only the most minimal belief in magic and the supernatural. Besides, if the Egyptians possessed magic so powerful, how would we manipulate them so easily?

A trumpet sounded and all the soldier-engineers dropped their tools and left their engines. The duty day was over. Perhaps twenty men filed out of the tower. Last of all came about thirty oxen from the interior. Then a gang of slaves went in with baskets and shovels to clean up after the oxen. So much for magic.

"Seen enough?" Hermes asked.

"Our boatman won't be back for us until tomorrow. I want a closer look. Let's go back to the orchard. It will be dark enough soon." We reversed our earlier progress, slithering rearwards until we were safely among the trees.

Two hours later, we passed through the grass again, walking this time, but crouched low. Slowly and with great caution, we made our way to the edge of the parade ground. Had this been a Roman encampment, we would have been challenged by sentries, but these were barbarians, lazy and incompetent, for whom soldiering was scarcely more professional than the tribal warrioring of their native lands. That they were within their own territory with no enemy for a thousand miles was no excuse. The legions fortify every camp even if they are within sight of the walls of Rome. Still, it was convenient for us.

The machines stood like dead monsters in the moonlight as we walked up to them. They were made of wood that had been painstakingly cut and shaped, then sanded smooth and in some cases painted. War engines are usually built at the site of a siege and are made of rough-hewn wood and are often abandoned when the fighting is over, after the ironmongery and the ropes have been salvaged.

Even with my inexperienced eye, I could see that these machines were held together by pins and wedges, so that they could be disassembled for transport. That, I guessed, was an innovation of Iphicrates. Egypt has little native wood save for palm, a soft and fibrous material unsuitable for such work. All of this wood had to be imported, shiploads of it.

We walked to the base of the tower, which gave off a powerful, disagreeable smell.

"What's that stink?" Hermes asked.

"It takes a lot of oil to keep this much iron from rusting," I told him. "There's enough here to make armor for three legions." I fingered a plate that had pulled a little loose from the frame. It was good metal, about the thickness of body armor. I walked up the back ramp and looked inside, but it was far too dark to see, only a little moonlight coming through the ports that had been left open. Despite the efforts of the slaves, the interior smelled strongly of oxen. This, mixed with the stench of rancid olive oil, finally drove me away.

The other machines told me little more. They were all as ingeniously designed and lovingly built. I assumed that the more commonplace machines all incorporated some improvement of Iphicrates's design. If only in their ease of transport and reassembly.

"What do we do now?" Hermes asked as I stepped off the ramp.

"We could have a look at those buildings," I said, "but they're probably just barracks and storerooms. Whatever is going on is happening in Alexandria. This is just a training facility and arsenal." I thought for a while. "It might be fun to set fire to all this."

"Let's do it!" I could hear the grin in his voice. "I could sneak a torch from one of those buildings, and there must be plenty of oil jars in the storehouses to keep all this metal greased. We could have everything alight before they know what's going on!" Arson was an unthinkable crime in Rome, so it was one he might never get a chance to commit at home.

"But then they'd sweep the area to find the culprits. They may not be much as soldiers, but they probably know how to make a search for fugitives."

"Maybe we'd better not, then."

"And I might need all this as evidence."

"Evidence of what?"

It was a good question. Rome would look with great disfavor upon this development, but would the Senate take action? I rather doubted it. And what had it all to do with the murder of Iphicrates? With these questions unanswered, we made our stealthy way back to the lakeside.

8

One of the requirements for a career in roman politics is an onerous but necessary apprenticeship in the civil service. Nobody likes it, but at least it teaches you how a state *works*. This is why kings so often rule badly. They know public life only from the top. They like the enjoyable parts: fighting and killing their enemies, lording it over everybody else, being above the law. But the rest of it bores them, and they leave it to men or sometimes eunuchs who may have ambitions of their own. Since the kings don't know how the business of government operates, they don't know that their flunkies are incompetent, or are robbing or even subverting them.

Washed free of mud and soot and dressed decently once more, I presented myself at the Land Office, a sizable government building near the Palace. I knew that here I would find the exact boundaries and ownership of every square inch of land in Egypt. The Egyptians invented the art of surveying out of necessity, since their lands are inundated yearly and boundary markers are often swept away. Like most conquerors, the Ptolemies had adopted the most beneficial practices of the conquered people, and this office was staffed almost entirely by native Egyptians. In the first room I entered, a public slave hurried over, bowing.

"How may I help you, sir?"

"Where might I find maps and documents concerning the lands nearest Alexandria?"

"Please come with me." We walked past rooms where scribes sat cross-legged in the Egyptian fashion, papyrus resting on their tight-stretched kilts, brushes in their hands, inkpots resting on the floor next to them. Others labored over maps spread on long tables.

"This is the Office of the Royal Nome, Senator, and this is Sethotep, Royal Overseer of the Northern Survey."

The man rose from his desk and came forward. He was a native and simply dressed, but by now I had learned to judge status by the quality of a man's wig and the weave of his kilt. Sethotep was a high-ranking functionary, about equivalent to a Roman *equite*. We made the expected introductions and I launched upon the story I had made up.

"I have embarked upon a work of geography concerning Egypt. There has been none in Latin in more than fifty years, and the earlier works are translations from Greek and consequently riddled with errors. I think we need an original book of our own."

"A commendable project," said Sethotep.

"I have already embarked upon my work concerning the city of Alexandria, and I want to begin my study of the nearby lands. I propose to start with Lake Mareotis and the lands surrounding it. Have you any maps of the lake? I would prefer survey maps, listing the estates of the district and their owners."

"Certainly, Senator," said Sethotep. He stepped over to a rack like the ones in the Library and took out a large scroll. "Of course, ail land in Egypt is the property of his Majesty King Ptolemy, but, after ancient custom, the king grants dominion over broad estates to his loyal nobles." That was just what I wanted to hear.

He took the map to a long table and slipped it from its leather tube. To clear a space for it, he picked up some scraps of papyrus, glanced at them, then tossed them into a huge box at the end of the table. The box was half full. The Egyptian bureaucracy generated ten times the waste papyrus of its Roman equivalent. The stuff was cheap in Egypt and they didn't even try to reuse it.

"Where does all the waste papyrus go?" I asked him idly.

"Every month the coffin-makers come to empty the bins," he answered.

"Coffin-makers? Really?" Another strangeness out of Egypt.

"Oh, yes. Wood is very precious in Egypt. Only the wealthy can afford wooden mummy cases. The coffin-makers mix the papyrus with glue and mold it into mummy cases for the poorer and middling classes. As long as the tomb is sealed it will last as well as wood, or so they claim. Personally, I prefer to trust wood. My own tomb is almost finished, and I have provided coffins for myself and my wife made of the finest Lebanese cedar." Romans are fond of funerals and mortuary preparations, but the subject is a veritable mania with Egyptians, who believe in an attractive afterlife. Give them a chance and they'll chatter on about it for hours.

"This is the lake," he said, his map now spread and its corners weighted. The lake thus displayed was irregular in shape, as most lakes are. Lines drawn at intervals defined the estates that bordered it, but the lettering was the sort called Demotic, a simplified form of hieroglyphic that represents phonetic sounds like the Greek or Latin alphabets, but only Egyptian is thus written. Thus did the Egyptians assure their place in the Ptolemaic service. Only they could read their maps or surveys.

"Are these the names of the landowners?" I asked him. "I shall be taking a tour of the lake, and I may wish to call upon some of them."

"Well, let me see. Going from the canal westward . . ."

"Actually, I was planning to begin by going east. Who is the landlord of this estate?" I put my finger on the area where I had been that very morning.

Sethotep considered the inscription for a moment. "That estate belongs to the Lord Kassandros. It has been held by direct inheritance from an ancestor who was a companion of Ptolemy Soter, first of the royal line."

This was bitterly disappointing. I had never heard of the man.

"So it is to this Lord Kassandros that I must make representation if I wish to visit this estate?"

"For some years now, Lord Kassandros has lived in retirement on his estate in the Arsinoene Nome, on the shores of the Faiyum."

"He has more than one estate, then?" I said.

"Like many kings, the Ptolemies have held to the policy of giving the greater lords a number of estates scattered about the kingdom, rather than one large holding. It reduces jealousy among the great men and assures that each gets some of the best land as well as some of the middling and some of the barren land."

It also keeps them traveling among their estates and prevents them from having a large base of power, I thought.

"Very wise. Then to whom should I speak?"

He adjusted his wig, which had come somewhat askew. "That estate may be overseen by a steward, or it may be supervised by one of Lord Kassandros's sons. The Lord Philip is the elder, but he is Steward of the Royal Quarries, and spends most of his time near the first cataract. The younger, the Lord General Achillas, is usually to be found here in Alexandria. You might apply at the Macedonian barracks or at Lord Achillas's town house, but I am sure that his Majesty will be pleased to send a messenger on your behalf. To please Rome is always our most ardent desire."

I could have kissed him. "I shall do as you advise at once, friend Sethotep. And now, I must be off."

"But there is still much to learn of the lake," he said.

"Another time. I have an appointment at the Palace that cannot wait."

He looked unhappy to see me go. I could sympathize. A bureaucrat often has few people to talk to, save the toilers in his own office. The visit had not been wasted. Now I felt I had something to report.

Creticus looked up from his desk grumpily. Apparently I had missed a party the previous night.

"That was a short hunting trip. Did you kill anything?"

"No, but I spotted some promising quarry. Do you have a little time, and is it safe to discuss sensitive matters here?"

"Found a plot to your liking? Oh, come on, then, let's take a turn around the garden. I suspect that some of the embassy slaves aren't as ignorant of Latin as they pretend."

In the olive orchard I told him of my findings and my suspicions. He nodded gravely, but that was just habit. It's a skill every Roman politician learns. He might have been calculating odds on the next races, as far as I knew.

"This sounds ominous," he admitted when I was finished. "But why are you so happy to find out that it was Achillas's land, other than having knocked out his lieutenant, a fact which secretly delights much of the court?"

"Why, because this means it's not Ptolemy," I said.

"And why does that make you happy?"

"First of all, it means that Ptolemy can discipline his own fractious nobleman, and Rome need not take too open a hand in it, sparing Egyptian feelings. And second—well, I just like the old buffoon. He's harmless and good company when he's conscious, and I don't think he's hostile to Rome."

Creticus shook his head. "Decius, you have a fine nose for the devious and underhanded, but your grasp of the obvious leaves much to be desired."

"What do you mean?" I asked.

"Several shiploads of timber, you said?"

"At least."

"And that tremendous tower is *entirely* plated with iron?"

"Do you think I exaggerate? It's covered with the stuff—oh, I see."

"Exactly. How rich do you think Achillas is? There are no nobles in Egypt as rich as Crassus, and that much iron bought all at once would bankrupt a small kingdom."

I should have thought of it. When Sethotep told me that Achillas was a younger son, I should have realized that Achillas probably owned little more than his arms and his arrogance. There was great wealth behind those military contraptions.

"But Ptolemy is a beggar!" I protested.

"Makes you wonder where all that money we've given him went, doesn't it?"

My mind darted around. Somehow, even discounting my rueful affection for the old winebag, I couldn't picture Ptolemy as the mastermind behind this absurd bid for power through superior machinery. Another thought came to me.

"Perhaps Achillas is front man for a horde of those disaffected satraps and nomarchs we've been hearing about," I hazarded.

"That's more like it. But I can't see them pooling their wealth and keeping it secret at the same time. Support with words, yes, and promises of aid and alliance once war is joined, that I can imagine. But parting with substantial money? These little Macedonian and Egyptian lordlings are too jealous of one another for that. Each would think he was giving more than his share, that the others were cheating him. And, Decius, you must learn one thing about all large-scale foreign conspiracies against Rome. Heed me, now, because you'll run into it many times if you live long enough." This was the older generation of Metelli teaching the younger, so I listened respectfully. I also knew that it would be damned good advice, because the elders of my family knew domestic and world politics as few other people did.

"If many men of small power are asked to combine against us, there are *always* some who know that their future lies in bringing word to us and aiding us against their fellows. Many a little chieftain has become a subject-king that way." I was to recall these words in later years when I encountered Antipater and his ferocious, gifted son, Herod. "No one has come to us with news of this conspiracy, expressing a willingness to replace Ptolemy on the throne in Alexandria."

"Then what *could* it be?" I demanded. "Someone has decided

that Roman might can be challenged with these ridiculous machines, and has expended vast wealth on the possibility."

"Well, that's the sort of thing you're supposed to be good at ferreting out. Get to it." With that, he left me pondering among the olives. That was where Julia found me.

"You look unusually grave this morning," she said.

"This is what I look like when I'm torn between elation and distress," I said. Then I brought her up to date on my discoveries of the previous day and that morning.

"Why didn't you take me on your spying mission?" she said, which was just like her.

"For one thing, you've limited experience of guerrilla warfare."

"You just wanted to go off adventuring by yourself," she retorted.

"It could have turned very dangerous. I don't want you hurt over this matter. The Caesars would never forgive me."

"As if you cared about them." Having established some form of verbal victory, she went on. "Have you seen the streets this morning?"

"They seemed rather crowded. Is there some sort of religious holiday being celebrated?"

"People are streaming in from the countryside. It seems that Ataxas has had another vision. Baal-Ahriman will speak very soon, ushering in a new age for Egypt and the world. People are dropping everything else to be there."

"If it's this crowded near the Palace, what must the Rakhotis be like?"

"I expect to find out. Berenice and a large party of her social set will be going to the temple this afternoon. She has invited Fausta and me to go with her. Would you like to go as well?"

"I wouldn't miss it for anything!" I said.

Her eyes narrowed. "I'll bet you think those priestesses will flog themselves again."

"No, far from it. The poor dears aren't recovered from last time. It's something else."

Even narrower. "What?"

"I'll have to muse it over for a while," I said, unaware at first of my unintended wordplay.

"Muse? Who is the Muse of snoops and investigators?"

"A good question. Clio comes the closest, I suspect. She is the Muse of history, and I try to uncover the truth behind historic lies. Or perhaps there's another Muse, a nameless one for men like me."

"Your *genius* is a strange one. Uncle Caius has often said so." Always Uncle Caius.

I rounded up Rufus and some of the livelier members of the embassy staff and told them of the upcoming sport. We had the huge official litter brought and loaded it up with enough food and wine for a minor banquet. We ended up with a party of six, each man bringing a personal slave to attend to his needs. Then we waited by the main Palace gate for Berenice's party.

"If the streets are so crowded," Rufus said, "these land-going triremes are going to take hours just to get to the Rakhotis." He should have known that would be taken care of.

When Berenice's party arrived, it was preceded by a flying wedge of a hundred Macedonian soldiers to help ease its passage. The men were dressed in the flashing bronze armor and towering scarlet plumes of the Palace guard. Behind them came Berenice's massive palanquin containing her personal favorites, including Julia and Fausta, a horde of slaves, dwarfs and dancers, plus numerous hissing cheetahs and frolicking baboons.

"I am so happy you have decided to join us!" Berenice yelled over the noise. "Just fall in behind my conveyance. The others will make room for you."

We did as directed, and the riders in the two other litters looked annoyed at being thus separated from their deity. I got a particularly ferocious glare from Achillas, who rode in the second litter. I was not surprised to see him there. Then, amid a shrilling of flutes and a pounding of drums, the twang of harps and the rattle of sistra, we were off.

Even with the soldiery clearing the way, our progress through the streets of Alexandria was leisurely. Densely packed mobs can get out of the way only so fast. From the Palace we took the Street of Argeus south to the Canopic Way, where we turned west like a line of warships veering into harbor on a still day. The crowds cheered us and sang praises to Berenice even as the soldiers' spears poked them out of our path. Flowers showered us, for everyone seemed to be wearing garlands. A good many were also draped with snakes, which I was grateful they did not throw at us.

"It's shaping up to be a lively day," Rufus said, his head now sporting a rose wreath.

"Things must be getting really raucous at the temple," I said, holding out my cup, which Hermes promptly filled.

"At this rate we may miss the statue speaking," said one of the staff.

"Have no fear," I told him. "That god is not going to speak until the princess and all the most important dignitaries are present."

"If this god has such a regard for royalty," Rufus said, "why does he operate through a greasy little Asiatic prophet?"

"Alien gods are strange, are they not?" I agreed. "Our gods make their will known through omens sent to the augurs: an orderly and sensible system. Asian deities are altogether an emotional and irrational lot. They depend much on enthusiasm, oblique utterances and coincidence. Although sometimes those coincidences can turn out to be convenient for certain parties."

"Eh?" Rufus said. "You're babbling again, Decius."

"I'll make you a little wager," I said. "Five hundred *denarii* says this god is about to predict a sudden shift in Egyptian-Roman relations."

"You know something, Decius," he said. "You can't fool me. You bet on chariots and gladiators because you fancy yourself an expert. You wouldn't offer a wager like that if you weren't privy to

133

some inside information. What is it? Have you been seeing one of those priestesses for a bit of clandestine flagellation?"

"Not at all," I said, my dignity offended. "I have arrived at this conclusion through a process of deduction." They all laughed and hooted at me.

"You've been hanging out with those old philosophers too much, Metellus," one of them said. "You've begun to fancy yourself one of them. Deduction, indeed!"

"And," I went on, ignoring them, "I want you all to testify to Creticus that I predicted it beforehand. He'll think I made it all up afterwards, otherwise."

"You've delved too deep into the wine, Decius," Rufus insisted. The rest of them agreed loudly, pelting me with some of the rose blossoms that littered the palanquin.

"Then," I said through my teeth, scenting blood, "you won't *all* mind betting me five hundred *denarii* that I'm wrong."

That gave them pause, but Rufus assented and the others, not wishing to appear timid, one by one agreed to the wager. Hermes leaned forward and refilled my cup.

"Where are you going to get twenty-five hundred *denarii?*" he muttered in my ear.

"Have no fear. Just start planning how you're going to steal it from me."

As we passed the Great Serapeum we saw the crowds backed up on its steps, so dense was the crush in that part of town. This, I thought, was the result of more than a sudden, flying rumor. Some real advance planning had gone into getting this mob assembled here on this day. The whole polyglot fabric of Alexandria was there, people of every nation present to enjoy the spectacle, but there was a huge majority of native Egyptians, more even than one would expect of a district like the Rakhotis. Most looked like peasants out of the fields, but there were a good many townsmen of the merchant, artisan and scribe classes. The only group that seemed conspicuously absent were the priests of the traditional gods, although some might have been present in disguise, which for an Egyptian priest consisted of doffing his leopard-skin cape and donning a wig.

At our arrival, the acolytes and priestesses flocked from the Temple of Baal-Ahriman and shoved the mob aside to clear a space for the royal party. Then they prostrated themselves on the pavement and yowled praises of the princess and the royal family. As we descended unsteadily from our litter, they screeched slightly more moderate praises to Rome in the aggregate and to ourselves in particular. We walked ankle-deep through flower petals across the pavement and up the steps of the temple.

Atop the stone platform musicians played endlessly and dancers twirled, sending their skimpy white garments flying. The music was an ear-grating racket, but the dancers were restful to the eye. We assembled atop the stops, waiting for Ataxas to appear. I saw Achillas and edged over toward him.

"Taking time out from your military duties for the good of your spirit, General?" I said.

"When one is a servant of the king," he answered, "then one humors the whims of princesses."

"Nothing else could have dragged you here, eh? Any idea what old Baal-Ahriman is going to say?"

He frowned. "How should I know that?"

"Did you know," I said, exaggerating my tipsiness a bit, "that a man answering your description was seen in Iphicrates's chambers just before his murder?"

"Are you accusing me of something?" His leather harness creaked with tension.

"Just sharing with you some of the fruits of my investigation."

"Roman." He stepped close and all but hissed his words. "Many here are sick of your arrogance and your meddling. Egypt would be far better off without your kind. Your absence would not be difficult to arrange."

"Why, General Achillas," I said, "one might almost suspect

your devotion to King Ptolemy's pro-Roman policy."

"Careful, Senator," he said. "You'll need more than a *caestus* and a trick punch to deal with me."

I had goaded him as far as I dared. "Look!" I said, pointing to the arriving Ataxas. "The spectacle begins!" Achillas backed off. This was more important to him than our feud.

Ataxas strode from within the temple like a man sleep-walking. His arms were crossed over his breast and his long, ring-leted beard trembled as if in ecstasy at divine visitation. His eyeballs were rolled back in their sockets so that only the whites showed, perhaps another reason for his cautious gait. He stopped before us and everything fell silent.

"Great Baal-Ahriman will speak!" he shouted. "Come within, all ye that are chosen!" He turned around and sleepwalked back into the interior. The acolytes and priestesses quickly sorted out the chosen from the unchosen. The whole royal party went in, of course, cheetahs included. That included the Roman presence. A great crowd tramped after, and soon the whole inside of the temple was jammed with the faithful.

The interior smelled somewhat better than the last time I had been there. Thankfully, the god no longer wore his cape of bulls' testicles, and the blood had been washed off the pavement. The air was smoky from the volume of burning incense. A single skylight admitted a narrow shaft of light that struck just in front of the idol. The only other light was provided by a few flickering candles and the incense braziers.

Ataxas stood before the statue and began a high, wailing, sing-song chant in some foreign language. At least I presumed it was a language. It might have been a string of nonsense syllables selected for their eerie sound. A subdued thumping of tambours and rattle of sistra began, and the acolytes commenced a low, almost whis-pered chant of likewise incomprehensible words or sounds.

"I'm going to watch to see if his lips move when he talks," said one of the embassy party.

"How could you tell?" Rufus said. "It looks as if his lips have rotted off from leprosy."

"Shh." This from at least a hundred bystanders.

We exalted ones stood in a circle defining a cleared space before the idol. A brazier of hot coals burned just in front of the thing, sending up a thin stream of smoke. An acolyte, head bowed, gave Ataxas a small silver bowl, then backed away. Ataxas raised the bowl high overhead and intoned, in Greek this time:

"Great Baal-Ahriman! Heed your trembling, suppliant worshippers! Visit them as you have promised! Favor them with your divine words, guide them in the path you have chosen. Great Baal-Ahriman, speak to us!"

With that, he emptied the bowl into the brazier before the god and a cloud of smoke went up, carrying with it the smell of frankincense. Then Ataxas fell to his knees and bowed deeply, clutching the bowl against his belly. The shaft of light from the single skylight fell directly upon him.

There was utter silence. I do not think anyone even breathed. The tension stretched, then stretched again, until it was like an overturned lyre-string about to snap. There came an instant when a single laugh would have destroyed the whole carefully constructed edifice of stage setting, but, with impeccable timing, the god spoke.

"AEGYPTOI!!" This in Greek, of course, and I have rendered the first word in that language because it sounds so impressive that way. The word seemed to thunder from every corner of the temple, a deep, stone-shaking voice that roared like a waterfall. There was a collective gasp and several people fainted. We Romans, made of sterner stuff, gulped a quick drink and listened to the rest.

"EGYPTIANS! I, BAAL-AHRIMAN, SPEAK TO YOU AS THE NEW VOICE OF THE GODS OF EGYPT! I SPEAK WITH THE VOICE OF THE ANCIENT GODS, OF AMON, HORUS, ISIS AND OSIRIS, APIS AND SUKHMET, THOTH, SEBEK, ANUBIS, NUT AND SET! I SPEAK WITH THE VOICE OF HAPI OF THE

UPPER NILE AND HAPI OF THE LOWER NILE, I SPEAK AS THE DJED PILLAR AND THE FEATHER OF MA'AT! I SPEAK WITH THE VOICE OF THE GODS OF GREECE: ZEUS, APOLLO, ARES, DIONYSUS, HERMES, HADES, APHRODITE, HERA, ATHENA, HEPHAESTUS, PAN. I SPEAK FOR ALL THE PHARAOHS OF EGYPT, AND FOR THE GODS OF ALEXANDRIA, SERAPIS AND THE DIVINE ALEXANDER!"

And, through all these pronouncements, the mouth of the idol *actually seemed to move!* The jaws did not move on mechanical hinges. Any fabrication so crude we would have detected instantly. Instead, the fanged mouth worked in some subtle manner that seemed to coincide with the spoken words. Tiny flashes like pale lightning seemed to come from the mouth as well, as if a god's words could be seen as well as heard. I knew that somehow we were being duped, but my scalp prickled anyway. I glanced at my companions and wondered whether I looked as foolish as they did, with their jaws hanging and their eyes bugged out.

Many of the worshippers prostrated themselves on the floor Berenice groveled with her face to the marble. Julia and Fausta stood beside her, looking both concerned and embarrassed. Achillas looked on with a smug smile.

"BEHOLD!" the hideous god boomed forth. "BEHOLD! I PROCLAIM A NEW DAWN FOR THE RED LAND AND THE BLACK! HORUS THE SUN RISES FOR EGYPT! IT IS NIGHTFALL FOR THE BARBARIANS!"

"Barbarians!" Rufus huffed. "We're not the barbarians, they are!"

"EGYPT IS FIRST AMONG THE NATIONS OF THE WORLD. EGYPT IS THE MOST ANCIENT OF LANDS. FOR THREE THOUSAND YEARS EGYPT WAS THE ONLY CIVILIZED NATION OF THE WORLD. EGYPT WILL BE FOREMOST AGAIN! I, BAAL-AHRIMAN, THE NEW, SUPREME GOD OF EGYPT, PROCLAIM IT SO! I SHALL SPEAK TO MY PEOPLE AGAIN! THEY MUST PROVE THEMSELVES FIT TO

HEAR MY WORDS!" The god fell silent and his mouth no longer moved, if indeed it had in the first place.

People began to get shakily to their feet. Some stayed prone, wailing and shaking their heads. Others ran outside, presumably to spread the good news among the faithful. The Egyptians muttered among themselves, and some of them cast dark looks toward us Romans.

"I think it might be a good idea to return to the embassy," Refus said. He and the others looked a bit shaken, although not exactly awestruck. It was the ominous implications of the god's message that disturbed them. I was not quite ready to leave, though. As they filed out, I went over to where Achillas stood.

"Do you think old Baal-Ahriman meant to include Macedonians among those barbarians for whom night comes on apace?" I said.

He smiled, showing long, sharp teeth. "But we Macedonians have ruled in Egypt since Alexander. We're virtual Egyptians ourselves now. No, it is my opinion that the god wants the overbearing Romans expelled from our midst. However, I am a mere humble servant of the king. I leave the interpretation of divine prophecy to the priests." He nodded in the direction of Ataxas.

Ataxas himself had sprawled on his back and lay jerking and thrashing about, foamy spittle flying from his lips. The silver bowl lay by him on the floor, the rays from the skylight gleaming from its polished interior.

"And now, Roman," Achillas said, "it might be best if you and your friends were to vacate this area. Alexandrian crowds are emotional and given to enthusiasm. Should they choose to interpret this event as a call for the expulsion of Romans, I would not be able to answer for your safety."

"You have a hundred soldiers. What is the rabble outside to that?"

He shrugged, making his harness creak once more. "Our duty is to guard the princess, not some band of Roman sightseers who tagged along for the fun."

"You have two patrician ladies in your party," I said. "They are under the princess's protection, surely." We looked to where Julia and Fausta were helping Berenice to her feet. The princess was in only marginally better condition than Ataxas. Her hair and clothes had become extremely disheveled in an amazingly short time, and it looked as if the acolytes had been somewhat lax about dusting the floor.

"Of course, I shall be most diligent in guarding the princess's honored guests." Achillas said. "Safe journey, Roman."

I turned my back on him and went to Julia.

"Things may get rough outside," I said quietly. "This is a scheme to stir the Egyptians up against us. Stay close to the princess. Achillas says he'll keep you safe, but we men are going to have to run for it."

She frowned. "But nothing was said about Rome."

"Yes. Very innocent. What do you want to bet that's not the word being spread outside? Goodbye, dear. See you at the Palace." With that, I ran. I thought they would be safe enough. Their gowns were all but identical to those of Greek ladies. As long as they didn't yell something in Latin, nobody would take them for Romans. It was different for the men. Our togas, short hair and clean-shaven faces were unmistakable.

Outside, the rest of my party gestured impatiently for me to ascend our litter. The crowd was muttering and jabbering away, everyone confused about exactly what had happened. As yet, there was no concerted action.

"Get aboard, Decius!" Rufus called. I climbed up and settled in. The bearers hauled us to their shoulders and started to push their way through the crowd.

"What was that all about?" asked one of the staff. "What does it mean?"

"What it means," I said, pouring myself some refreshment, "is that you each owe me five hundred *denarii*."

"I protest," someone said. "That leper-god never mentioned Rome!"

"I said, if you will recall, that his words would proclaim a sudden change in relations between Rome and Egypt," I pointed out. "He said in there that Egypt was to be the foremost nation in the world. If that isn't a change in Roman-Egyptian relations, what is?" Where only lately we had been pelted with flowers, we began to be pelted with fruit peels.

"It was an awfully short message," Rufus said, ducking a handful of camel dung. "I rather expected something longer."

"You have to keep it short when you're employing conjurer's mummery," I said. "Another minute and we would have figured out that trick with the idol's mouth."

"How *did* he do that?" said a secretary. "It was awfully impressive."

"I propose to find out," I said. People were pointing fingers at us from all over the plaza. We were not yet into a street.

"I haven't heard any anti-Roman slogans yet," said the secretary. These men were used to hearing such slogans in various parts of the world.

"That's because none of us speaks Egyptian," I told him. "The acolytes are spreading a highly colored version of Baal-Ahriman's words."

"You seem to know an awful lot about this, Decius," Rufus groused.

"All it takes is intelligence," I told him. "That's something best left to me. Can't these bearers go any faster?" We weren't under attack yet, but the jeers and pelting were getting more ominous.

"I suppose they can," Rufus said. He began to rummage among the cushions. "Let's see, there ought to be a whip in here someplace. Aha!" He came up with a long, snakelike lash of braided rhinoceros hide. He leaned out over the railing of our platform and brought his arm down in a mighty swing "Get a move on, you scum!" Not the most adroit of whipmen, he managed to back-lash himself, drawing a stripe from his left buttock to his right shoulder. He fell back howling and the rest of us laughed until tears ran down our faces.

"This is rare sport," said the secretary, "but this crowd is getting meaner."

By this time we were in a street and were almost past the Great Serapeum. The people ahead of us had not yet been told of the divine word, but they were ignorantly blocking our progress.

"That's it," someone said. "Time to lighten ship. You slaves get off."

"Not on your buggering life!" Hermes said stoutly. "That mob's ready to eat anything with a Roman haircut."

"Insolent little bastard," the same someone said. "He needs discipline, Metellus."

"And you need sobering up," I told him. I picked up the whip and climbed over the railing and went down the steps until I stood just above the carrying-poles. I sent the whip whistling through the air and made it pop thunderously. I had taken whip lessons from a charioteer of the Red faction in my youth.

"We are already going as fast as we can, master!" protested the pacesetter.

"Then get ready to run," I said. I slashed the whip over the heads of the crowd in front of us.

"Make way!" I bellowed. "Make way for the majesty of Rome, you silly foreigners!" I popped the whip like a madman and the crowd melted away before us magically. I have no idea where they went. Into doorways and windows, possibly. When their blood was not up, there was nothing more instantly responsive to authority than the Alexandrians.

The bearers began to trot, then to run as I continued to flail the air as if bringing down a harpy with every blow. The Romans in the litter clapped and cheered me on. Soon I was wishing we had another litter to race against, for I think we made it back to the Palace in record time. After the first quarter-mile there was no crowd to speak of, since nearly everyone in the city had gone to the Rakhotis, but this was so much fun it seemed pointless to slow down.

When we were safe within the Palace precincts, the litter almost tipped over as all the right-hand bearers collapsed at once, coughing and vomiting. Somehow disaster was averted, though, and we dismounted safely.

"I didn't know you were so handy with a whip," Hermes said uneasily.

"Keep it in mind," I advised him. The rest of the Roman party congratulated me and clapped me on the shoulder.

"Just don't forget the five hundred *denarii*," I told them. Then I went to seek out Creticus.

9

THE LEADERS OF THE ROMAN COM-
munity in Alexandria gathered in the assembly hall of the embassy
to address their complaints and concerns to Creticus and the other
officers of the Roman legation. There were quite a few of them,
merchants for the most part. It was customary for upper-class Romans to despise merchants, but these were a force to be reckoned
with. The wealthy grain traders were among the most influential
men in our Empire. The moneylenders were similarly powerful,
although if anything even less loved. There were many other merchants as well. Exporters of papyrus and books were numerous, as
Egypt was virtually the only source of papyrus and the Library was
the greatest book-producing organization in the world. There were
dealers in ivory and feathers, in exotic animals and slaves. There
was even a man whose sole business was the export of high-quality
sand for the Circuses and amphitheaters of the Roman world.

"Ambassador," said the spokesman for the group—a big-
nosed, bald-headed individual named, as I recall, Fundanius—

"the situation here quickly grows intolerable. We Romans are publicly insulted as we seek to carry out our business in the streets of Alexandria. We are pelted with offal, and our wives are assailed with the vilest of language. Are you going to wait for open violence against us before you take action?"

"What action would you have me take?" Creticus demanded. "I am an ambassador, not a proconsul. I have no imperium and therefore no legions. I cannot whistle up a military force because you are getting nervous. May I remind you that Egypt is an independent nation, a friend and ally of Rome? I will carry your message to his Majesty, but that is all I am empowered to do. I will send a letter to the Senate describing the situation here."

"What cares this mongrel king for our welfare?" Fundanius said, sneering. "And what good will a letter to the Senate do? If you sent it today, it would not reach Rome before we were all massacred in our beds."

"A massacre of Roman citizens would probably stir the Senate to action, if that is any comfort to you," I said helpfully.

"This is an outrage!" Fundanius shouted. "We are treated with disrespect by the Egyptian rabble. Roman citizens!"

"Sir," said Creticus, "you are a moneylender, and men of your trade are universally hated. You should be grateful that you've escaped crucifixion all these years."

"You can speak thus!" Fundanius said scornfully. "You patricians can huddle safely here in the Palace, gorging yourselves, while we who do the real work of the Empire are exposed to every peril!"

"For your information," Creticus said, "the gens Caecilia is plebeian. I admit there is little pleasure in sharing the same class designation with moneylenders and tax-farmers."

A book exporter stood. He was a tall man of dignified appearance.

"Gentlemen, this is unseemly. We need not refight the brawls of the Gracchi when we are in danger from without. In any case, this is not a conflict between Egypt and Rome, but rather the doing of a malignant religious fraud from Asia Minor. Honored Ambassador, can the king do nothing about this man? With his supposed divine revelations he has whipped up the ignorant multitude against us, and it is no more to the advantage of the Ptolemaic house than it is to Rome."

"Well, at least one of you can talk sense," Creticus grumbled. "Just now our situation is delicate. King Ptolemy would like to take action, but he worries that rioting here could spread to the nomes and bring about fullscale civil war. For years Luculius and Pompey had their legions in Asia, within easy striking distance of Egypt. For all those years the Egyptians had to tread softly Now such Roman forces as remain under arms are preparing for trouble in Gaul. It could be a long time before we are in a position to intervene in Egyptian affairs."

These were sobering words, and the men in the hall were Roman enough to understand their import. Whether in business, government or the legions, Romans were accustomed to thinking in terms of the world rather than just a tiny corner of it as most people did.

"What about Antonius in Macedonia?" someone asked.

Creticus snorted. "First off, the Macedonians beat him. Last word we had, he hadn't yet been relieved. It's a bad time of year to move troops by sea, and Macedonia is a long way from here by land."

"Then what is to be done?" said the book exporter

"If you men feel all that concerned," Creticus said, "perhaps now would be a good time to take a vacation from Alexandria. Cyprus is a pleasant place, as is Rhodes or Crete. Take your families there and leave your business interests in the hands of your freedmen."

"But we cannot just leave!" protested Fundanius. "We are men of substantial property. Our homes and warehouses will be looted and burned. Most of our freedmen are Romans, too. They will be killed."

"Gentlemen," Creticus said, "there is no need to grow so

alarmed. Events may not take so grievous a turn. I shall continue my efforts to get Ptolemy to take action against this absurd cult." He rose and, on that unsatisfactory note, the audience ended.

"How is Ptolemy really acting?" I asked when they were gone.

"Like a flute-player," Creticus said. "He refuses to believe that this activity presages anything important. He says he has instructed Berenice to have nothing further to do with Ataxas, but I doubt that bubblehead pays much heed to the old drunk."

"Have you sounded him out about that arsenal on the lake?"

"I have. He professes total ignorance and insists that Achillas is the most loyal of his servants. Funny thing about that . . ."

"What?"

"Well, whenever he spoke of Achillas, he had the unmistakable air of a man who speaks of someone who terrifies him."

"Achillas is overweening and ambitious. Even little Cleopatra says he and Memnon behave insolently, and she's only ten years old. What do you think are the chances of Achillas pulling a coup?"

Creticus cogitated for a while. "The Egyptians are resistant to any sort of change. There hasn't been a change of dynasty since the first Ptolemy. They don't like rule by non-natives, but they haven't much choice in that. Before the Macedonians it was the Persians and even the Nubians. Conquest by Alexander wasn't so bad, since they think he was a god. In any case, they're used to the Ptolemies now, and they don't want to see anyone else on the throne. Achillas is just another Macedonian upstart to them. Even if he married one of the princesses, they wouldn't recognize him as legitimate ruler."

"And with the nomes in a state of unrest, the whole country could dissolve in civil war."

"That makes it all the more unlikely that he's planning a takeover, doesn't it?" Creticus said.

"If he could build a reputation as a great general," I pointed out, "he would be more palatable to the Egyptians. And the only people left for him to fight are the Romans. How many of our recent wars have begun with an uprising of the local populace against Romans?"

"Most of them," he admitted.

"Mithridates did it, and so have others. It's what will precipitate the war with Gaul, if that comes. The local king or chief or whatever sends out agitators to stir up bad feelings against the local Romans—never difficult to do at the best of times. The next thing you know, there is riot and general massacre. By the time people have come to their senses, it's too late. They're at war with Rome and they have no choice but to support the leader who encouraged their folly in the first place."

"It's effective," Creticus allowed. "The Roman public is always for war when foreigners slaughter Roman civilians. If Egypt wasn't so damned rich and tempting, I wouldn't mind a quick war of conquest myself. But it's the wrong time for a war in Egypt. Macedonia's a fiasco and we're preparing for war in Gaul. Even Roman legions can get spread too thin, and there would be that many more veterans to settle."

"Keep working on Ptolemy," I advised. "If he's afraid of Achillas, he might not be upset to see the man out of the way."

"What are you suggesting?" Creticus demanded.

"Just that one less troublesome, subversive soldier would be infinitely preferable to riot and war, both civil and foreign."

"Why, Decius, I never took you for an assassin." There was something akin to family pride in his voice.

"Nothing underhanded about it," I said. "As far as I'm concerned, it's open warfare between me and Achillas now, and the better man will walk away from it."

"Spoken like a true Roman," he said, chuckling.

Back in my quarters, I made preparations for a foray into the city. First I laid out my weapons: *caestus*, dagger and sword. I decided against the rather bulky legionary *gladius* I wore when in uniform. Instead I had a very nice short sword of the sort favored in the arena by certain types of gladiator. It was about three-fourths the size of the military sword, light, wasp-waisted with a narrow point for stabbing and edges so sharp you could cut your eyes just looking at them.

"You're not really going out in the streets, are you?" Hermes asked with a touching concern for my safety.

"I'll be safe enough," I assured him. "As long as I'm not dressed as a Roman and don't speak Latin, nobody will notice me." In our travels down the river I had picked up some good desert garments for protection from the sun. I had an excellent striped robe with a hood that would conceal my Roman coiffure. I kicked off my Roman sandals and slipped my feet into a pair of light, camel-skin slippers such as the caravaneers favor.

"Got your will made out?" Hermes said. "The one where you give me my freedom in the event of your death?"

"If I ever made such a will, I'd live in fear every day of my life. Don't worry, I'll come back safe." Actually, I'd long since made out my will and registered it at the Temple of Vesta, with manumissions and stakes for all my slaves. But you must never allow a slave to think you softhearted.

With my weapons concealed about my person, I slipped on the long desert robe. I fought the temptation to darken my skin. Such subterfuges are rarely convincing and would make me that much more likely to be uncovered. The fact is, fair-skinned people are not all that rare in the East, what with the mercenaries who had policed Persia's far-flung empire and Alexander's rampaging armies and the equally polyglot Successor armies, which for the last two hundred years had included Gauls from Galatia. My typically Italian features would pass easily enough, as long as I watched my tongue. I could butcher Greek with the best of them.

"Good luck, then," Hermes said.

"Stay out of the wine," I cautioned.

Out in the street, I made an effort not to walk like a Roman. This was not too difficult as the desert men also have a very erect posture, but they walk more slowly. We are accustomed to the quick legionary pace, while they adopt a stride calculated to avoid heat stroke. My main worry was that I might encounter real desert men who would want to converse, but that was no great danger. There are a number of languages spoken in the dry parts of the world, and I could always pretend to speak one of the others. In any case, the desert people are very haughty and rarely deign to acknowledge someone of another tribe.

I walked casually, as if I had already sold my goods and was engaged in a little sightseeing before mounting my camel for the caravan homeward. In a city like Alexandria such a one was all but invisible, which was what I most desired.

Most of the city streets through which I walked were quiet, if a bit uneasy. Few of these people were Egyptians and they did not look like good material for a rampaging mob.

In the Rakhotis it was different. Here there was an air of tension. People spoke in mutters instead of their usual cheerful babble. They drew away from foreigners and generally exhibited the mannerisms of people who were on the verge of violence directed against outsiders. I had seen it at work elsewhere. I had seen much the same in my recent visit to Gaul, although we had managed to temporarily calm matters there.

But I was not merely tasting the mood of the city. I had a specific goal in mind. My mission also contained a certain amount of dangerous foolhardiness, and I took pleasure in that. Before long, I stood at the steps of the Temple of Baal-Ahriman.

Many people lingered around the courtyards, as if waiting for something to happen. I mounted the stairs unnoticed, just another sightseer. Then I stood on the platform before the sanctuary of the god himself. I passed within.

As I had anticipated, the inner sanctum was deserted. In Egypt the temples are not places of assembly. When there are rites to be performed, the priests go within and perform them. The rest of the time the inner temples are deserted. The occasion of Baal-Ahriman's address to the faithful had been an exception.

The shaft of sunlight still illuminated a small space before the ugly idol. I avoided the light and circled until I was within touching distance of it. I looked around to make sure that I was unobserved; then I put out my hand and gripped its jaw. There was no movement whatever. It was carved from solid stone. But I did feel something odd, and I leaned close and squinted to make out the anomaly.

Near the thing's putrid-looking lips and paralleling them were ridges of stone, also in the shape of those lips but not so prominently carved, as if the sculptor had begun one set, then changed his mind and carved another without destroying the first effort. Then I ran my fingertips over the lion's teeth and found there were two sets. The easily visible teeth were much longer. In front of them were shorter teeth, offset in serried order like legionaries standing in open formation. I felt the interior of the mouth. The tongue was oddly rippled and I noticed that the roof of the mouth had been painted black. Why black? So as not to reflect light?

I looked to the pool of light where Ataxas had knelt, his hands clasped to his belly. And what had he been doing? Holding a silver bowl. A silver bowl much like the ones I had seen in Iphicrates's study.

I searched the sanctum and found a table that held boxes of incense and the silver bowl. I took the bowl and walked back to the pool of light. Another quick scan for watchers, and I held the bowl low and directed its reflected light to the face of Baal-Ahriman. Carefully, I shifted the bowl, making the spot of light move along the god's mouth and jaws. The ridges and false lips and serried teeth had been exquisitely placed to reflect light alternately, so that only one set at a time showed. The effect was that the jaw seemed to move as the light played across it. But what of the flashes of light that had seemed to shoot from the mouth? Even as the thought occurred to me, a wisp of incense smoke drifted past the statue's face, and the light reflected startlingly from the white smoke. The silver bowl had contained frankincense, and Ataxas had dumped it into the brazier before going down on his knees. Every aspect of the effect had been carefully planned.

"What are you doing here?"

I almost dropped the bowl as I whirled around. It was Ataxas, flanked by a pair of brawny acolytes. It is never a good idea to get too absorbed in your work, however fascinating it may be.

"Why, I was just admiring your handiwork. First-rate design; you have my congratulations."

"I have no idea what you are talking about, but you profane our holy of holies. And, Roman, why are you dressed as a desert nomad?" It seemed to me that his heavy Eastern accent was slipping a little.

"The streets aren't safe for Romans these days." I looked for a fast-exit route. "Something about your god's predictions."

His eyebrows went up in exaggerated puzzlement. "But my Lord said nothing about Romans."

"No need to. Your message came across well enough."

"You talk in riddles. You are not wanted here, Roman. Go while you still have your life."

"Do you threaten me, you Oriental fraud?" I demanded.

He smiled, placed spread fingertips against his breast and bowed. "But how could a humble priest out of Asia Minor constitute a threat to an envoy of the mighty Roman Empire?"

"Sarcasm should be left to those with the wit to deliver it well."

He turned to his flankers. "My sons, expel this man." The two unfolded their arms and came for me.

I would never have accounted myself as any sort of professional swordsman, but I always took a certain pride in my capacity as a brawler. As the one on the right closed. I floored him with a left hook to which my *caestus* gave added authority. The man went down with a splintered jawbone.

The other fancied himself a wrestler and went for the classic cross-buttock throw, which I foiled by sticking the point of my dagger into his left armpit. He jumped back howling. I did not wish to complicate an already deteriorating situation with homicide, which I thought displayed admirable restraint on my part. I could have gone for my sword and killed both of them easily.

Now Ataxas was yelling, calling for guards and acolytes and priestesses and the legions of the faithful to come and slaughter this impudent Roman for him. I took the hint and deemed myself unwelcome. On winged heels I flew from the Temple of Baal-Ahriman, stashing my weapons beneath my clothes as I did so. Ataxas pursued me, but his long, heavy robes hampered him. I was down the steps and heading for a side street before he even got out of the sanctum. The people I passed were too far from him to hear his words and only blinked in puzzlement as I ran past them. But I could hear sounds of pursuit beginning behind me.

Alexandria, I found, was not an easy place in which to shake pursuit. It was all those straight, wide streets. My beloved Rome was different. A veritable rabbit warren of a city, Rome featured so many twisting streets and narrow alleys that a few paces would carry you out of sight of those who thirsted for your blood. I ran from many a rampaging mob in my day, and no few assassins, and even a jealous husband or two, and I knew that the best way to lose pursuers was to get lost yourself. After all, if you didn't know where you were, how could they be expected to find you?

Not so Alexandria. Luckily, I had a long head start on my pursuers. I made random turns down side streets and never went more than a block without making a turn. To my great relief I chanced upon the Alexandrian Salt Market. In that part of the world, salt is the monopoly of caravaneers who carry blocks of it loaded on camels from the Dead Sea in Judaea. Among so many long, hooded robes my own did not stand out. Of course, mine was a good deal cleaner than theirs, but one had to get close to notice that.

I worked my way well into the crowd, pretending an interest in salt and the price thereof. The buyers were many, so the market was quite crowded when Ataxas's mob, mostly shaven-headed acolytes, stormed in looking for me. One of them grabbed a nomad and jerked his hood down, which proved to be a mistake. Not only was the man not me, but the nomads are a very proud and touchy people who consider it a mortal offense for a stranger to lay hands upon them. This one drew a short, curved knife from his sash and slashed the acolyte across the face.

The desert men thought they were attacked, which made sense, what with the recent anti-foreign sentiment that gripped the city. And, indeed, the mob may have been unclear about Ataxas's instructions and thought that he wanted them to attack *all* men they saw in desert robes. It is little misunderstandings such as this that enliven the days of any city, and soon there was a full-scale riot going on in the Salt Market. The followers of Ataxas were greater in number, but few of them carried any weapons save for staves, whereas no adult male nomad ever goes unarmed. All had daggers, some had swords and many of them employed spears as walking sticks.

It made for a fine bloodletting, but I thought it imprudent to stay too long to enjoy the show. I quietly slipped away down a side street and began to make my way back toward the Palace. I restrained myself to a leisurely pace. No one pursued me now, and I did not wish to attract attention. As I ambled past the Macedonian barracks, I saw men forming up hastily, scrambling into their armor as they did so. With a series of barked commands, they were marched out into the street and set out for the Rakhotis at the double. Apparently, a runner had come to bring news of the riot in the Salt Market.

As I neared the Palace I stepped into a small public garden and pulled my robe off over my head. With my weapons rolled up in the robe and the bundle thrust beneath my arm, I strolled through the gate dressed in my tunic, I acknowledged the salutes of the guards and made my way to the embassy. In my quarters I stashed arms and robe and practiced looking innocent.

The summons from Creticus was not long in coming.

He looked decidedly impatient when I walked into his study.

"Decius, you were seen this morning leaving the Palace compound dressed, for some reason, as a desert nomad. I have just received word that the desert salt caravaneers and an Egyptian mob are fighting a pitched battle and troops have been sent to restore order. This cannot be mere coincidence. What have you done now?"

"Just engaging in a bit of investigation, sir." I described to him what I had discovered.

"Do you mean to say," he began, in that long-suffering voice that superiors always use to dress down subordinates, "that you put on a childish disguise, went out and committed mayhem and got a riot started, just so you could satisfy yourself how a foreign mountebank accomplished one of his cheap tricks?" The written word fails to do justice to this speech, which began in a near-whisper but which ascended with each word until the last few were delivered in something very much like a shriek.

"There's more to it than that," I maintained. "In the first place, I didn't make those fools attack the nomads. Anyway, I am certain that it wasn't Ataxas who designed the talking idol. It was Iphicrates of Chios. He was working with the properties of reflected light, using concave mirrors identical to Ataxas's frankincense bowl. I wouldn't be at all surprised if he designed the system of pipes or whatever that transmitted and magnified the god's voice."

"Are you still fixated on that dead Greek? With all the problems we now have, with Roman-Egyptian relations in a shambles and anti-Roman riots in the offing, you are still concerning yourself with a dead foreign mathematician?"

"It isn't just him anymore," I said. "It's what he was up to! Somehow, everything that has been happening here is tied in to Iphicrates, and he was murdered because of it."

"Decius, these fancies of yours get wilder as the years go by. It was hoped that you could stay out of trouble in Alexandria, but you would find trouble if you were locked up in the Mamertine."

Like most men of my acquaintance, he lacked the facility for building evidence into a solid image of what has happened. In fact, I am the only man of my acquaintance who has ever had that quality.

"Decius," Creticus said. "I want you to forget about that Greek. I want you to concentrate on helping me, which means quieting the fears of the Roman community here and being agreeable to Ptolemy and his family. You are not to investigate any murders. You are not to go near Ataxas or his temple. You are to avoid General Achillas. Is all this clear?"

"Perfectly, sir," I said.

"And you agree to my rules?"

"Absolutely, sir."

He looked at me for a long time. "I don't believe you."

"You wound me, sir."

"Get out, Decius. Allow me not to hear about you for a long time."

I left, relieved at getting off so lightly. Back at my quarters, I found that my adventures for the day were not yet over. Hermes came to me with a tiny, sealed scroll.

"A slave girl came here this morning and gave me this. Said it was extremely important and you were to read it at once."

"Did you recognize the girl?"

He shrugged. "Just some little Greek."

"Did she identify her owner?"

"Didn't say a thing except what I've told you. Gave me the letter and ran off."

"I've taught you better than that."

"She was well-dressed, but all the slaves in this Palace wear good clothes. She was small, dark-haired and -eyed, like most Greeks. I think her accent was Athenian, but I don't know Greek all that well."

Of course, all the elocutionists teach the Athenian mode of speech, but if a slave spoke that way, she was probably actually from Athens. That told me little, slaves being an international sort of people.

"Well, are you going to read the damned letter?" Hermes said impatiently.

"These things require a sense of pace," I informed him as I broke the seal and unrolled the little note. It was on fine papyrus and was written in excellent Greek penmanship with what appeared to be a split-reed pen rather than a quill or an Egyptian brush. All of which was amusing but not terribly relevant. The message, however, was. It read:

> *To Decius Caecilius Metellus the Younger, Greeting. We have not met. I am Hypatia, concubine to his Excellency Orodes, Ambassador of King Phraates III of Parthia. I have urgent information to convey to you concerning Parthia, Rome and Iphicrates of Chios. Meet me tonight in the Necropolis, in the tomb of Khopshef-Ra. It is the largest tomb on the south edge of the plaza dominated by the Obelisk of the Sphinx. I will be there at moonrise and will await you for one hour.*

"I suppose you'll go," Hermes said. He'd been hanging on every word, naturally. "It's the most foolish thing you can do, so you'll just have to do it."

"You think it's a trap?" I said.

He gaped. "You think there's a possibility it *isn't?*"

"It's conceivable. The woman has already told Julia that she was privy to correspondence between Iphicrates and the Parthian court. She may well have something she believes is valuable."

"Why should she betray Parthia?"

"She isn't Parthian, she's Greek, and Greeks will betray anybody. Besides, she's a *hetaira*, a companion hired for the ambassador's stay here. He'll go home to his wife and she'll be looking for another patron, only this time she'll be a few years older than last. It's not the sort of relationship that builds strong loyalty."

"You just want an excuse to go out and seek trouble again," Hermes said.

"Admittedly, that's a part of it. Creticus has forbidden me to pursue this matter any further, and that, to me, is like a *bestiarius* in the Circus, waving his red kerchief at the bull."

"The purpose of the kerchief," Hermes pointed out, "is to lure the stupid bull onto the spear."

"Don't trifle with my metaphors. Or was that a simile? I am going."

And so, forbidden by a Roman official and warned by a slave, I went forth at dusk to meet with a high-class Greek prostitute.

10

N O DESERT ROBE THIS TIME. AFTER
dark, a simple traveler's cloak was sufficient. A cool wind blew
from the sea across the city, making the street-torches flutter. These
illuminations are something that would benefit Rome, where the
streets are so dark that a man out in them and struck suddenly
blind wouldn't know it until morning. At intervals of about fifty
paces along the broad streets, these torches burned atop ten-foot
poles. They were made of tow or hemp soaked in oil and were
tended all night long by public slaves. Between the torches and a
fine, full moon, one could walk the streets of nighttime Alexandria
as swiftly and assuredly as during the day. More swiftly, in fact, for
at night the usual crowds were absent.

Individuals and small parties walked about, going to and from
dinner parties and symposia, visiting, carrying out assignations and
so forth. Alexandrians don't always go to bed at sunset the way
Romans are supposed to.

For much of the route I took the street that paralleled the

harbor. On my right hand the Pharos sent its plumes of flame into the night sky, a most impressive sight. I passed the Temple of Poseidon and the northern periphery of the Macedonian barracks, the two huge obelisks, the rows upon rows of warehouses that smelled strongly of papyrus, Alexandria's chief export. At the Moon Gate I turned south along the Street of the Soma, then turned west at the Canopic Way.

Canopic ended at the Necropolis Gate. There I paid the guard to open the gate for me. His was a lucrative duty, because in Alexandria the Necropolis was the popular meeting-place for clandestine lovers.

"How do I find the Obelisk of the Sphinx?" I asked him.

"Just through the gate you'll be on Set Street. Go west for three blocks and turn left on Anubis Street. You'll find the Obelisk of the Sphinx two blocks down. You can't miss it." I thanked him and passed on through.

A necropolis may seem an unlikely place for lovers to meet, but the Necropolis of Alexandria is not like others. It is laid out just like the city, with broad, straight streets. The difference is that the streets are lined with tombs instead of houses. The other factor in its favor is the nature of Egyptian tombs. They are like miniature houses. Whether the chosen architecture and decoration be traditional Egyptian, Greek, Persian or other, the layout was always in the old Egyptian style. You entered a small room like the atrium of a house, where offerings were left for the dead. On the back wall of this room was a tiny window allowing visitors to look into another room which contained a portrait statue of the dead, which the Egyptians believed to contain one of the souls of the dead, or at least a place for the soul to visit when offerings were made. It also provided a refuge for the soul should the mummy be destroyed.

It was the entrance rooms of these cozy buildings that made the Necropolis a resort for lovers, and as I walked through the streets I heard all the usual, passionate sounds of a trysting-place.

There were no torches in the Necropolis, but the full moon provided more than adequate light. The Necropolis swarmed with the inevitable Egyptian cats. I was told that the place was full of mice that came in to eat the food-offerings left in the tombs, and the cats in turn hunted the mice. This seemed to be an equitable arrangement.

As the guard had said, I had no difficulty in finding the Obelisk of the Sphinx. The granite shaft rose from a base that also supported a human-faced lion carved from white marble. The curling ram's horns flanking the human face told me that this was yet another portrait of Alexander, done up for Egyptian tastes.

I scanned the southern edge of the little plaza and saw an imposing tomb of the antique mastaba style said to be even older than the pyramids. The oldest pyramid still standing is just a series of mastabas stacked atop another in diminishing sizes. Old fashions were always being revived in Alexandria, just as lately, in Rome, there has been a revival of Etruscan art and decor. I went to the tomb and stood before the door.

"Hypatia?" I said in a low voice.

"Come inside," came a feminine voice in an urgent whisper, I was determined to be foolhardy, but on the worst day of my life I was never that stupid.

"You come out here," I said. "If there's anyone else out here, you brought them." I gripped my sword hilt, ready to draw at the first sign of danger. The uncertain light did not bother me. To one accustomed to running fights in Roman alleys at midnight, this was like the Forum at high noon.

There was a stirring from within; then a slight figure came outside. She wore a long gown of some pale color, with a dark *palla* drawn over her head. As she emerged she lowered the *palla* to reveal a face of classic beauty. She had the straight, level brows and high-bridged nose so admired by the old Greek sculptors. Her lips were generous, albeit set in a rather hard line. Her eyes were large and they darted around the little plaza.

"I wasn't followed," I told her. "I am knowledgeable at this sort of business."

"That is what Julia told me. She said that you hunt down any

who conspire against Rome as relentlessly as the Friendly Ones."
She used the euphemism for the dreaded demons because to pro-
nounce their real name can call them down upon the speaker.

"She speaks flatteringly, but I have been of some service to
the state in the past. What have you for me?"

"A certain book, a large book of Pergamese skin-paper with
vermilion handles."

"I've read it in copy, but I'm sure the Librarian of the Pergamese Collection will be grateful for its return."

"But you will find the original far more interesting. It contains
more than the text in the copy."

"And what might that be?"

"First, my price."

I was expecting that. "How much?"

She laughed. "I have all the money I need. But you belong to
the great family of Caecilia Metella."

"They have no choice but to acknowledge me."

"Plebeian, but with a line of Consuls and generals and great
magistrates almost to the founding of the Republic."

"You are well educated."

"So you have great influence. I want to go to Rome. A woman
without a protector is less than a slave anywhere in the world except
Rome. In Rome, a woman of property has the protection of the law,
even if she is not a citizen. In Rome, as a resident foreigner with
the patronage of a Caecilius Metellus, I will be secure even when
my beauty fades."

"Commendable foresight," I said. "You would do even better
to contract a marriage of convenience with some impecunious citizen. There are men who do so regularly for a fee. That way, even
if he divorces, you will have full citizenship rights, except, of
course, for such as are restricted to men—the vote and the right to
hold office and so forth. Your children would be citizens."

"I may do so. But first I must get to Rome. A simple sea
passage would get me that, but I don't wish to be expelled from the

city because your Censors decide that immoral foreigners are corrupting the good citizens."

"It could be done," I said. "If one of my family or an ally holds the office of Praetor Peregrinus, it would be made easier. Elections come along every year and someone suitable should be in office before long. I can't protect you from the courts should you operate a house of prostitution, but otherwise you should be safe. Assuming, that is, that the book contains important evidence."

"Oh, it does!"

"You have it with you?" I asked.

"No. It is too bulky to carry through the city. But I can bring it to you. Will you be at the Roman embassy tomorrow night?"

"To the best of my knowledge."

"There is to be a reception at the Palace for the new Armenian ambassador. Orodes will be there, with most of the Parthian embassy staff. I can get the scroll at that time and bring it to you."

"Do so. You will not regret it."

She came close and for the first time I noticed her perfume. Jasmine, I think. "Just what sort of obligations does Roman patronage demand?" she asked.

"Nothing a man can't do in public," I said.

She chuckled. "Well"—she gestured toward the dark entrance—"we could seal our bargain in there, even if it isn't required by law. It seems to be an old Alexandrian custom."

I have never been overfastidious, but somehow a quick stand-up in a tomb didn't appeal to me. Especially with Julia in the same city. She had preternatural senses where other women were concerned. I didn't really think she could set her uncle Caius Julius on me but there was no sense in taking chances.

"Our bargain depends upon your evidence being what you say it is," I said. "I wouldn't want to take advantage."

"When did a Roman ever fail to use every advantage he could get? Suit yourself, but it's your loss. I'll bet you've never been with a real Athenian *hetaira*."

That was true, but I had never been impressed to know that their accomplishments were in the areas of conversation, eloquence and quick wits. It suggested that they might neglect the important things.

"Another time, perhaps," I said. "Come, let's go back to the city." We walked back like another couple returning from a visit with the dead, my arm about her shoulders and hers around my waist. The guard at the gate opened the little sally port at our knock and collected another fee.

"If they just made this a toll-gate," I remarked, "Ptolemy wouldn't be such a beggar."

She laughed musically, but that might just have been another of her accomplishments. "Are you enjoying your stay in Alexandria?"

"Except for the odd murder and attempt on my life, yes. If one cannot be in Rome, this is the place to be. How did you come to be here?"

"Seeking opportunity. I was raised and trained in the house of Chrysothemis, the most famous *hetaira* in Athens. It was a good life, as women's lives go in Athens, but that isn't saying much. Athenian men can't perceive even noble ladies as any better than slaves, and there's little satisfaction in entertaining men who just like an occasional change from their usual boys. So I saved my money and came to Alexandria. Here, among the foreign ambassadors, a genuine Greek *hetaira* is a mark of status, especially if she's Athenian. I've been in turn concubine to the Libyan, Armenian, Bithynian and Pontic ambassadors, the last back when Mithridates was still king. Now I serve the ambassador from Parthia."

"I've never met a woman of such impressive diplomatic credentials," I said. "But I cannot blame you for finding Rome more congenial."

"Yes. Mine is an unforgiving profession. One's desirability lasts only as long as youthful beauty. Once that fades, the road downhill is steep. I've known women to go from highly paid *hetaira* to mere streetwalking *porna* in two years."

"It is a hard world," I agreed.

"But it is looking better now," she said. "Tell me, have you visited the Daphne of Alexandria?"

"I'll confess, the diversions of the court have been too exhausting to seek out the more strenuous amusements of the city."

"It isn't as famous as the one in Antioch, but it is more than lively. You've been living the high life thus far, Roman. Why not come with me and sample the low?"

"Now?" I said, looking up at the full moon. "It must be near midnight!"

"Then things should just be getting lively," she said.

I was never one to hold out against temptation for long. "Lead on!" I said.

In Rome, it was easy for people to forget that some other cities have what is known as a night life. When Romans feel in a mood for debauchery, they begin their parties early so everyone can get properly paralytic before it gets too dark for their slaves to carry them home. In other places, they just light the torches and carry on.

The Daphne of Alexandria, named for the famous pleasure-garden of Antioch, was located in a beautiful grove in the Greek quarter, near the Paneum. Lines of torches led to its entrance, and between the torches vendors wandered, selling the wherewithal necessary for an evening of revelry. To my surprise, we were expected to wear masks. These were cleverly made out of pressed papyrus, artfully molded and painted to resemble various characters from mythology and poetry. They were rather like theatrical masks save that they left the mouth uncovered to facilitate eating, drinking and whatever other uses to which one wished to devote that orifice. I took one with a satyr's face; Hypatia, one with the licentious features of a nymph.

Then we had to have wreaths. Around our necks went wreaths

of laurel and vine leaves, and Hypatia wrapped a garland of myrtle around her beautiful black hair. I chose a generous chaplet of acorn-studded oak leaves to help disguise my Roman haircut. Not that I was greatly worried in this place, where the crowd consisted mainly of Greeks and other foreigners. There were few if any Egyptians.

At the entrance a fat fellow dressed as Silenus came to greet us. He wore the white chiton, carried the flowing bowl and wore the chaplet of vine leaves complete with dangling bunches of grapes. He recited verses of welcome in the rustic Greek of Boeotia.

> *"Friends, enter these sacred precincts*
> *In peace of heart and expectation of joy.*
> *Here dread Ares has no home,*
> *Nor does hardworking Hephaestus toil.*
> *But only Dionysus of the grape, Apollo of the lyre,*
> *Eros and the gentle Muses reign.*
> *Here each man is a swain,*
> *Each woman a carefree nymph.*
> *Leave care and sorrow behind you*
> *For these have no place here.*
> *Welcome, doubly welcome, and rejoice!"*

I tipped the man handsomely and we entered. The grove consisted of a series of interlocking arbors in the form of a maze. Torches burned, perfumed to give a fragrant smoke. There was just enough light to make everything clear and to reveal rich colors, but no more than that. A step would carry you from plain view to dark intimacy as desired. Everywhere were small tables on which little lamps burned, the low-level light making the masked faces nearby look like something from another world. Among the tables wandered women in the abbreviated tunics of mythical nymphs, men costumed as satyrs, boys with the pointed ears and tails of fauns, wild-haired women in the leopard skins of Bacchantes. All of them poured wine from amphorae or served delicacies from trays or danced or played wild music upon the syrinx and double flute and tambour. It was all quite licentious and abandoned to Roman eyes, but its joyous exuberance utterly lacked the fanatic hysteria of, say, the rites in the Temple of Baal-Ahriman.

"Come on, let's find a table," Hypatia urged. We wandered into the maze, taking so many turns that I despaired of ever finding a way out again. It is the virtue of such a place that you don't really care if you ever get out. Eventually we found a table with a top no larger than the thumping tambours of the musicians. A bright-eyed girl placed cups on our table and filled them. As she bent over, her breasts nearly fell out of her brief tunic. Hypatia eyed her as she danced away.

"A pity it's so cool," she said. "Most of the year they wear less."

We raised our cups and saluted each other. The cups were of finely polished olive wood, in keeping with the air of poetic rusticity. The wine was Greek, sharply resinous. A boy dressed as a faun brought a platter of fruits and cheeses. After the fanciful fare of the Palace, which was a delight to the eye and palate and a disaster to the digestion, this simple food was a distinct relief.

A troupe of Argive youths and maidens came through, performing the very ancient crane dance. Then came a huge, brawny man dressed as Hercules with a lion skin, who entertained the crowd with feats of strength. Then came singers who sang erotic verse or praises of the nature gods. There was no epic verse or songs of the deeds of warriors. It was as if all such unpleasantness had been banished for the night.

I found that one becomes a different person when wearing a mask. One is no longer constrained by the rigid views of one's upbringing and may instead adopt the persona of the mask, or else dispense with all such coercion and see the world as a god looking down from a passing cloud. Just so a gladiator, in donning the anonymity of the helmet, ceases to be the condemned criminal or the ruined wretch who sold himself to the *ludus*, and becomes instead the splendid and fearless warrior he must be out on the sand. Without my accustomed cosmopolitan, not to say cynical, poses, I could see these revelers and these performers as the very characters from pastoral poetry they pretended to be.

Hypatia, the hard-mouthed professional woman, became an exotic, flower-haired creature, her hands on the olive-wood cup like lilies made animate. I had always thought pastoral verse one of the silliest forms, but I was beginning to understand its attractions.

And I? I was growing rapidly drunk. The setting and the company provided an unwonted abandon, one to which I was not accustomed. At home, I always had to consider the possible political consequences of even my most private indiscretions. In a place like the Palace, I had to be ever mindful of who was behind me, as a matter of self-preservation. But here there was no one behind me. And, in any case, I was no longer Decius Caecilius Metellus the Younger, slightly disreputable scion of a prominent Roman family. I was a character in one of those poems where all the women are named Phyllis and Phoebe and the men are not men but "swains" and *they're* all named Daphnis or something of the sort.

In short, I let my guard down completely. I realize this sounds like the utmost folly, but a life lived cautiously is a dull one. All the really careful and cautious men I ever knew were drab wretches, while those who eschewed caution had interesting if brief lives.

Before long, I had our serving-girl, or one just like her, seated in my lap, while a faun-boy occupied the same place on Hypatia. They sang and popped grapes into our mouths as general liberties were taken by all. I learned more ways to drink someone's health in Greek than I ever dreamed could exist. Versatile language, Greek.

At some point during the night I found myself standing behind Hypatia, my hands on her lissome hips, and someone else's on mine. This might have been alarming, but it turned out that we were all doing the crane dance under the tutelage of the Argive youths and maidens. Like the bird for which it is named, the crane dance is a blend of grace and awkwardness. Hypatia supplied one and I the other. I had never danced before. Roman men never dance unless they belong to one of the dancing priesthoods. It seemed to me that these Greeks had happened upon a good thing.

The moon was very low when the whole reveling crowd poured out of the Daphne and wound its way up the spiral path of the Paneum. Live creatures mixed with the bronze ones along the path, cavorting and disporting themselves in the time-honored fashion of rural worshippers. In the heat of their exertions, many had divested themselves of clothing along with their inhibitions and sense of decorum.

In the sanctuary we all sang traditional hymns to Pan in the Arcadian dialect. The flickering light of the torches played over the bronze god and I thought I saw him smile, a real smile, not the fraudulent grimacing of Baal-Ahriman. The women draped their garlands around his neck and over his outsized phallus, and a few of the masked ladies begged him to help them conceive. If the fervor of the worship were of any help, they would all surely bear twins.

It was an easy walk from the Paneum to the Palace, but I was sorry to see the place again. I was weary of its plots and intrigues, and for all its luxuries it seemed a grim place after a magical night spent in the Daphne.

"I must leave you here," Hypatia said as we approached the gate nearest the Roman embassy. "My protector keeps me in a house close by. It is forbidden for women to be housed in the Parthian embassy."

"How will you come to me tomorrow?" I asked, reluctant to see her go despite my better instincts.

She pushed back her mask, came into my arms and kissed me. She was like a sack of wriggling eels, and I was ready to carry her into a doorway and make good on the offer I had turned down in the Necropolis. But she pulled away and placed her fingers across my lips.

"It is too late now, the time is past. But look for me to come tomorrow evening. One with the right friends can go about freely within the Palace, and I have more friends than most. I will bring the book, and you will help me to establish myself in Rome."

"I have given my word," I said.

"Good night, then. Until tomorrow." She turned and was gone.

With a sigh I staggered toward the gate. I remembered to take off my mask and stuck it inside my tunic. The guard at the gate sleepily returned my equally sleepy salute. The Palace was as lifeless as the Necropolis as I made my way across its elaborate pavements.

The embassy was, if anything, even more devoid of life, not even a slave stirring. That suited me perfectly. I was sure that, by this time, my appearance must confirm Creticus's worst fears about me. I made my way to my quarters undetected and dropped my cloak to the floor, let my weapons clank onto a table, then thought better of that and locked them away in my chest. The mask I hung on the wall.

I left my tunic where it fell and brushed the vine leaves from my hair before collapsing into my bed. It had been one of the most eventful days of my life. Had it really started out with my visit to Baal-Ahriman? It seemed more like weeks ago. First the fine intellectual exercise of deciphering the trickery of Ataxas, then my flight through the Rakhotis, culminating in the Salt Market riot.

Then the night, which had begun in a city of the dead and ended in a veritable Arcadian fertility rite. Even at my most adventurous, I was unaccustomed to so many changes of venue and circumstance. In this place death lurked in many places and took many guises, but I would never die of boredom.

The memory of Hypatia writhing against me was unsettling,

but I knew that I would see her again the next night. Perhaps there was some other site of exotic debauchery we could try. And perhaps what she was to bring me would solve the mysteries surrounding the death of Iphicrates.

I was well pleased with the events of the day and the prospects for the morrow. It was just as well that I could go to sleep in such a state of complacency, because when I woke up, there was a dead woman in bed with me.

11

I COULD NOT UNDERSTAND WHY A LE-
gion of cocks was crowing in my ear. Surely, with all their strange
tastes, these pseudo-Egyptian Macedonians didn't keep livestock
in the Palace. Then my head began to clear and I realized that it
was the embassy slaves raising the racket. Some of them were eunuchs and these added a falsetto quality to the uproar. What on earth
had them so upset?

I struggled to a sitting position, rubbing my eyes to get them
into focus. Right away, I knew that I had the sort of hangover that
makes you certain that the gods robbed you of your youth in your
sleep. My mouth tasted like the bottom of a *garum* vat. The resin
from the Greek wine lent a certain dockside element to the foulness,
as if my mouth had been tarred and caulked.

I glared blearily at the slave who stood in the doorway pointing
at me and gabbling something in Egyptian. Others behind him
stared wide-eyed.

"What are you pointing at?" I demanded. I intended to sound

forceful. But my voice came out in a croak. "Have you all gone mad?"

Then I realized that he was not pointing at me. He was pointing just to one side of me. With a prickling scalp I turned to see, then squeezed my eyes shut. It didn't help. When I opened them again, she was still there. It was Hypatia, and she was quite dead. Were I a poet, I would say that her staring eyes were full of reproach, but they expressed nothing at all. The eyes of the dead never do.

She was naked, and the bone hilt of a dagger protruded from just below her left breast. There was a small wound below her left ear, and her lovely black hair was matted with blood. I saw her bloodstained gown on the floor by her.

"What is this?" Creticus came storming in and went pale when he saw the little tableau. Behind him were Rufus and the others.

"It isn't . . ." I cursed my thick tongue.

Creticus pointed at me. "Decius Caecilius Metellus, I arrest you. Bind him and throw him in the cellar."

A pair of burly, shaven-headed men came forward and laid hands on me. These were the Binder and the Whipper, the slave disciplinarians belonging to the embassy. They didn't often get a chance to practice their skills on a free man and they made the most of it. They jerked my arms behind me and slapped manacles around my wrists. Then they hauled me to my feet.

"At least let me get dressed!" I hissed.

"Decius, you are not only a degenerate but a madman," Creticus said. "I will go to talk to the king. Since you are part of the embassy, he can't call for your head, but rest assured I'll have you tried before the Senate and banished to the smallest, most barren island in the sea!"

"I'm innocent!" I croaked. "Bring Asklepiodes!"

"What?" Creticus said. "Who?"

"Asklepiodes, the physician! I want him to examine that body before these Greeks cremate it! He can prove that I am innocent!" Actually I was confident of no such thing, but I was desperate.

"Rufus! Go to the Museum and fetch him." His shocked face nodded minutely. I was not even sure he understood my words.

The Whipper and the Binder hustled me through the halls and past goggling slaves, then down a flight of steps to the cellar. There they bolted a neck-ring on me and chained me to the wall. They talked to each other merrily in some barbarous tongue, their bronze-studded belts scraping my abused hide as they disposed of me. With their big bellies and thick, leather-banded arms, they looked like apes imitating men. Well, one doesn't employ disciplinarians for their refinements. With a final test of my bonds, they left me to my thoughts. These were not pleasant.

Somehow, I had been neatly bagged. I was not sure how this had been done, but it seemed to have been done with my fullest cooperation. I was now assumed by everyone to be a murderer. The victim had been a free woman and a resident of Alexandria, although of foreign origin. At the very best, Ptolemy would allow me to be quietly shipped off to Rome. I had no doubt that Creticus would make good on his threat to impeach me before the Senate. Roman officials were allowed a certain license in foreign lands, but for a member of a diplomatic mission to disgrace the Republic was unconscionable.

How to get out of this? It had all been so sudden, and my mind so benumbed, that I had not been able to take in the circumstances, much less devise a defense. I knew a few basic facts: The woman was Hypatia, she was in my bed and she was unquestionably dead. What, if anything, was in my favor?

The knife buried in her body was not mine. I remembered with relief that I had locked my weapons away before retiring. Perhaps something could be made of that. I certainly had no reason to kill her, but I had enough experience with murder trials to know that a motive is the least of considerations, especially when evidence of culpability is strong. It was certainly strong in this case.

How had this been carried out? All too easily. The whole Palace had been sound asleep, and I had been too sodden to notice the arrival of marauding Gauls. Poor Hypatia had simply been deposited in my bed and the murderers or their lackeys had strolled away, all of it as casual as tradesmen making a delivery.

But why had they not simply killed me? If Achillas and Ataxas were determined to put an end to my investigation, it seemed to me that the simplest thing would have been to deposit the dagger in *my* heart, not in some innocent woman's. Not that Hypatia had been terribly innocent, either in her professional life or in her intentions toward the conspirators. A dungeon is an excellent place to mull over questions like this, free as it is from distractions. I don't recommend it as a regular practice.

I wished that I could consult my friends Cicero and Milo on this. Between Cicero's legal expertise and Milo's criminal genius, they would have cracked this problem within minutes. Cicero had once told me that many men in legal difficulties failed to understand their situation because they always assumed themselves to be the focus of the problem. Each man exists at the center of his own personal cosmos and believes that he must be the foremost concern of gods and men. This is a grievous fallacy and must be guarded against.

I suspected that Achillas was behind everything. Ataxas was his accomplice and cat's-paw. Milo had told me that he overcame the other gang leaders in Rome by simply thinking like them. In this way he could anticipate their every attack. The difficult part, he said, was in duplicating the thought processes of someone more stupid than oneself, which was always the case.

Achillas wanted me out of the way, but was I all that important? This was a man who lusted for the throne of Egypt. My investigation was causing him annoyance, threatening to upset his plans, but what was that in the context of his greater agenda? For more than a century it had been understood that the ruler of Egypt would be the one favored by Rome, and Rome had, for the sake of stability and consistency, opted to support the weak, foolish but traditional Ptolemies.

I was not Achillas's problem. Rome was his problem.

And I had very thoughtfully given him a wonderful weapon to

use against Rome. I, a Roman diplomat, had murdered a free woman of Alexandria. And I had done it, not merely in the city, but within the Palace itself. The city was already poised to erupt in anti-Roman riots, and I had poured oil on the coals.

And there was that old Gaulish saying about two birds with one arrow or something of the sort. The traitorous Hypatia had to be disposed of anyway, so why not let her be my poor, innocent victim? And that turned my mind down other channels. Had her treachery been detected, or had it been planned by Achillas from the start? She might have been given a role to play, not understanding, of course, that she was to be paid with a dagger through the heart. An Athenian *hetaira* receives training comparable to an actor's, and she knew well how to keep me off guard, lusting for the mysterious book and her skilled body alternately. And she knew that a beautiful woman cannot fail to control a young man by letting him know that she finds him irresistible. Or an old one either, for that matter.

I was distracted by a noise from the top of the stairs. The door opened and shut and there was a glow from the top step.

"Whoever you are, I hope you've come to let me go. I am innocent!"

"It's Julia."

"How did you get here?" I asked.

"I walked, idiot."

"Oh. Ah, Julia, it might not be a good idea to bring that lamp too close. They dragged me from bed and didn't give me a chance to dress. I'm, well, the only way to describe my condition is naked."

She came on relentlessly. "If we're to be married, I'll have to learn the awful truth sooner or later. Besides, I believe that was also the state of that poor woman they found in your bed. Oh, Decius, what have you done now? I knew that you were reckless, but you've never murdered anyone before."

"Do you believe I did?" If my betrothed thought I was a murderer, I was really in trouble.

"I know it can't be, but the circumstances are so damning! The story is all over the Palace."

"And I'll bet I know who's spreading it. Julia, Asklepiodes has to examine that woman's body while it's still in my room, if it hasn't been moved already. I think Rufus has gone to get him, but I can't be sure."

"I'll see about it," she said. "Now tell me everything that happened." So I did. She frowned deeply when I got to the part about going to the Daphne.

"You are telling me that you took a prostitute to Alexandria's most notorious scene of debauchery?"

"Julia," I protested, "she was my informant! I had to keep her happy!"

"How convenient! Would you have felt so compelled if she had been old and ugly?"

"Julia, don't speak foolishly. Would the Parthian ambassador have an old and ugly concubine?"

"Listen to me, Decius. I will do what I can to get you out of this alive, but I am beginning to doubt your sanity. A man who can get himself into a situation this grotesque makes a very doubtful prospect as a husband, even without consorting with prostitutes."

"I have to get that book, Julia," I insisted. "It must be the key! With that I can prove the conspiracy, I will earn the gratitude of Ptolemy, I'll be the latest savior of Rome and all will be forgiven!"

"You are pinning a lot of hopes on very little. The woman may have been lying about the book."

"I don't think so. I think this was a case where telling the truth was the easiest lure."

"You are in no position to get hold of it," she pointed out.

"Alas, yes. Not only am I chained like a recalcitrant slave, but security is probably tighter at the Parthian embassy than it is at the Roman." Then something occurred to me. "Julia, didn't the Parthian ambassador depend on Hypatia to help him in translating correspondence?"

"According to her, yes."

"Well, *women are not allowed in the Parthian embassy!* So where did they carry out all this work?"

"You tell me."

"He kept her in a house somewhere near the Palace. That is most likely where they went over the book from the Library, and it may still be there!"

"Surely Achillas would have collected it by now if it is so incriminating."

"Not necessarily. Achillas thinks he had solved all his problems. He has no need to move swiftly now. I have to get that book!"

"How?" she said, practically.

"If this were Rome, I could just ask Milo and he would put a dozen experienced burglars at my disposal."

"You will have noticed that this is not Rome."

"That means I'll have to do it myself."

Idly, she fingered the chains that hung from my limbs.

"Yes, I admit that there are complications. I have to get free. Let me concentrate on that. You just find out where the house of Hypatia is to be found. The court women gossip a lot; some of them must know. She said she had many friends in the Palace."

"I'll do what I can, but I have a feeling that the safest thing for you would be a swift ship for Rome and a nice, safe trial before the Senate. My uncle's influence . . ."

"I don't want to be beholden to Caius Julius," I snapped. "Besides, what good is the influence of a Consul if my own family wants me exiled for disgracing them? Just find out where that house is. I'll bribe a slave to file these chains off if I have to. Now go. And see about Asklepiodes!"

She leaned forward and kissed me, then she whirled and was gone. She was a sweet, brave girl, but I knew that business in the Daphne would plague me for the rest of my life.

She left the lamp, and after a while this feeble light was sufficient for me to see my abode. It was the wine cellar. An open channel of running water passed through the room, and the amphorae of wine were set in the water to keep cool. An ingenious system of underground channels connected Alexandria to the Nile, and the water ran through the basements of most of the buildings and houses of the city, supplying them with water and giving them drainage for the sewers.

Using this room for disciplinary purposes had a certain fiendish ingenuity, for the length of the neck-chain kept the wine forever out of reach, inflicting the punishment of Tantalus. Luckily, wine was the last thing on my mind. But the smell of the river water increased my already raging thirst.

After a while the door opened again and several men came down the steps. Some of them were armed. Creticus was with them. At his gesture the Whipper and the Binder unlocked my bonds and hauled me to my feet.

"Decius," Creticus said, "I've arranged for a hearing before King Ptolemy, before this situation gets completely out of hand. He's given us safe-conduct to the throne room and back."

"Water," I said. A slave dipped a bowl in the river water and brought it to me. Hoping it wouldn't make me deathly ill, I drank until I thought I could speak without choking.

"Wouldn't it be safer to have him come here?" I asked. "This is Roman territory."

"A king does not go out of his way to do favors for a degenerate murderer, even one from Rome. Count yourself lucky."

"Achillas is behind this," I said.

Creticus turned to the others. "Wash him up and get him dressed. Be quick about it and don't let him out of your sight."

He went back up the stairs and I was dragged up behind him. In the bathhouse I washed and was barbered and I drank a great deal more water. Cleaned up and in fresh clothes, I felt infinitely better. Even a guilty man looks good in a toga. The Roman party was assembled in the atrium. I didn't see Rufus there.

"Let's go," Creticus snapped. "And act like Romans!" We descended the steps of the embassy. At the bottom of the steps, the extent of Roman territory, a double file of Macedonian soldiers extended from embassy to Palace. All the usual gawkers gawked as we made our stately way.

In the throne room, we found Ptolemy decked out in full monarchial fig. It was a typically Alexandrian mixture. He wore a Macedonian royal robe of Tyrian purple heavily embroidered with gold, much like a Roman triumphal robe. On his head was the double crown of Egypt, the white crown towering from within the red crown. On its forepeak were the heads of the cobra and the vulture. Everything in Egypt is doubled, for Upper and Lower Egypt. In his hands were the crook and the flail, and attached to his chin was the silly little false beard that signified the power of the Pharaohs. For a wonder, he appeared to be sober.

Achillas was there as well, along with a number of men in Parthian clothing. Berenice was there but had, thankfully, left her cheetahs behind, along with the baboons and dwarfs. There was a great gaggle of court hangers-on, and I saw Julia among them, chatting up the ladies. Fausta stood by Berenice, looking as sardonic as usual.

"Quintus Caecilius Metellus Creticus," Ptolemy began, "grave charges have been brought against your kinsman Decius Caecilius Metellus the Younger. A free woman, a resident foreigner residing in Alexandria, was found murdered in his bed this morning. All evidence points to his guilt. What have you to say?"

"Your Majesty, my kinsman Decius is a rash and foolish young man, but I hardly think him capable of coldblooded murder. Be that as it may, the embassy is by ancient custom Roman territory, and by rights it is a Roman court which should try him."

"Your Majesty," cried Achillas, "this cannot be set aside so easily. Another embassy is involved. The woman Hypatia, murdered by the younger Metellus, was the bound concubine of my good friend, his Excellency Orodes, Ambassador of King Phraates III of Parthia."

Ptolemy looked at the head of the Parthian delegation. "Is this true?"

183

The man came forward. "It is, your Majesty." He unrolled a scroll and held it before the king's eyes. "This is her contract of concubinage. You will note that it had more than a year to run, and that man"—he pointed a long finger at me—"owes me for the balance of her contract!"

"I see," Ptolemy said. "In this case, Ambassador Metellus, since it involves another foreign embassy, I must have a further inquiry. Does Decius insist upon protesting his innocence?"

"I do, sir," I said, not waiting for Creticus to step in.

"Your Majesty," Achillas said, "not only was the woman's body in his bed, but nearby were a mask and garlands of the sort peddled at the Daphne. If you wish, I will produce witnesses to testify that the murderer and the woman were seen cavorting there last night."

Creticus turned scarlet and began to swell like a bullfrog. Now his anger was directed at Achillas rather than at me.

"May I ask your business in all this, sir? And how is it that you know what was in Decius's room? That is Roman territory!"

"As for my business, I am a loyal servant of King Ptolemy and I want no violent foreigners anywhere near him. As for my knowing what was found this morning, everybody in the Palace knows by now. Your staff is a talkative lot."

"Paid spies is more like it!" Creticus said.

At that moment a door opened and Rufus came in, closely followed by Amphytrion and Asklepiodes, I could have fainted with relief. Asklepiodes gave me a smile as he passed. Save me, old friend, I thought. Rufus joined the Roman party and leaned toward me.

"I no longer owe you five hundred *denarii*," he whispered.

"With all my heart," I said fervently. I knew I would get it back. The man was a miserable judge of horses and charioteers.

"And what might you gentlemen be doing here?" Ptolemy asked.

"Your Majesty," Amphytrion said with a bow, "this is the

physician Asklepiodes, a visiting lecturer attached to the School of Medicine of the Museum."

"I remember him," Ptolemy said.

"Sir, Asklepiodes is acknowledged to be the world's foremost expert on the subject of wounds violently inflicted by weapons. We have just come from examining the murdered woman, and he has information of interest of these proceedings."

"Your Majesty!" Achillas yelled. "Must we endure the mumbling sophistry of these philosophers?"

"Majesty," Creticus said, "noble Amphytrion speaks truly. Asklepiodes is a recognized authority in this field and has testified before Roman courts many times in the past."

"Speak, then, learned Asklepiodes," said Ptolemy.

Asklepiodes took the center of the room and did a bit of actor's business with his robe, then began.

"Your Majesty, your Excellencies of the embassies, noble gentlemen and ladies of the court, what I am about to say I swear by Apollo Silverbow, by Hermes Thrice Great and by Hippocrates, founder of my art."

"Got great style, doesn't he?" Rufus whispered.

"Shhh!" I said.

"The woman identified as Hypatia, *hetaira* of Athens, died sometime in the very early hours of this morning. A knife was found thrust between her ribs just below the left mammary, but this blow was delivered postmortem. The death-wound was a small cut to the carotid just beneath the left ear." Everyone leaned forward to hear his words, delivered with a sonorousness of voice and a subtlety of gesture that is difficult to describe.

"The body was nearly devoid of blood, as is frequently the case after such a wound. Yet there was no blood in the room or on the bed, save for some on the gown which lay on the floor, and some soaked into the woman's hair, neither in sufficient quantity to account for the condition of the body."

"This meaning?" Ptolemy said.

"The woman was killed elsewhere, and then brought to the embassy and deposited in the bed of the accused." A prolonged sigh went through the room.

Achillas shrugged. "So he killed her somewhere else and then took her to bed. Romans are necrophiles. I've always said so."

"And this," Asklepiodes said, "is the knife thrust into the body of the unfortunate woman." He held up a bone-handled weapon, its blade about eight inches long, somewhat curved and single-edged. Now there was a gasp from the Roman party.

"Is this significant?" Ptolemy asked.

"Your Majesty," Creticus said, "this changes things! I am now far more inclined to support my troublesome young relative's assertion of his innocence."

Ptolemy examined the knife with bloodshot orbs. "It looks ordinary enough to me."

"Perhaps in Alexandria," Creticus said, his lawyer's blood up, "but not in Rome! Sir, in Rome such a weapon is called a *sica*. You see that it is curved and has but a single edge. Under Roman law it is defined as an infamous weapon. It is the favored weapon of common cutthroats and of Thracian gladiators. The honorable weapons are the straight, double-edged *pugio* and *gladius*. These are the honest weapons of free men!"

"You mean," Ptolemy said, "that mere shape of blade makes one weapon honest and the other infamous?"

"Exactly," Creticus affirmed. "I am reluctant to believe that a kinsman of mine would commit cowardly murder. But if he did, he might use a *pugio* or a *gladius*, or even his bare hands, but he would *never* stoop to killing with a *sica!*"

"Hear, hear!" shouted the Roman contingent, myself included.

"Your Majesty," Achillas said, "are we not only to lend credence to sophists but to consider the impenetrable nonsense of Roman law? This man has brought dishonor on the whole court of Egypt, and has shown likewise the contempt in which Rome holds our nation!"

"Lord Achillas." Ptolemy said, "you are making a great deal of fuss about a dead whore. You are to cease this instant." It was good to see the old sot show a little iron. Churlishly, Achillas nodded. Ptolemy turned toward us.

"Your Excellency, I am now inclined to credit your kinsman's claim of innocence, although this is mystifying. Your legal customs are strange to us, but I have no doubt that they are perfectly sensible to you. Lord Orodes"—he turned to the Parthian—"if it will help to settle things, I will buy up the remainder of the dead woman's contract myself. Since her body is in my house, even though she may not have died there, I will even see to her funeral. Is that satisfactory?"

Orodes glowered. "Perfectly, your Majesty."

Now Ptolemy turned back toward us. "Tell me, young Decius, how did you happen to be in this woman's company, romping about in the Daphne?"

"Actually, sir," I said, feeling that I was all but clear, "we met in the Necropolis." At this the whole court roared with laughter.

"Your Majesty," Creticus said, "what is the meaning of this unseemly mirth?"

Ptolemy wiped tears from his eyes. "Excellency, the Necropolis is the resting place for our honored dead, but it is also the most popular fornicating-place in Alexandria. Why, in my younger days . . . well, never mind. Go on, young Decius. This was worth getting up early for."

"Sir, I was engaged in that investigation for which you yourself commissioned me."

"I have not forgotten."

"The woman set the assignation to tell me something of great importance. I thought the opportunity was worth the effort and I met her as directed. She wanted to make her home in Rome but needed a patron there to give her legal support. I agreed to this if her evidence proved to be of sufficient importance."

"And the nature of this evidence?" the king asked.

"She was supposed to deliver it to me tonight, but she did not

live to do so. I do not know what the evidence was supposed to be."
This was not quite a lie. The book itself was not the incriminating
item. I hadn't studied law for nothing.

"And how did you end up at the Daphne?" Ptolemy asked.

"She expressed a desire to go there," I said.

"And?"

"The night was yet young. Why not?" At this everyone erupted
in laughter again, except for Achillas and Orodes. And Julia.

"Quintus Caecilius Metellus Creticus."

"Yes, your Majesty?"

"I find sufficient grounds to doubt your kinsman's guilt. I re-
lease him to your custody. Keep him out of mischief. I bid this
court disperse." A chamberlain clanged his iron-shod staff on the
polished marble and everyone bowed to the king, the Romans in-
clining slightly, the other foreigners deeply, the Egyptians all the
way to the floor.

"Back to the embassy," Creticus said. We turned and walked
from the court with great dignity. Asklepiodes fell in beside me.

"That was an excellent performance, even for me," he said
complacently.

"I won't forget it. Was there anything else you didn't tell the
king?"

"I told all that reinforced your innocence. Innocence of murder, that is. But there were other things. There were many bruises.
The woman was killed with considerable violence."

"Torture?"

"I saw no sign of it. I found this in her mouth." He handed
me something that looked like a piece of soggy leather, brownish
on one side, pinkish on the other.

"What is it?" I asked.

"Human flesh. Assuming that the lady was not a cannibal,
this is a piece of her murderer. One of her murderers, anyway. A
man in his late forties or early fifties, of one of the fair-skinned
races, but he has spent much of his life exposed to sunlight."

"Asklepiodes, you surpass yourself. Any idea which part it came from?"

"A part habitually exposed to the sun. There isn't enough of it to tell much more than that. It did not come from the face, hands, feet or penis. My guess would be the shoulder or upper arm, but even my art cannot guarantee that."

"It's sufficient," I assured him. "I'll get them all and this will help."

"No, you won't," Creticus said. "You are going nowhere except to your quarters. From there you are going onto the first ship to sail from here for Rome. You may not be a murderer, but you are more trouble than a cohort of Sicilian auxiliaries! I want to hear nothing further of you save the welcome news that you have sailed out past the Pharos. Good day to you!" With that he stormed up the steps of the embassy. I followed, the others patting me on the shoulder.

"I never thought you did it, Decius," was the usual comment.

Asklepiodes went with me to my quarters. Hypatia's body had been taken away, along with the bloody gown. I knew I would never be able to get into that bed again. I called for some slaves.

"Take that bed out and burn it," I ordered. "Fetch me another." You could do things like that in Egypt. Then, remembering that I hadn't eaten, I called for some food.

"Any progress on the death of Iphicrates?" Asklepiodes asked. While our table was set and while we ate, I told him what had happened, always pausing when a slave was within hearing. Some of them, at least, had reported to Achillas. Asklepiodes heard me out, nodding and making wise sounds.

"Clever about the reflector," he said. "Iphicrates was into more realms of knowledge than he let on. I wonder what Achillas promised him."

"What? I suppose he paid him with money."

"Possibly, but Iphicrates never struck me as a man with a great love of wealth. But many scholars want high prestige and honors among their fellows. If Achillas made himself king of Egypt, he would be in a position to make Iphicrates the head of the Museum. He could use all its facilities and endowments to further his grandiose projects. For the sort of scholar who actually likes to *do* things, to see his plans transferred from papyrus into reality, that is a heady prospect."

"Asklepiodes," I said, "I've known men to fight and scheme and commit all sorts of treachery for the sake of wealth, or for revenge. I've seen them devote their lives to war and politics and even to commit treason in order to gain power over their fellow men. I confess it never occurred to me that they might do all these things for . . . for a sort of intellectual preferment."

He smiled benignly. "It has been your good fortune that you have never had to deal with professional philosophers."

12

I WAITED UNTIL NIGHT, WHICH I CON-
sidered to be a display of commendable restraint. After Asklepiodes
left, I was not without visitors. To my surprise, one of them was
Fausta. She came shortly before dusk, cool and imperious as ever.
She was a woman I always found intimidating. The Cornelians always considered themselves favored even among patricians, and on
top of that, she was the daughter of Sulla, the most feared Dictator
in the history of Rome. But these things were not enough. She was
a twin, and one of an identical brother-sister pair. This was a combination so portentous that she was not merely respected but genuinely feared. Despite her great wealth, she had remained
unmarried until the unexpected suit of Titus Annius Milo, perhaps
the only man of my acquaintance who was utterly without fear.

I knew that he would come to regret this match. For all his
great charm and penetrating intellect, poor Milo lacked experience
with women. His fixation, like that of so many, was power. In its
pursuit he had neglected what were, to him, lesser matters, such

as the necessary but sometimes bewildering relations between men and women. Milo had no use for bewilderment.

The fact was that Fausta was an acquisition for Milo. He was a nobody from Ostia who had come to Rome to win the city. He had started from nothing to become a prominent gang leader and had now started up the ladder of office. He wanted a wife, and the wife had to be noble, preferably patrician. It would not come amiss if she were presentable as well. Fausta was perfect, as far as he was concerned. He neglected the fact that Fausta was Fausta. It was like buying a horse for nothing but its looks and its bloodlines, forgetting that it might throw you and cheerfully trample and kick you to death for the fun of it. But all that was in the future.

"I begin to see what Julia finds attractive in you, Decius Caecilius," she said by way of preamble.

"That I get locked up in dungeons and put on trial for my life?" I said.

She sat in a spindly Egyptian chair. "What is it like to be chained naked to a wall? Is it exciting?"

"If you wish," I said, "I can call in the Binder and the Whipper. They can take you to the cellar and chain you up nicely. Any special services you'd like to request first?"

"Oh, it's such a bore when it's voluntary."

"Fausta, surely you didn't come here to discuss your singular tastes in entertainment?"

"No, I came to bring you this." She held out a folded papyrus. "It's from Julia. Are you going to do something foolish?"

"At the first opportunity." I took the papyrus from her and opened it. "Why didn't Julia bring it herself?"

"Berenice insisted that Julia help her choose a gown for the banquet tonight. She owns several hundred, so don't expect to see Julia any time soon. Julia said she was very pleased with the way you looked without your clothes."

"She has excellent taste." I read the note. *The house where Hypatia lived is on the Street of the Carpenters, opposite the eastern end of the theater. It has a red front and the doorposts are carved with acanthus leaves. Don't do anything foolish.*

"You read this?" I said.

"Of course I read it. I'm no slave messenger. Why do you need to know where that poor woman's house is?"

"My reasons are sufficient to me. Why are you so curious?"

"If you are so hated by so many powerful men, there must be more to you than I thought."

"How good it is to enter your charmed circle. Yes, I, too, am the coveted target of assassins."

"I think that always makes a man more interesting and exciting. But not poor Julia. She actually worries about you." To my relief, Fausta rose. "I must go now, Decius. I think, should you live, you might turn out to be an interesting man." And so she left.

Rufus came by to tell me that Creticus was making inquiries about ships leaving for Rome. Failing Rome, for anywhere at all. I clearly had little time to settle matters in Alexandria. Fortunately, Creticus hadn't set armed guards over me. This might have been because the embassy had no armed guards. There were always the Whipper and the Binder, but now that I was no longer charged with murder, it would have been unfitting to set slaves over me.

So when it was fully dark and everyone had retired, I just put on my cloak and walked out.

Once again, I was on the streets of Alexandria at night. The theater was one of the landmarks of the city, and I made for it. The theaters of Greece were cut into hillsides, taking advantage of natural terrain features. Since Alexandria was flat, the theater of Alexandria was a free-standing building, much like the one Pompey was even then building on the Campus Martius in Rome. It was visible from a long distance, and I could see it almost as soon as I left the Palace enclosure.

The theater in Alexandria was the great resort of prostitutes, as was and is the Circus Maximus in Rome. There is something about dark archways that is conducive to their trade. There were practitioners of both of the usual sexes, and some who seemed to be a combination of both.

I made a show of strolling about, examining the wares to be had, making comparisons of appearance, price and specialty (I truly was not interested), all the while keeping an eye on the red-fronted house with the carved doorposts. In the torchlight it was actually possible to distinguish color. I had to assume that the leaves adorning the doorposts were of the acanthus. I wouldn't know acanthus from poplar. A person of enormous, liquid-brown eyes and indeterminate gender noticed my preoccupation and sidled over to me.

"You can't afford that one," she said (I use "she" for lack of an adequate pronoun).

"How do you know?" I asked.

"She is kept by some very rich men. They keep her well, and I doubt that they would like it if she were to spread herself too thin."

"Men?" I said. "She is kept by more than one?"

"Oh, yes. At least three who go there in turn; sometimes all three are in there at once. She must have some sophisticated tricks to keep all three amused at once."

"Who are they?" I asked.

"Why are you so curious about her?" she said suspiciously.

I almost told her about the murder, but she would clam up if she thought she might be hauled in for an investigation.

"I have reason to believe she's a slave who ran away from her master in Syracuse."

"Then there is reward money involved."

"I am willing to pay for information."

"I've already given you some," she said petulantly.

"That was your miscalculation." I held out two silver *denarii* and dropped them into the soft palm. "Describe the three regulars."

"One is an Eastern foreigner, a Syrian or Parthian, I think. He's the one who's there almost every night. There's a big, good-looking man who favors clothes with a military cut. The third is a little Greek. Not from Greece, I don't think, but from one of the Eastern colony cities."

"How can you tell that?"

"He's bought the services of a few of the boys. I've heard him talk. He tries to speak like an Athenian, but he can't quite pull it off. Fine voice, though, like a trained orator."

"Are any of those boys here tonight?" I asked.

"I don't think so. They're a pretty transient lot, runaways mostly, both slave and free. They don't last long."

I tossed her another *denarius* and went toward the house. I had expected Orodes and Achillas, but who was the Greek? A woman like Hypatia might keep any number of lovers on the side, but the catamite had said that all three of these had been in the house at the same time, upon occasion. No matter. My business was with a certain book in that house.

There were no lamps showing, but that meant nothing. The only windows on the street side were two small ones on the second story. The flanking buildings appeared to be private houses as well. I walked around the block. On the opposite side was a row of small shops. Most were shuttered for the night, but there was a small wine-shop right in the middle of the block. As near as I could make out, it was directly opposite Hypatia's house. I went in and found a place much like its Roman equivalent, only better lit and ventilated. A half-wall separated it from the street, its upper half bearing top-hinged shutters that were propped open to catch the evening air.

Inside, a long counter ran the length of one wall. The other side was devoted to a number of small tables at which a dozen or so patrons sat, drinking and talking in low tones. None of them paid me any heed when I entered. I went to the bar and ordered a cup of Chian. There were platters of bar food, and I remembered that it had been a while since I had eaten, and it is always a mistake to commit burglary on an empty stomach. So I loaded a plate with bread, cheese, figs and sausage.

As I annihilated everything on the plate, I pondered my next move. I had to get into that house, and the easiest way seemed to be through the back of this one. I took my empty cup and plate to the bar.

"More, sir?" asked the barkeep, a one-eyed man in a dirty tunic.

"Not just now. Is there a public latrine out back?"

"No, there's one just down the street."

"That won't do," I said. "I need to get out back. The truth is, I'm visiting a lady's house and I'd rather not be seen going in." I'd actually told the truth.

He grinned lopsidedly and took the silver *denarius* I held out. "Come this way, sir."

He led me through a curtained doorway into the rear of the shop. There was a storeroom with amphorae, full on the right, empties on the left, and miscellaneous goods and supplies. A stairway led to the upper floor, undoubtedly the shopkeeper's home. He unbolted a rear door and let me through.

"Will you be coming back this way?" he asked.

"Probably not, but it's possible."

"I can't leave it unbolted, but if you pound loud enough. I'll come and open it up for you."

"There will be another *denarius* for your trouble should it be necessary," I assured him.

"Good evening to you, then, sir." I got the impression that he had performed this service before.

Behind the shop was a large courtyard shared by most of the houses on the block. As in Rome, few buildings actually fronted on the streets in Alexandria. The yards were separated by head-high, gated walls. I scrambled atop a wall and surveyed the scene. No one appeared to be in the yards or on the second-story balconies. All was quiet. Cats walked silently along the tops of the low walls like spirits.

The house that I judged to be Hypatia's showed no lights. I walked along the wall and jumped down into its courtyard. The space was filled with planters in which flowers bloomed. A marble table stood in its center, circled by bronze chairs. It was undoubtedly a pleasant spot in the daytime. Poor Hypatia must have taken great pleasure in it.

I made my way past the flowers and tried the ground-floor door. It opened quietly. I went in cautiously, afraid there might be slaves somewhere about, sleeping lightly. I didn't dare try to fetch a light from one of the street torches until I was sure I was alone, so I spent the next hour or more tiptoeing through the house, guiding myself by touch. I found no one on either floor. I took a lamp and began to descend the stairs, congratulating myself on my ingenuity and good fortune. Then I heard a sound at the door. Somebody was fumbling at it with a key. I tiptoed back up the stair and to the largest room on the second floor. It was a bedroom, and I scrambled beneath the bed like the wife's young lover in a farce.

I heard men's voices downstairs, and saw faint lights flickering on the walls of the stairwell. Then the voices were in the room. From my point of limited vantage I counted three pairs of feet, one in slippers, one in Greek sandals, one in military boots.

"It is in that cabinet," said a heavily accented voice. "I could have fetched it myself."

"There are many things we could all do individually, if we trusted one another, which we do not." This was a cultivated Greek voice with a faint accent. The mystery man.

"We don't have all night," said a third voice, brusque and military. "Let's go over it."

This had to be Achillas, I thought, although his words were somewhat tightly spoken, as if suppressing some resentment. Well, conspirators hardly ever get along very well. There came a shuffling of feet and a scraping of furniture. A loud rustling announced the unrolling of a heavy scroll.

"Most interesting work," said the Greek voice. "Only the first part is Biton's treatise on war engines, you know, written in his own hand. It also contains the work of Aeneas Tacticus and a unique

work by one Athenaeus concerning the mechanical school established by the tyrant Dionysus I of Syracuse to improve military
engineering, all of it profusely illustrated."

"I read it all years ago," said Military Boots. "Valuable stuff,
but that's not what's important."

"So it isn't," said Greek Sandals. "But . . ." There was a sound
of more rustling. ". . . here are the original plans by Iphicrates for
his new machines, including the propulsion system for the great
tower, the reflectors for firing enemy ships . . . note that it only
works on a sunny day . . . and so forth. Why is King Phraates so
anxious to have these?"

"The Parthians are horse-archers," Military Boots said. "That
gives them the edge against the Romans on an open battlefield.
Romans are heavy infantry and little else, on the field. But they are
masters at both besieging and defending fortified positions, and you
can't take those with horses and arrows. A war between Rome and
Parthia would be fought to a bloody draw, with Parthia victorious
in the field and Rome taking and holding the forts, the cities and
the harbors. With these machines, and the trained engineers we'll
send them, Parthia has nothing to fear from Rome."

"I see. Ah, here are the earlier drafts of the treaty, since we
no longer have the services of the late Hypatia . . ."

"Was it really necessary to kill her?" hissed Asiatic Slippers.

"Oh, absolutely," said Greek Sandals. "She was about to sell
us all out to the Roman."

"We don't allow treachery," said Military Boots. "Not from an
Athenian whore, and not from a Chian philosopher."

"Yes, I suppose the man had to die," said Asiatic Slippers.
"Dealing with the kings of Numidia and Armenia might have been
overlooked, but not blackmail. Still"—he sighed—"he was a
unique resource and we shall miss him."

"I shall read through the treaty clause by clause," Greek Sandals said. "You may then translate into the Parthian tongue. In the
absence of your lamented concubine, I fear that you must trust the
accuracy of my reading."

"At this stage," Asiatic Slippers said, "I have no fear of double-dealing. However, you must understand that all of this hinges upon Lord Achillas making himself king of Egypt."

"You need have no doubt of that," said Greek Sandals. "We Greeks invented the concept of the self-fulfilling prophecy. Very shortly the god Baal-Ahriman shall prophesy that the Lord Achillas is actually the son of the late King Ptolemy, and is the true heir to the double crown. He shall put aside the usurper, the false Ptolemy. He shall marry the Princess Berenice, and possibly Cleopatra and Arsinoe as well. He will then lead Egypt back to its ancient position of glory."

"As long as he does not move into Parthian territory," Asiatic Slippers said.

"That is what this treaty concerns," said Military Boots. "Let's be about it. I would like to be out of this house by dawn."

And they went over it, clause by clause. It was an alliance of Egypt and Parthia against Rome. Iphicrates and Achillas had convinced Phraates that, with these silly engines, he could defy the Roman legions at will. Far more ominously, it established an Egypt-Parthia axis complete with a war plan. At a time to be agreed upon, Egypt would invade up the Sinai and into Judaea and Syria as far as the Euphrates. Phraates would send his horse-archers (with all those splendid new machines) westward into Pontus, Bithynia and Asia Minor as far as the Hellespont, between them pushing Rome entirely out of all those territories. The plan was incredibly ambitious and would have been unrealistic except for one thing. We were readying for war with Gaul. Since Mithridates had died, we had been lulled into the idea that the East was utterly pacified. They might, I realized, just get away with it.

But I could not allow this. I had heard everything. I was on the spot and had the documents and the conspirators within my grasp. Most of all, I had the most agonizing need to urinate.

Just keeping quiet under a bed for hours is difficult enough, trying not to shift, scratch or sneeze. It is far worse when you've indulged in a bit of Chian beforehand.

"I think that concludes our business," said Military Boots, his voice still oddly strained. "It's getting light outside."

"I shall send the book with the documents enclosed to King Phraates," said Asiatic Slippers.

"And I am for the temple," said Greek Sandals. "A good day and a fine new era to you gentlemen."

"Not so fast!" I said, bursting up from beneath the bed, letting the delicate Egyptian fabrication smash back against the wall as I drew my sword. "I have you all . . ." The three had backed away, eyes going wide, startled. The first thing I noted was that Military Boots was not Achillas. It was Memnon, and he wore a bandage about his jaw where I had marked him with my *caestus*. No wonder his voice sounded strained. He had his sword out, too.

Orodes was just who I thought he was, but the other man I did not know, although he seemed decidedly familiar. He was a Greek with a close-trimmed beard and hair that just covered his ears. His hand went into his tunic and came out with an odd axe, its blade deeply curved with a short spike on the opposite side. The handle had been crudely cut to about a foot in length. I grinned at him.

"You look better without the wig and false beard, Ataxas," I said. "But why the axe? Is it what you kill bulls with? I suppose a slave like you never learned to use a freeman's weapons."

"The Roman!" Memnon said, giving me a smile that must have hurt. "I swore I'd avenge the blows you struck me!"

Orodes darted toward the book. It had been rerolled and a small stack of papers stood beside it—undoubtedly the earlier drafts of the treaty. He reached for the book and I flicked out with the point of my *gladius*, opening his forearm from wrist to elbow. He squawked and jumped back.

"No, no," I said. "That's mine. We're going to see some treason trials and some crucifixions when I present those, first to King Ptolemy and then to the Senate."

Memnon chuckled. "Roman, you're assuming that you're going to get out of here alive. You're wrong." He came toward me in that flat-footed, shuffling crouch that denotes the practiced swordsman. I moved toward him as I had been taught, gladiator-style, balanced on the balls of my feet. I picked up a spindly chair to use as a shield. Memnon whipped his cloak around his left forearm for the same purpose.

Memnon aimed a stab at my face, but his sword was a Greek type, longer than mine, with a swelling point. It was just a bit slow and I sidestepped it, sending a thrust in return. When you thrust with a *gladius*, your arm becomes a target. That is why gladiators wear armor on the weapon arm. So my arm snapped out and back, quick as a snake's tongue. I meant to put the blade right through Memnon's throat, but he pulled back and ducked his head and I only nicked his chin. I had my arm back so fast that he didn't have an opportunity to cut at it, but he thrust low at my belly. I jerked backward, a little clumsily because of my long stay beneath the bed. I rotated the chair down, caught the sword and swept it aside as I stepped in and thrust at his chest. No Thracian in the amphitheater ever executed the move as neatly.

But Memnon was no mean swordsman. He brought his cloak-wrapped forearm up and across and batted my blade past his left shoulder as he slid in and sent his own blade at my belly. I brought the chair down and made an unexpected catch. His point jammed into one of the legs, split it and lodged there. I yanked the chair aside, sweeping his sword wide and stepping in to thrust my point into his belly, just below the breastbone, and lancing upward into the heart. To make a thorough job of it, I twisted the point before I withdrew it, causing a great effusion of blood to follow my blade.

Memnon crashed across the table, taking the lamps with it. This did not plunge the room into darkness, for the sun was up and light came in through the single window. For the first time since Memnon had come for me, I had a chance to see what the other two were doing.

Orodes had disappeared. I hadn't heard him going down the stairs, but then I had been preoccupied. A fight to the death narrows one's focus considerably. I stuck my head out the window and saw

Orodes headed toward the Palace, hugging his wounded arm to his body. Just below me, Ataxas burst out the front door and began sprinting toward the Rakhotis. He carried something bulky. I pulled back in and looked at the smashed table. The book was gone.

I had to give chase, but I had some urgent business to transact. I was tempted to piss on Memnon, but it is inadvisable to abuse the bodies of the dead. I have never been superstitious, but it always pays to be cautious. Look at what happened to Achillas after he dragged Hector behind his chariot. A vase served adequately, and I resheathed my sword without bothering to wipe it off. Another job for Hermes.

I was out the door in time to see Ataxas's dwindling form disappear around a corner of the theater. I ran after him, to the great curiosity of the citizens who were beginning to populate the streets.

It was an interesting race. Each of us had certain advantages and disadvantages. And the stakes were very high. Ataxas was encumbered by the heavy book, but he had a head start. He was an ex-slave who had probably never spent an hour in the *palaestra*, much less in the stadium, whereas I had had all the usual military training, although I was out of condition. If he could get to his temple, he would be safe. I was a Roman in a city where Romans were rapidly growing unwelcome and were soon to be targets of hostility.

Here the streets of Alexandria worked to my advantage. The wide boulevards, the long, straight blocks, made it virtually impossible for him to get out of my sight for more than a few seconds. I was gaining on him, impatient to catch him but knowing better than to put on a sudden burst of speed that would leave me gagging on the pavement before we even reached the Rakhotis.

We passed market stalls and rumbling farm carts, braying asses and groaning, ill-smelling camels and even a couple of elephants bound for some ceremonial in the Hippodrome. Chickens scattered before us and cats watched us warily. People looked at us with interest and then went back to what they were doing. Alexandria is a city of many spectacles, and we made a sorry spectacle, indeed.

I noted that the complexion of the crowd had grown darker. White kilts and black wigs came to predominate. We were in the Rakhotis. Now I became acutely conscious of my Roman haircut and generally Latin features. If I had been chasing an Egyptian, I would probably have been mobbed immediately. I had to catch Ataxas and get out of there before they decided to do it anyway.

I reached him just before the street we were on opened onto the huge plaza surrounding the Great Serapeum. I was tempted to spit him with my sword, but something that public and that outrageous would undoubtedly result in my death, probably on the altar of some disgusting god with the head of a warthog. So instead I grabbed his shoulder and spun him around.

He was red-faced and gasping, trembling with exhaustion as I shoved him back into a space between two buildings. A couple of cats paused in their contest over the remains of a fish long enough to hiss at us. Triumphantly, I snatched the scroll from his arms. He made a halfhearted grab for his shortened axe, but I kicked him in the crotch and that made him change his mind.

"Don't mistake me for some helpless mathematician, Ataxas," I said to him as he writhed on the cobbles. "It takes more than some jumped-up runaway slave to kill a Caecilius Metellus."

"How much do you want, Roman?" he gasped. "I will make you rich beyond your wildest ambitions. There is a whole country here to loot."

"I just want to see what Ptolemy does to you. Or possibly your own followers when they see Ataxas is a runaway Greek slave in a wig and a false beard. The king's soldiers will go into your temple with sledgehammers and smash your trick statue and tear up the floors and walls to find the pipes you used to fake the sound of Baal-Ahriman's voice. You'll probably be pulled apart and devoured by priestesses with lacerated backs to avenge."

"You place great faith in Ptolemy, Roman," Ataxas said. "His time is over, as is the ascendancy of Rome in Egypt." He had worked his way back up to his knees.

"Not after I get back to the Palace with this," I said, shaking the document in his face.

"That may not be as easy as you think, Roman," he said, with no small measure of truth. I was in the Rakhotis, and these were bad times to be a Roman in that part of the city.

"Farewell, Ataxas," I said. "I'll come to your execution, should you live long enough to be sentenced." I turned and walked to the mouth of the alley. Before going out, I stopped and looked out into the street. It was getting crowded, but nobody was paying me any attention. Just as I stepped out into the street, I heard a horrible squalling sound that cut off suddenly. I could only think that it was Ataxas making some inarticulate sound of rage. Then something hit me squarely between the shoulder blades and flopped to the pavement. I turned, bewildered. Something gray and furry lay at my feet, inert. It was all so unexpected that at first I didn't recognize the thing. Then Ataxas ran past me into the street, pointing at me, his eyes wide with horror.

"The Roman has killed a cat!" he shouted, then, in a hysterical shriek: "THE ROMAN HAS MURDERED A CAT!"

The people in the street stared, mouths agape. They stared at me, then looked down at the wretched beast, as if they could not comprehend the sheer sacrilegious horror of what they saw.

"He killed a cat!" they began to murmur, in both Greek and Egyptian. "The Roman killed a cat!" It did not take them long to get over their shock as I sidled away from the little corpse. Then:

"KILL THE ROMAN! KILL THE CAT-MURDERER!"

I began to retrace my steps at great speed. This time I was encumbered with the heavy book, and it was my second life-and-death race of the morning. I thought of that Greek with the interminable name who had run from Marathon to Sparta and back to Marathon and then all the way to Athens, where he dropped dead, which served him right. After all, *he* didn't have a rampaging Alexandrian mob on his heels.

Every time I looked back over my shoulder, the mob was getting bigger. News of the enormity I had committed flew faster than I would have credited possible. They were calling not just for my death but for the death of all Romans. But they wanted to start with me.

It seemed ridiculous to me to be rent asunder by a rampaging mob for killing a cat. But to have this happen over a cat-slaying of which I was entirely innocent was beyond endurance. I had little love for the slinky beasts, but it never would have occurred to me to slaughter one.

I was out of the Rakhotis as if I wore the winged sandals of Mercury, but I was far from safe. The mob rampaged into the Greek quarter and picked up strength even there. There are Egyptians in all the quarters of Alexandria, and there are always people in any city who will jump at any chance to join a riot. I had done it myself, when the riot was in a good cause.

I ran by the Macedonian barracks, screaming, "Riot! Riot! Turn out the troops! The city is aflame!" The soldiers on parade looked bewildered, but officers barked orders and the drums began to beat and the trumpets to bray.

I looked behind me to see the soldiers boil out of the gates and collide with the following mob. Many got through, and they continued to pursue me. I tried to turn up a street that led northward, toward the Palace, but members of the mob had got there ahead of me and cut me off. That was more of Ataxas's doing. Why hadn't I killed the fiend when I had him at my mercy?

There was nothing for it but to continue fleeing east, all the way to the delta if need be. I was gasping heavily by this time, bringing up phlegm with every wheeze. I began to see men in long robes wearing pointed caps and their hair loose about their shoulders. That meant I was in the Jewish quarter. These were the traditional Jews, for most of the Jews of Alexandria were dressed and barbered like Greeks, and many of them spoke no language except Greek.

With a final burst of speed I got far ahead of the cat-avengers and darted down an alley. It was intersected by another alley and I took that one. This was refreshing, almost like Rome. I pounded on a door.

"Let me in!" I begged.

"What is it?" The voice came from overhead. It belonged to a man with thin features, dressed in a red-and-white robe. His eyes had a slightly fanatic gleam.

"The Egyptians are after me!" I said.

"I don't like Egyptians," the man remarked. "They kept my people in bondage for many generations."

"Then you'll save me from them! They think I killed a cat!"

"The Egyptians are uncircumcised idolaters," he said. "They worship animals and animal-headed gods." That was certainly true, although I had no idea what the state of their penises had to do with anything.

"The Macedonians went out to suppress the riot," I said, "but some got through and they're after me. Let me in!"

"I don't like the Macedonians either," he said. "King Antiochus Epiphanes killed our priests and befouled the Holy of Holies!"

I was growing impatient.

"Listen. I am a Senator of Rome, attached to the diplomatic mission. Rome will reward you richly if you will just let me in!"

"And I don't like Romans!" he screamed. "Your General Pompey stormed the Temple Mount and violated our Holy of Holies and seized the Temple treasury!" I had to run into one who held a grudge. Somebody tugged at my shoulder and I turned to see a man in Greek dress.

"Come with me," he said urgently. "They are no more than a street away." I followed him down the alley and through a low doorway. The room we entered was modest, with spare furnishings. "Amos is the wrong man to ask for aid," he said. "He's half cracked. My name is Simeon son of Simeon."

"Decius son of Decius," I said. "Pleased to meet you." My breathing grew a bit less ragged. "This is all too complicated to explain, but it's all part of a plot to turn the Egyptians against Rome. I have to get to the Palace, but I can't until the streets are safe."

"I will go out now," Simeon said. "I'll spread the word that you were seen heading out the Canopic Gate and past the Hippodrome. We don't want that mob in our quarter."

"A very sensible attitude," I told him. "Let me rest here and regain my wind. Then perhaps I can borrow some clothes from you. You will be well rewarded."

He shrugged. "There is no sense thinking of rewards while your life is still in danger. Worry about that later." With that he left.

For the first time in what seemed like forever, I had nothing to do. So I went up the stairs and found an upper room much like the lower one. No sign of a wife or children. Another stair led to the roof, so I went up to it. I kept well back from the parapet as I listened. The sounds of the mob and the clank of arms seemed to come from all directions. In any other city, a riot of this magnitude would have featured plumes of smoke as building after building caught fire until a full-scale conflagration was in progress. Usually, the fires kill far more than the rioters.

Not in Alexandria, the fireproof city. I could follow the progress of major segments of the mob up and down the streets, just by the sounds they made. They did seem to be dwindling toward the Canopic Gate. Then I heard soldiers heading that way. After a couple of hours, the whole cacophony came back toward me, then dwindled to the west. Apparently the soldiers had lined up across all the streets shield-to-shield and were driving the rioters all the way back to the Rakhotis.

I wondered what would happen in this city if anyone ever killed *two* cats.

It was well past noon when the city seemed to be at peace again. This did not mean that I was out of danger. Even without rioting mobs, Achillas was out there somewhere. I heard sounds from below.

"Roman? Senator Decius? Are you up there?"

"Simeon?" I said. "Is all clear in the streets?"

He came out onto the roof. "The mob was driven back. Heavy squads of soldiers patrol the streets, but it was bloody. Once a mob turns on one sort of foreigner, it soon turns on all foreigners. We've been here as long as Alexandria has existed, but the Egyptians still regard us as foreigners."

"They lack the enlightened Roman attitude toward citizenship," I told him. "And now, I must get to the Palace. Can you lend me some clothes?"

"Easily enough, but no adult male Jew goes clean-shaven, nor do we cut our hair as short as yours. Let me see what I can find."

We went down into his house, and he rummaged through his chests until he came up with a very coarse cloak and one of those Egyptian head-scarves that follow the shape of the wig.

"These belonged to a slave I freed after his seven years," Simeon remarked. "Let's see what you look like in them."

"Seven years?" I asked as I donned the itchy cloak and the ridiculous scarf.

"My religion forbids chattel slavery," he said. "We allow bond servitude for seven years only; then the servant must be given his freedom."

"We could use a custom like that," I said. "It would probably spare us no end of trouble. Never get the Senate to accept it, though."

He lent me a bag of coarse sacking to conceal the scroll, and I felt as disguised as I could, under the circumstances. It occurred to me that the streets would be full of Achillas's men, who would undoubtedly have orders to deliver me to the Palace in small pieces.

"What is the most direct way to get to the sea from here?" I asked.

"If you walk from here to the city wall and turn north along it, you will reach the Fishermen's Gate."

"I think that is my best course, rather than back through the city Farewell, Simeon. You may look for tangible evidence of my gratitude soon."

"Just do what you can to put a stop to the anti-foreign hysteria, Senator. This used to be such a wonderful city."

I stepped from the front door and found the alley empty. A very few steps brought me to an east-west street and I turned east. The district was all but deserted, the inhabitants huddling behind bolted doors. That suited me admirably. I reached the city wall without incident and found an especially heavy guard patrolling along its crest, their eyes scanning the city for signs of disturbance. Following the wall north brought me to a small gate. It stood open for the day, and nobody along my route had so much as a glance to spare for another slave carrying another load on his shoulder.

On the other side of the gate I found a paved embankment from which several small stone jetties protruded into the shallow, greenish water. Most of the fishing boats were out for the day, but a few night-fishermen sat on the jetties repairing their nets. They were native Egyptians and I approached them warily.

"I need boat transport into the Great Harbor," I told an industrious-looking pair who sat near a well-maintained boat. "I will pay you well."

They eyed me curiously. "How could you pay anything?" asked one without hostility. He spoke passable Greek. I took out a purse and let them hear the clink. That decided them. They folded their net and placed it in the boat, and in minutes we were rowing up along the peninsula of Cape Lochias.

With a little talk, I learned that they were not true Alexandrians; rather, they lived in the little fishing village that stood on the water just to the east of the city wall. They had no interest in the disturbances of Alexandria save as those affected the fish-market. That being the case, I removed my scarf and cloak. It was all one to them. They probably wouldn't have known a Roman from an Arab.

We passed beneath the fort of the Acrolochias, then rounded

the point, passing between it and the nearest of the little islands that stood off the cape, each bearing its tiny shrine to Poseidon. The Pharos was a great smoking pillar to our right as we came back down the cape. The fishermen began to pull for the docks, but I stopped them.

"Put me in there," I said, pointing to the strait between the base of Cape Lochias and the Antirrhodos Island.

"But that is the royal harbor," said one. "We will be executed if we go in there."

"I am a Roman Senator and a part of the Roman diplomatic mission," I said grandly. "You will not be punished."

"I don't believe you," said the other.

I drew my sword, crusted with black blood. "Then *I* will kill you!" They pulled for the royal harbor.

Only a couple of guards in gilded armor decorated the royal pier. They shuffled down to where the boat pulled up and made indignant noises as I was paying my boatmen.

"I am Senator Decius Caecilius Metellus of the Roman embassy!" I shouted to them. "Lay hands on me at your mortal peril. I must see King Ptolemy at once!"

"We can't let you in and we can't leave our post, Senator," said one. "We'll have to pass word for the Captain of the Watch."

One of Achillas's men, no doubt. "Why?" I said, scanning the harbor like a slave in a comedy. "I see no enemy fleet rounding the Pharos. Let me by."

"Sorry, sir. It's our standing orders."

"You are behaving like fools," I insisted.

"Would you let Roman soldiers get away with neglect of duty, Senator?" said the younger of the two. He had a point.

"Can't leave your post, eh?" I said.

"Sorry, sir no," said the elder.

"Then you can't chase me." I dashed between them and sprinted for the Palace. As they hollered for more guards behind me, I thought that I must take up this running business seriously. This was my third hard run of the day. My prolonged relaxation in

Simeon's house had taken its toll, though. My legs had grown stiff and sore. My motions were wobbly, like one just ashore after a long, rough sea voyage.

I ran past the royal menagerie, where the lions and other predators set up a roaring and yowling. Anything running meant food to them. Slaves jumped from my path, alarmed at this wild-eyed apparition with his mysterious burden. Then I saw the stair leading to the throne room before me. Ptolemy would be somewhere near, and I vowed a goat to Bacchus if he would just be sober.

I charged up the stairs and came to a halt as the guards closed rank before me, their spears leveled, but with the inevitable look of uncertainty worn by soldiers everywhere when confronted by an unexpected situation.

"Senator Metellus of the Roman embassy demands audience with King Ptolemy!" I shouted. They muttered and shuffled; then someone came through the shadowed portico behind them. But it was not Ptolemy. It was Achillas.

"Seize that madman," he said coolly. "And bring him inside."

Ah, well. It had been worth a try. Luckily for me, even parade armor is heavy. I kept a few steps ahead of the clattering guardsmen all the way to the Roman embassy. If the servants and hangers-on had scattered before me on my way to the throne room, they were doubly swift to do so with all that pointed and sharp-edged steel bearing down upon me.

Then I was in sight of the Roman embassy. But it was not the placid scene I had grown used to. The steps were crowded with men dressed in togas and women in Roman dress and even children, the boys in purple-bordered togas. More to the point, in front of them stood a line of grim soldiers, their spears leveled outward. I was certain I was doomed until I recognized the shape of the big old-fashioned, oval Samnite shields. These were Roman soldiers, not legionaries but marines.

"Save me!" I shouted. "I am a Senator!" Their spear points wavered not a single inch.

"Arrest him!" yelled Creticus from the top of the steps. "Tie him up and bring him in here!" The line of soldiers parted just enough to let me through and then closed smoothly. Behind me, the royal guards came to a halt in a screech of hobnails on pavement. Hands grasped me and dragged me up the steps. I had just run from this very situation, only to have it inflicted upon me by my own countrymen. I was thrown to the steps at Creticus's feet, still hugging my scroll.

"Chain him up!" Creticus screamed. "Flog him! We may have to find a priest to *purify* the evil little monster!" He was quite beside himself.

"If you'll just get a grip on yourself . . ."

"Get a grip?" he shrieked, his face going scarlet. "Get a grip! Decius, have you any idea what you've done? Roman citizens have been attacked! Their houses have been destroyed, their property plundered! And why? Because you skulked away from the embassy, against my orders, and killed a cat! A cat!" I thought he was sure to have a seizure.

"I have saved Rome!" I insisted. "A big, wealthy part of the Empire, anyway."

"Enough of these vaporings! Bring the chains."

"Just a moment." Julia pushed her way past him, her face white and drawn. She knelt beside me and wiped my sweaty face with a corner of her scarf.

"Decius, did you really kill that cat?"

"Absolutely not!" I told her. "I love the sneaky little beasts. It was Ataxas. He killed it and blamed it on me. He started it all, and I have the evidence here to convict the lot of them."

She stood and faced Creticus. "Listen to what he has to say."

"Listen to him! That's what caused all this trouble! I listened to him! No more! I will have him tried for treason and flung from the Tarpeian Rock! I'll have his traitorous corpse dragged on a hook down the Tiber steps and thrown into the river!"

She didn't flinch. She stood with her face three inches from his, and her voice didn't waver in the least.

"Quintus Caecilius Metellus Creticus, if you do not hear him out, my uncle, the Consul-elect Caius Julius Caesar, will have some words for you when we return to Rome."

Creticus stood for about five minutes while his normal color returned. Then he snapped: "Bring him inside." We went into the atrium. "Make it fast and convincing."

"War," I gasped, at the end of my resources. Suddenly Hermes was at my elbow with a brimming cup, the blessed boy. I emptied it in one gulp. "War with Parthia. Revolt in Egypt. This is the stolen book."

"Book!" Creticus shouted. "You started a riot over a cat, now you want a war over a book?"

I'd had enough of this. I held one end of the scroll and tossed the bulk of it to the floor. It unrolled for the whole length of the atrium and continued into a hallway, displaying fine Greek writing, exquisite drawings, and spilling documents. I held out the cup and Hermes took it, returning in seconds with a refill. I went to the spilled documents and scooped them up, then handed them to Creticus.

"The secret treaty between Achillas and Phraates of Parthia, plotting to overthrow King Ptolemy and divide up Rome's Eastern possessions between them. Not just the final treaty, but the earlier drafts as well." While Creticus studied it, I glared at the other embassy officials who stood tensely by. "You weasels don't get out of paying me five hundred *denarii* that easily."

Creticus grew very, very white as he read. "Explain," he said at last. I gave it to them, quickly, from the murder of Iphicrates to my appearance at the bottom of the embassy steps.

By the end of it, somebody had shoved a chair beneath me and I was making quick work of my third cup.

"All right," Creticus said grimly. "I grant you a temporary reprieve. In your insane fashion, you may have done the state some service. Let's go outside."

There was now a great crowd of the Palace guard filling the courtyard, but we felt safe enough behind our line of Roman marines. I staggered out to stand wearily beside Creticus. Julia stood by me. I saw Fausta in the crowd of Romans, looking on happily, as if this spectacle were being staged just for her amusement. Achillas stood at the head of his soldiers. I expected him to bluster, but I had underestimated him. He was biding his time in silence, waiting to see which way he should jump.

"You think he'll storm the embassy, Decius?" Creticus said, maintaining that haughty demeanor for which Roman officials are famed all over the world.

"Wouldn't dare," I whispered, looking equally lofty. "It would precipitate war too soon. He needs that alliance with Parthia, and the treaty hasn't been delivered."

Then there was a disturbance at the rear of the crowd. It looked as if a ship were sailing toward the embassy.

"Here comes Ptolemy," Creticus said. "Let's hope he's sober."

Achillas and his soldiers bowed as the tremendous litter was set down in the courtyard. Its ramp was lowered and slaves unrolled his long carpet, dyed at fabulous cost with Tyrian purple. When Ptolemy descended he was sober, and he was not alone. Behind him came his newly pregnant queen, who was followed by a nurse carrying the infant Ptolemy. Behind them came the princesses: Berenice, then solemn Cleopatra, last of all little Arsinoe, holding the hand of a court lady. The marines parted to let them pass, then reformed, their spears steady.

The message was plain: Ptolemy was putting himself and his family under the protection of Rome. As he reached the top of the steps, Creticus handed him the treaty wordlessly. The king perused it as his family filed within the embassy. Then he turned to face the crowd.

"General Achillas, come here," Ptolemy said.

I must hand it to the man: I never saw anyone so coolly brazen. He walked up the stairs with perfect confidence and bowed deeply.

"What would my king have of me?" he asked.

"An explanation," Ptolemy said. He held the condemning document before Achillas's face. "You sought to arrest young Senator Metellus when he tried to bring this to me. Can you tell me why?"

"Of course, your Majesty. He was obviously deranged, a danger to both himself and the community. Alexandria is not safe for Romans at this time, and I wanted to subdue him for his own protection."

"And this little document?" Ptolemy asked.

"I have never seen it before," he said quite truthfully. Ptolemy raised an eyebrow in my direction.

"It was his henchman Memnon who arranged the final draft, along with the Parthian ambassador, Orodes, and the fraudulent holy man, Ataxas, acting as scribe."

"Memnon was found murdered this morning," Achillas said. "What does the Senator know about that?"

"It was a fair fight. He was conspiring against King Ptolemy and against Rome. He deserved to die. But he was acting in your name, Achillas."

He studied the document with mock seriousness. "Then he did so without my knowledge. I see neither signature nor seal to indicate my participation. I protest that anyone should regard my name written by another's hand to be incriminating evidence."

"Fetch the Parthian ambassador!" Ptolemy called.

"Unfortunately," Achillas said, "Lord Orodes was found dead near the Palace gate this morning. It seems he bled to death from a cut on the forearm."

"Ridiculous!" I said. "I didn't cut him that badly. There would have been more blood on the floor when he ran away."

"You've been busier than a gladiator at a *munera sine missione*," Creticus commented.

"And what would be the response," Ptolemy said, "should your king summon the priest Ataxas?"

"My officers report that he was killed in the rioting this morning. You know how these things are, sir. First the mob wants to kill Romans, then any foreigner will do. It seems that he was dressed and barbered like an Asiatic Greek and nobody recognized him as the Holy Ataxas. Tragic."

Ptolemy sighed. "General Achillas, the nomes near the first cataract are in revolt. My markets on the Elephantine Island are in great danger. You shall gather your troops and set out southward before nightfall. You are not to come back until I send for you."

Achillas bowed. "Your Majesty!" I protested as Achillas descended the steps and began barking orders to his troops. "That man is a deadly danger to you! He plotted against you and against Rome. He had Iphicrates murdered when he learned that the man was making the same promises to other kings. He had Orodes and Ataxas silenced before they could be arrested and made to talk. He should be crucified forthwith."

"His family is a very important one, young Decius," Ptolemy said. "I cannot move against him just now."

"I beg you to reconsider," I said. "Remember how your ancestors would have handled this. They were perfect savages and they would have killed him, then annihilated his family, then gone all the way back to Macedonia, found his ancestral village and leveled it with the ground!"

"Yes, well, the world was younger and simpler then. My problems are very complicated. I thank you for your services, but leave the statecraft to me." Then he turned to Creticus. "Excellency, we must go inside and discuss important matters. I must have Roman protection from my domestic enemies. I will pay full reparations for damage suffered by Romans in Alexandria."

The two went inside and the rest of the embassy staff went with them. I was left alone at the top of the steps, above the crowd of Roman refugees. Achillas finished giving his orders and he came up the steps, grinning at me. I itched to draw my sword and kill him, but I was so tired, he would have taken it away from me and skewered me with it. Then he stood a foot from me, wearing a strange expression of hatred, puzzlement and grim respect.

"Why did you do it, Roman?" he asked.

That was simple. "You should not have committed murder within the sacred precincts of the Temple of the Muses," I told him. "That sort of behavior angers the gods." He regarded me for a moment as if I were truly insane; then he whirled and went back down the steps. Weary to my bones, I turned and staggered back within the embassy. They attacked me as soon as I was inside.

Laughing and whooping, the embassy staff bore me to the floor and tied my hands behind me; then they bound my feet at the ankles.

"You still think you can get out of paying me!" I gasped, too weak to do anything else.

"Don't forget to gag him," Creticus said. A rag was stuffed in my mouth and tied securely behind my head. Creticus came over and nudged me in the ribs with his toe.

"Decius, in case you were wondering where those marines came from, the war galleys *Neptune*, *Swan* and *Triton* are in the harbor. I've sent orders for the *Swan* to come to the royal harbor, and that's where you are going right now. The marines from the *Neptune* are going out on a little mission of arson on Lord Achillas's nearby estate; then the flotilla sails for Rhodes. That is as far as they take you."

"Beautiful place, Rhodes," Ptolemy said. "A bit dull, though. No army, no politics. In fact, nothing there except schools."

"Maybe you can attend a few lectures, Decius," Creticus said gleefully, nudging me with his toe again. "Learn a little *philosophy*, eh?" Then the two of them laughed until the tears ran down their degenerate old faces.

I was carried down to the harbor and thrown aboard the ship. Julia accompanied me tearfully, holding my bound hands, which were already growing numb. She said she would follow me to Rhodes as soon as possible. Probably just wanted to meet all those scholars, I guessed. Hermes carried my weapons and a jug of wine, muttering and cursing, already missing the soft life in Alexandria.

As the ship backed away, Creticus came down to the dock

and yelled across the water, "If we hear that Rhodes has sunk beneath the sea. I'll know who was responsible. Captain, don't untie him until you're out past Pharos!"

By the time we rounded the lighthouse, another column of smoke rose to the east of the city, a short way inland. I knew that much wood should make a fine fire. I was glad we were too far away to smell the stench from those human-hair ropes.

Before long, Alexandria was out of sight. I would not see it again for twelve years, but when I returned, it was with Caesar, and Cleopatra was queen and events made my little adventures of my first sojourn there seem dull and uneventful, and I finally got to settle matters with Achillas.

These things happened in Alexandria in the year 692 of the City of Rome, the Consulship of Metellus Celer and Lucius Afranius.

GLOSSARY

(Definitions apply to the last century of the Republic.)

Acta: Streets wide enough for one-way wheeled traffic.

Aedile: Elected officials in charge of upkeep of the city and the grain dole, regulation of public morals, management of the markets and the public Games. There were two types: the plebeian aediles, who had no insignia of office, and the curule aediles, who wore the toga praetexta and sat in the sella curulis. The curule aediles could sit in judgment on civil cases involving markets and currency, while the plebeian aediles could only levy fines. Otherwise, their duties were the same. Since the magnificence of the Games one exhibited as aedile often determined election to higher office, it was an important stepping-stone in a political career. The office of aedile did not carry the imperium.

Ancile: (pl. ancilia) A small, oval sacred shield which fell from heaven in the region of King Numa. Since there was a prophecy that it was tied to the stability of Rome, Numa had eleven exact copies made so nobody would know which one to steal. Their care was entrusted to a college of priests, the *Salii* (q.v.), and figured in a number of ceremonies each year.

Atrium: Once a word for house, in Republican times it was the entry hall of a house, opening off the street and used as a general reception area.

Atrium Vestae: The Palace of the Vestal and one of the most splendid buildings in Rome.

Augur: An official who observed omens for state purposes. He could forbid business and assemblies if he saw unfavorable omens.

Basilica: A building where courts met in inclement weather.

Caestus: The Classical boxing glove, made of leather straps and reinforced by bands, plates or spikes of bronze.

Caliga: The Roman military boot. Actually, a heavy sandal with hobnailed sole.

Campus Martius: A field outside the old city wall, formerly the assembly area and drill field for the army. It was where the popular assemblies met. By late Republican times, buildings were encroaching on the field.

Censor: Magistrates elected usually every fifth year to oversee the census of the citizens and purge the roll of Senators of unworthy members. They could forbid certain religious practices or luxuries deemed bad for public morals or generally "un-Roman." There were two Censors, and each could overrule the other. They wore the toga praetexta and sat in the sella curulis, but since they had no executive powers they were not accompanied by lictors. The office did not carry the imperium. Censors were usually elected from among the ex-Consuls, and the censorship was regarded as the capstone of a political career.

Centuriate Assembly: (comitia centuriata) Originally, the annual military assembly of the citizens where they joined their army units ("centuries"). There were one hundred ninety-three centuries divided into five classes by property qualification. They elected the highest magistrates: Censors, Consuls and Praetors. By the middle Republic, the centuriate assembly was strictly a voting body, having lost all military character.

Centurion: "Commander of 100"; i.e., a century, which, in practice, numbered around sixty men. Centurions were promoted from the ranks and were the backbone of the professional army.

Circus: The Roman racecourse and the stadium which enclosed it. The original, and always the largest, was the Circus Maximus, which lay between the Palatine and Aventine hills. A later, smaller circus, the Circus Flaminius, lay outside the walls on the Campus Martius.

Client: One attached in a subordinate relationship to a patron, whom he was bound to support in war and in the courts. Freedmen became clients of their former masters. The relationship was hereditary.

Coemptio: Marriage by symbolic sale. Before five witnesses and a *libripens* who held a balance, the bridegroom struck the balance with a bronze coin and handed it to the father or guardian of the bride. Unlike conferreatio, coemptic was easily dissolved by divorce.

Cognomen: The family name, denoting any of the stirpes of a gens; i.e., Caius Julius *Caesar*. Caius of the stirps Caesar of gens Julia. Some plebeian families never adopted a cognomen, notably the Maru and the Antonii.

Coitio: A political alliance between two men, uniting their voting blocs. Usually it was an agreement between politicians who were otherwise antagonists, in order to edge out mutual rivals.

Colonia: Towns which had been conquered by Rome, where Roman citizens were settled. Later, settlements founded by discharged veterans of the legions. After 89 B.C. all Italian coloniae had full rights of citizenship. Those in the provinces had limited citizenship.

Compluvium: An opening in a roof to admit light.

Conferreatio: The most sacred and binding of Roman forms of marriage. The bride and groom offered a cake of spelt to Jupiter in the presence of a pontifex and the Flamen Dialis. It was the ancient patrician form of marriage. By the late Republic it was obsolete except for some priesthoods in which the priest was required to be married by conferreatio.

Consul: Supreme magistrate of the Republic. Two were elected each year. Insignia were the toga praetexta and the sella curulis.

Each Consul was attended by twelve lictors. The office carried full imperium. On the expiration of his year in office, the ex-Consul was usually assigned a district outside Rome to rule as proconsul. As proconsul, he had the same insignia and the same number of lictors. His power was absolute within his province.

Curia: The meetinghouse of the Senate, located in the Forum.

Dictator: An absolute ruler chosen by the Senate and the Consuls to deal with a specific emergency. For a limited period, never more than six months, he was given unlimited imperium, which he was to lay down upon resolution of the emergency. Unlike the Consuls, he had no colleague to overrule him and he was not accountable for his actions performed during office when he stepped down. His insignia were the toga praetexta and the sella curulis and he was accompanied by twenty-four lictors, the number of both Consuls. Dictatorships were extremely rare and the last was held in 202 B.C. The dictatorships of Sulla and Caesar were unconstitutional.

Dioscuri: Castor and Pollux, the twin sons of Zeus and Leda. The Romans revered them as protectors of the city.

Eques: (pl. equites) Formerly, citizens wealthy enough to supply their own horses and fight in the cavalry, they came to hold their status by meeting a property qualification. They formed the moneyed upper-middle class. In the centuriate assembly they formed eighteen centuries and once had the right of voting first, but they lost this as their military function disappeared. The publicans, financiers, bankers, moneylenders and tax-farmers came from the equestrian class.

Faction: In the Circus, the supporters of the four racing companies: Red, White, Blue and Green. Most Romans were fanatically loyal to one of these.

Fasces: A bundle of rods bound around an ax with a red strap, symbolizing a Roman magistrate's power of corporal and capital punishment. They were carried by the lictors who accompanied the curule magistrates, the Flamen Dialis, and the proconsuls and pro-praetors who governed provinces. When a lower magistrate met a higher, his lictors lowered their fasces in salute.

Flamen: A high priest of a specific god of the state. The college of flamines had fifteen members: three patrician and twelve ple-beian. The three highest were the Flamen Dialis, the Flamen Martialis and the Flamen Quirinalis. They had charge of the daily sacrifices and wore distinctive headgear and were surrounded by many ritual taboos. The Flamen Dialis, high priest of Jupiter, was entitled to the toga praetexta, which had to be woven by his wife, the sella curulis and a single lictor, and he could sit in the Senate. It became difficult to fill the college of flamines because they had to be prominent men, the appointment was for life and they could take no part in politics.

Forum: An open meeting and market area. The premier forum was the Forum Romanum, located on the low ground surrounded by the Capitoline, Palatine and Caelian hills. It was surrounded by the most important temples and public buildings. Roman citizens spent much of their day there. The courts met outdoors in the Forum when the weather was good. When it was paved and devoted solely to public business, the Forum Romanum's market functions were transferred to the Forum Boarium, the cattle market, near the Circus Maximus. Small shops and stalls remained along the northern and southern peripheries, however.

Freedman: A manumitted slave. Formal emancipation conferred full rights of citizenship except for the right to hold office. Informal emancipation conferred freedom without voting rights. In the second or at latest third generation, a freedman's descendants became full citizens.

Genius: The guiding and guardian spirit of a person or place. The genius of a place was called genius loci.

Gens: A clan, all of whose members were descended from a single ancestor. The nomen of a patrician gens always ended with -ius.

Thus, Caius *Julius* Caesar was Caius, of the Caesarian stirps of gens Julia.

Gladiator: Literally, "swordsman." A slave, prisoner of war, condemned criminal or free volunteer who fought, often to the death, in the munera. All were called swordsmen, even if they fought with other weapons.

Gladius: The short, broad, double-edged sword borne by Roman soldiers. It was designed primarily for stabbing. A smaller, more antiquated design of gladius was used by gladiators.

Gravitas: The quality of seriousness.

Haruspex: A member of a college of Etruscan professionals who examined the entrails of sacrificial animals for omens.

Hospitium: An arrangement of reciprocal hospitality. When visiting the other's city, each hospes (pl. hospites) was entitled to food and shelter, protection in court, care when ill or injured and honorable burial, should he die during the visit. The obligation was binding on both families and was passed on to descendants.

Ides: The 15th of March, May, July and October. The 13th of other months.

Imperium: The ancient power of kings to summon and lead armies, to order and forbid and to inflict corporal and capital punishment. Under the Republic, the imperium was divided among the Consuls and Praetors, but they were subject to appeal and intervention by the tribunes in their civil decisions and were answerable for their acts after leaving office. Only a dictator had unlimited imperium.

Insula: Literally, "island." A large, multistory tenement block.

Itinera: Streets wide enough for only foot traffic. The majority of Roman streets were itinera.

Janitor: A slave-doorkeeper, so called for Janus, god of gateways.

Kalends: The first of any month.

Latifundium: A large landed estate or plantation worked by slaves. During the late Republic these expanded tremendously, all but destroying the Italian peasant class.

Legates: Subordinate commanders chosen by the Senate to accompany generals and governors. Also, ambassadors appointed by the Senate.

Legion: Basic unit of the Roman army. Paper strength was six thousand, but usually closer to four thousand. All were armed as heavy infantry with a large shield, cuirass, helmet, gladius and light and heavy javelins. Each legion had attached to it an equal number of non-citizen auxiliaries consisting of light and heavy infantry, cavalry, archers, slingers, etc. Auxilia were never organized as legions, only as cohorts.

Lictor: Attendants, usually freedmen, who accompanied magistrates and the Flamen Dialis, bearing the fasces. They summoned assemblies, attended public sacrifices and carried out sentences of punishment. Twenty-four lictors accompanied a dictator, twelve for a Consul, six for a propraetor, two for a Praetor and one for the Flamen Dialis.

Liquamen: Also called garum, it was the ubiquitous fermented fish sauce used in Roman cooking.

Ludus: (pl. ludi) The official public Games, races theatricals, etc. Also, a training school for gladiators, although the gladiatorial exhibitions were not ludi.

Munera: Special Games, not part of the official calendar, at which gladiators were exhibited. They were originally funeral Games and were always dedicated to the dead. In munera sine missione, all the defeated were killed and sometimes were made to fight sequentially or all at once until only one was left standing. Munera sine missione were periodically forbidden by law.

Municipia: Towns originally with varying degrees of Roman citizenship, but by the late Republic with full citizenship. A citizen from a municipium was qualified to hold any public office. An

example is Cicero, who was not from Rome but from the municipium of Arpinum.

Nobiles: Those families, both patrician and plebeian, in which
members had held the Consulate.

Nomen: The name of the clan or gens; i.e., Caius *Julius* Caesar.

Nones: The 7th of March, May, July and October. The 5th of other
months.

Novus Homo: Literally, "new man." A man who is the first of his
family to hold the Consulate, giving his family the status of nobiles.

Optimates: The party of the "best men"; i.e., aristocrats and their
supporters.

Patria Potestas: The absolute authority of the pater familias over
the children of his household, who could neither legally own property while their father was alive nor marry without his permission.
Technically, he had the right to sell or put to death any of his
children, but by Republican times this was a legal fiction.

Patrician: A descendant of one of the founding fathers of Rome.
Once, only patricians could hold offices and priesthoods and sit in
the Senate, but these privileges were gradually eroded until only
certain priesthoods were strictly patrician. By the late Republic,
only about fourteen gens remained.

Patron: A man with one or more clients whom he was bound to
protect, advise and otherwise aid. The relationship was hereditary.

Peculium: Roman slaves could not own property, but they could
earn money outside the household, which was held for them by
their masters. This fund was called a peculium, and could be used,
eventually, to purchase the slave's freedom.

Peristylium: An open courtyard surrounded by a colonnade.

Pietas: The quality of dutifulness toward the gods and, especially,
toward one's parents.

Plebeian: All citizens not of patrician status.

Pomerium: The line of the ancient city wall, attributed to Romulus. Actually, the space of vacant ground just within and without

the wall, regarded as holy. Within the pomerium it was forbidden to bear arms or bury the dead.

Pontifex: A member of the highest priestly college of Rome. They had superintendence over all sacred observances, state and private, and over the calendar. There were fifteen in the late Republic: seven patrician and eight plebeian. Their chief was the pontifex maximus, a title now held by the Pope.

Popular Assemblies: There were three: the centuriate assembly (comitia centuriata) and the two tribal assemblies: comitia tributa and consilium plebis, q.v.

Populares: The party of the common people.

Praenomen: The given name of a freeman, as Marcus, Sextus. Caius, etc.; i.e., *Caius* Julius Caesar; Caius of the stirps Caesar of gens Julia. Women used a feminine form of their father's nomen, i.e., the daughter of Caius Julius Caesar would be named Julia.

Praetor: Judge and magistrate elected yearly along with the Consuls. In the late Republic there were eight Praetors. Senior was the Praetor Urbanus, who heard civil cases between citizens. The Praetor Peregrinus heard cases involving foreigners. The others presided over criminal courts. Insignia were the toga praetexta and the sella curulis, and Praetors were accompanied by two lictors. The office carried the imperium. After leaving office, the ex-Praetors became propraetors and went to govern propraetorian provinces with full imperium.

Praetorium: A general's headquarters, usually a tent in camp. In the provinces, the official residence of the governor.

Princeps: "First Citizen." An especially distinguished Senator chosen by the Censors. His name was the first called on the roll of the Senate and he was first to speak on any issue. Later the title was usurped by Augustus and is the origin of the word "prince."

Proscription: List of names of public enemies published by Sulla. Anyone could kill a proscribed person and claim a reward, usually a part of the dead man's estate.

Publicans: Those who bid on public contracts, most notably builders and tax farmers. The contracts were usually let by the Censors and therefore had a period of five years.

Pugio: The straight, double-edged dagger of the Roman soldiers.

Quaestor: Lowest of the elected officials, they had charge of the treasury and financial matters such as payments for public works. They also acted as assistants and paymasters to higher magistrates, generals and provincial governors. They were elected yearly by the comitia tributa.

Quirinus: The deified Romulus, patron deity of the city.

Rostra: A monument in the Forum commemorating the sea battle of Antium in 338 B.C., decorated with the rams, "rostra" of enemy ships (sing. rostrum). Its base was used as an orator's platform.

Sagum: The Roman military cloak, made of wool and always dyed red. To put on the sagum signified the changeover to wartime status, as the toga was the garment of peace. When the citizens met in the *comitia centuriata* they wore the sagum in token of its ancient function as the military muster.

Salii: "Dancers." Two colleges of priests dedicated to Mars and Quirinus who held their rites in March and October, respectively. Each college consisted of twelve young patricians whose parents were still living. On their festivals, they dressed in embroidered tunics, a crested bronze helmet and breastplate and each bore one of the twelve sacred shields ("ancilia") and a staff. They processed to the most important altars of Rome and before each performed a war dance. The ritual was so ancient that, by the first century B.C., their songs and prayers were unintelligible.

Saturnalia: Feast of Saturn, December 17–23, a raucous and jubilant occasion when gifts were exchanged, debts were settled and masters waited on their slaves.

Sella Curulis: A folding camp-chair. It was part of the insignia of the curule magistrates and the Flamen Dialis.

Senate: Rome's chief deliberative body. It consisted of three hundred to six hundred men, all of whom had won elective office at least once. Once the supreme ruling body, by the late Republic the Senate's former legislative and judicial functions had devolved upon the courts and the popular assemblies and its chief authority lay in foreign policy and the nomination of generals. Senators were privileged to wear the tunica laticlava.

Servile War: The slave rebellion led by the Thracian gladiator Spartacus in 73–71 B.C. The rebellion was crushed by Crassus and Pompey.

Sica: A single-edged dagger or short sword of varying size. It was favored by thugs and used by the Thracian gladiators in the arena. It was classified as an infamous rather than an honorable weapon.

Solarium: A rooftop garden and patio.

Spatha: The Roman cavalry sword, longer and narrower than the gladius.

SPQR: "Senatus populusque Romanus." The Senate and People of Rome. The formula embodying the sovereignty of Rome. It was used on official correspondence, documents and public works.

Stirps: A sub-family of a gens. The cognomen gave the name of the stirps, i.e., Caius Julius *Caesar*. Caius of the stirps Caesar of gens Julia.

Strigil: A bronze implement, roughly s-curved, used to scrape sand and oil from the body after bathing. Soap was unknown to the Roman Republic.

Strophium: A cloth band worn by women beneath or over the clothing to support the breasts.

Subligaculum: A loincloth, worn by men and women.

Subura: A neighborhood on the lower slopes of the Viminal and Esquiline, famed for its slums, noisy shops and raucous inhabitants.

Tarpeian Rock: A cliff beneath the Capitol from which traitors were hurled. It was named for the Roman maiden Tarpeia who, according to legend, betrayed the Capitol to the Sabines.

Temple of Jupiter Capitolinus: The most important temple of the state religion. Triumphal processions ended with a sacrifice at this temple.

Temple of Saturn: The state treasury was located in a crypt beneath this temple. It was also the repository for military standards.

Temple of Vesta: Site of the sacred fire tended by the vestal virgins and dedicated to the goddess of the hearth. Documents, especially wills, were deposited there for safekeeping.

Toga: The outer robe of the Roman citizen. It was white for the upper class, darker for the poor and for people in mourning. The toga praetexta, bordered with a purple stripe, was worn by curule magistrates, by state priests when performing their functions and by boys prior to manhood. The toga picta, purple and embroidered with golden stars, was worn by a general when celebrating a triumph, also by a magistrate when giving public Games.

Tonsores: A slave trained as a barber and hairdresser.

Trans-Tiber: A newer district on the right or western bank of the Tiber. It lay beyond the old city walls.

Tribal Assemblies: There were two: the comitia tributa, an assembly of all citizens by tribes, which elected the lower magistrates— curule aediles, and quaestors, also the military tribunes—and the concilium plebis, consisting only of plebeians, elected the tribunes of the plebs and the plebeian aediles.

Tribe: Originally, the three classes of patricians. Under the Republic, all citizens belonged to tribes of which there were four city tribes and thirty-one country tribes. New citizens were enrolled in an existing tribe.

Tribune: Representative of the plebeians with power to introduce laws and to veto actions of the Senate. Only plebeians could hold the office, which carried no imperium. Military tribunes were elected from among the young men of senatorial or equestrian rank to be assistants to generals. Usually it was the first step of a man's political career.

Triumph: A magnificent ceremony celebrating military victory. The honor could be granted only by the Senate, and until he received permission, the victorious general had to remain outside the city walls, as his command ceased the instant he crossed the pomerium. The general, called the triumphator, received royal, near-divine honors and became a virtual god for a day. A slave was appointed to stand behind him and remind him periodically of his mortality lest the gods become jealous.

Triumvir: A member of a triumvirate—a board or college of three men. Most famously, the three-man rule of Caesar, Pompey and Crassus. Later, the triumvirate of Antonius, Octavian and Lepidus.

Tunica: A long, loose shirt, sleeveless or short-sleeved, worn by citizens beneath the toga when outdoors and by itself indoors. The tunica laticlava had a broad purple stripe from neck to hem and was worn by Senators and patricians. The tunica angusticlava had a narrow stripe and was worn by the equites. The tunica picta, purple and embroidered with golden palm branches, was worn by a general when he celebrated a triumph.

Usus: The most common form of marriage, in which a man and woman lived together for a year without being separated for three consecutive nights.

Via: A highway. Within the city, viae were streets wide enough for two wagons to pass one another. There were only two viae during the Republic: the Via Sacra, which ran through the Forum and was used for religious processions and triumphs, and the Via Nova, which ran along one side of the Forum.

Vigile: A night watchman. The vigiles had the duty of apprehending felons caught committing crimes, but their main duty was as a fire watch. They were unarmed except for staves and carried fire-buckets.